THE
RED LIGHT
DISTRICT

By Morgan Keyes

Copyright © 2025 Morris Lowery Jr

This is a work of fiction. All names, characters, places, and events are products of the author's imagination or are used fictitiously. Any resemblance to actual events, locales, or real persons, living or dead, is purely coincidental.

ISBN: 979-8-9999867-1-9

Cover design by Morris Lowery Jr.

"Duty and desire rarely share the same path. In war's shadow, love can feel like both security and sabotage."

- Anonymous

"Three may keep a secret, if two of them are dead."
- Benjamin Franklin

Principle characters

USS Daniel Shaw (DDG-148)

Chief Master-At-Arms Damion Jackson
Ensign Salina Maria Cabrera, ATFP Officer
Commander Jack Bates, Commanding Officer
LCDR Austin Jacobs, Executive Officer
Lieutenant Bartholomew Baker, CSO
Ensign Donna Reed, Main Propulsion Assistant
Ensign Stephanie Cheng, Cybersecurity Officer
Command Master Chief Beulah "Bucky" Buchanan
Chief Quartermaster Alvin Casanova Valentino
Chief Boatswain's Mate Mike Stein
Chief Electronic Warfare Specialist Sylvia Beechum

NCIS Resident Agency Rota, Spain

Special Agent Maya Torres

Chapter 1- A Glimpse of Liberty

It was one of those typical autumn days in Barcelona, Spain, where even time seemed to stand still in awe. The air was crisp and clear, with a comfortable temperature of 72°F. The sun filtered through the rustling green canopies above the narrow, cobblestone side streets, transforming the entire area into a picturesque scene like you see on a postcard. People flowed like paint strokes on a moving canvas - tourists with their selfie sticks and shopping bags, locals on scooters weaving through crowds like it was a dance, and street performers trying to earn a few Euros with juggling tricks or slightly off-key renditions of American pop songs played on keyboards and acoustic guitars.

Liberty call had started several hours before, at 07:45, and the USS Daniel Shaw (DDG-148) sailors who had been on duty the previous day wasted no time changing into their favorite civilian outfits to head out on the town. After rendering salutes to the Officer of the Deck and the American flag, they literally ran off the brow full of excitement and plans for what they imagined would be about 20 hours of freedom before having to return to the ship for another workday.

However, for U.S. Navy Master-at-Arms Chief Petty Officer (Surface Warfare) Damion Jackson, referred to in short as the MAC, he knew that he had several hours of routine work to accomplish before he could also go out and enjoy the much-anticipated liberty port. After finishing the tasks he deemed were most pressing, he was finally getting a taste of freedom after months at sea and two extra days stuck on the ship handling personnel rotations. He had taken a fellow Chief's duty the first day inport, so that they could see family who lived in the historic city, and now, at long last, this sunny slice of Spain belonged to him. No khakis, no rank, no duties—just a pair of jeans, his favorite faded T-shirt, and a pair of loafers that had been through too many airports and liberty ports to count.

Taking long, deep breaths, he walked with that slow, deliberate pace of someone in no rush for anything. Just taking it all in - the food smells, the noise, the way the city felt alive but relaxed at the same time. And for the first time in a long while, he wasn't thinking about inspections, duty rosters, or how many days were left in deployment.

No. Right here, right now, was all that mattered.

Turning a corner into a café-lined courtyard, he spotted them. A cluster of his fellow non-khaki-wearing Navy Chiefs seated under an umbrella, with drinks on the table. He would soon be close enough to hear the unmistakable buzz of off-duty banter in the air, filled with "sea-stories" of heroic deeds that each of the others would find questionable. As he drew closer to the usually rambunctious group, he sensed that something didn't sit right.

They weren't talking.
They weren't drinking.
They weren't even blinking.

Every one of them had their head turned in the same direction, eyes locked with laser focus, on something or possibly someone. And in that moment, Damion's gut told him everything he needed to know.
Something was up.

He stepped up to the edge of the table, but none of them even looked his way: no nods, no greetings, just thousand-yard stares.

GENERAL QUARTERS, he thought, hearing the silent alarm ringing somewhere deep in his brain.

Damion shifted his stance and began scanning the area with the methodical precision he had trained into countless security force lookouts over the years. Near-to-far, left to right, up and down—every quadrant accounted for.

First scan - nothing.
Second scan - still nothing.
Then, on the third scan, he froze.

Boom. Target acquired.

Roughly 300 yards and closing, a small, caramel-toned figure flowed through the crowd like she had somewhere important to be, but not in any rush. She glided, not walked. Long auburn hair spilled halfway down her back, swaying behind her like something out of a shampoo commercial. Her outfit wasn't flashy - dark sunglasses, a loose, tan blouse, white linen slacks, and sandals that showcased her well-manicured toes. The shopping bags in her hands and the drink with a straw only added to the whole "I'm not trying, but I'm still winning" look.

As she closed in—now about 200 yards away—Damion felt it more clearly. This wasn't just a beautiful woman passing by. This was a threat. Not to their lives, but to their composure. To every shred of discipline their Navy training had given them. A different kind of battlefield had opened, and none of them were winning.

Whatever she was, she wasn't just another tourist.

The entire courtyard seemed to hush around her, like the universe decided she was the main character for the next few minutes.

And then… something jolted in his brain—a bolt of recognition.

Realizing the implications of this unexpected revelation, he slowly blinked, then casually glanced to his left, then right, to see if his fellow Chiefs had observed his reaction and were silently reprimanding him for his lack of professionalism. To Damion's relief and surprise, no one had noticed what he imagined he looked like – a cartoon character wolf with his tongue hanging out, eyes bulging, and heart beating through his shirt. Heck, they still hadn't acknowledged that he was *even* there. They were still mesmerized by this alluring, mysterious, and unknown woman. Only she was no longer a mysterious, unknown woman. Not by a long shot.

She was Salina Maria Cabrera. Ensign - United States Navy. USS Daniel Shaw (DDG-148) Antiterrorism/Force Protection Officer. His boss.

No. Freakin'. Way.

He had worked side by side with her for the last 18 months on the ship. In operations briefings. Cleaning weapons in the armory. Always squared away, no-nonsense. Sharp as hell. And, she never hesitated to roll up her sleeves and do everything the enlisted security personnel did, a quality that quickly earned her deep respect from the crew. But this-this was not the version of Cabrera he'd ever seen on duty. This wasn't her coveralls with a handgun or M4 carbine rifle on the shooting range. This was something else entirely.

Turning her head as if she had sensed their presence, Cabrera looked directly at the group sitting at the cafe in the courtyard, and without hesitation, changed course directly towards the table. Her walk quickened, but her grace never faltered.

Damion snapped out of his trance just as she reached the table. Her sunglasses came off with casual ease, revealing warm mocha-brown eyes and a smile that could stop a bar fight.

"*Hello* Chiefs," she said casually, like she hadn't just derailed the mental stability of everyone in a 30-foot radius.

The group stumbled through a collection of throat-clears and awkward hellos. Damion, somehow, had found his voice.

"Hello, Ma'am", he answered respectfully, as was protocol when addressing a female military officer. "Looks like you are enjoying your liberty. Little shopping spree? Taking in the sights?"

Her grin grew wider, even brighter. "Yes, Chief. I *love* it here - first time in Barcelona. Everyone is so friendly. I wish we had more time to explore— another week would be perfect."

She continued talking about the *lovely* shops and her plans to test the local food later. He nodded but didn't speak right away, mainly because his brain was still busy trying to process what exactly had just walked up and smiled at him like they were old high school buddies at a 10-year class reunion.

He'd worked beside her and even trained her for months. Thought he knew her, but clearly, he did not.

"So," she asked, tilting her head a bit, "what's the plan for the rest of *your* day, Chief?"

Damion smirked. He could already feel the ears of every Chief at the table leaning into his response.

"Well, I figured I'd sit here for a bit with these old bastards, drink some overpriced beer, belch a lot, and later maybe find a local hole-in-the-wall with some native food that'll probably give me diarrhea by morning."

Cabrera burst out laughing - genuine laughter that turned several heads nearby. She clapped a hand over her mouth but didn't stop grinning. "Well, I hope the beer's good and the food isn't *that* bad," she replied, still trying not to laugh.

"Hey! Who are you calling a bastard?" came a beer-infused voice from the other side of the table. Damion looked over to see the Chief Quartermaster - QMC(SW)Alvin "Casanova" Valentino lightly holding a half-empty Estrella Galicia beer. His fellow Chiefs had affectionately given the QMC the nickname *Casanova* because of his last name and the fact that he mistakenly revealed that *it was necessary* for him to brush his fine hair, inherited from his mother, 100 times before leaving the ship to go on liberty. A mistake he regretted every day for ever sharing with his khaki brothers-in-arms. "I'll have you know, my parents were together when I was born!" followed by a small, resounding belch. This comment was quickly answered with a low grunt from the other side of the table by the Chief Boatswain's Mate – BMC(SW)Mike Stein of Texas, *the greatest state ever*, in his humble opinion.

"Cas, just because you were raised by a pimp living with three women in the middle of nowhere, doesn't mean you are legit! How many times I gotta' explain that to you?"

"What are you talking about, Boats? That's how we roll in Utah. You're just jealous 'cause I'm *prettier* than you."

"Yep, that's it. You got me, Brother!" A burst of laughter flowed around the table, followed by the clinking of toasting beer bottles, and gulps of the Spanish liquid losing another round to the thirsty group.

Turning from his two shipmates back to Cabrera, Damion shook his head and gave her a half-crooked smile. "Hmm, it looks like I've got my hands full. Well, you enjoy your liberty, Ensign Cabrera."

"Thanks, Chief. You, too." Then, with a polite turn to the rest of the group, "Bye, Chiefs."

And finally, as she walked away: "*Bye, Chief Jackson.*"

Damion nodded and added, "Stay out of trouble."

"Yes, Chief!" she said, mock-serious. Then, looking over her shoulder with a half-smile, "But, no promises."

With that, she disappeared back into the crowd like she had never even been there.

The silence around the table lasted exactly three seconds.

"Bye-bye, Sweetie-Chiefee," one of the Chiefs muttered in a singsong voice, cracking the dam on a wave of chuckles, elbow nudges, and crude jokes that were just getting started.

"Yo, DJ!" piped in one of the other Chiefs. "Why didn't you tell us your little Div-O looked like that in civvies?"

"That was your Division Officer?" responded another, letting out a long, slow whistle while still seeming oblivious to the whole interaction that occurred, as if he had just awakened from a long nap.

Damion didn't respond. He just leaned back in his chair, eyes still on the crowd where she had vanished.

The threat was gone. Finally.
But he felt in his gut that this battle was only just beginning.

Chapter 2 – Not a Date

After the laughter had died down and his first round of beers was halfway drained, Damion peeled himself away from the group. The courtyard was getting louder, and the Chiefs were already three jokes deep into a new round of *"Sweetie-Chiefee"* commentary that was going to get old real fast. He gave them a nod, tossed a few euros on the table, and walked off without saying much.

Sometimes, liberty meant cutting loose with your crew. Other times, it meant finding a little peace and quiet and remembering you are a human being outside of a uniform. Damion wanted the latter.

He found himself drifting through the narrow alleys of the old city, where the buildings leaned in close, as if whispering secrets to each other. The streets here didn't follow logic—they curved, narrowed, and branched off in unpredictable ways, like a maze built by poets. The tourists thinned out. The sounds changed. Less English. More Catalan. The locals moving at their own unhurried pace.

Passing by the many tourist establishments, he decided to pick up some items from a family-owned leather shop and a few small figurines resembling the famous Lladro porcelain brand, only these were not quite as exquisite or expensive. Nothing big. Just enough to send home—something that said "I thought of you" without sounding like an apology for being gone too long.

The sun was dipping lower now, hitting the rooftops with that burnished glow you only get right before dusk. That golden hour where everything looks like a memory before it even happens.

That's when he found the place.

A small café tucked between two quiet storefronts— one closed and faded, the other a florist that looked like it hadn't changed since 1950. No neon sign, no English menu posted out front. Just a small candle-lit lantern surrounded by fireflies and a hand-painted wood placard above the door: *La Flor del Barrio*. The Flower of the Neighborhood. Perfect.

He stepped inside.

Terracotta floors. Wooden beams overhead. Tables draped in white linens that didn't try too hard. Soft lighting that didn't try at all. Flamenco music playing low in the background from a speaker that probably had stories of its own.

A middle-aged woman greeted him without fanfare and motioned toward a table near the back, close to a window overlooking a quiet stone courtyard where ivy climbed the walls as if it were headed somewhere important.

Damion sat. No one asked for his name, his rank, or his ID. He liked that.

The waitress approached with a menu and a neutral expression—the kind you get after serving too many tourists who can't pronounce the dishes and tip like they're doing you a favor.

"Buenas tardes," she said flatly, setting the menu down. "Would you like something to drink?"

Damion looked up and gave her a polite, easy smile. "Buenas tardes," he said back with practiced Spanish. "I'll try something local. Whatever goes best with your favorite dish."

That caught her attention. Her eyes met his.

"You don't want what the Americans usually order?" she answered suspiciously.

"I'm not here for a cheeseburger. I'm a guest in *your* country, so I want to experience *your* culture."

Her mouth curled—just slightly. "Rabo de toro. Braised oxtail. Traditional. Heavy, but worth it."

"Perfect. And bring me a cold Estrella Galicia to go with it."

"Very well," she said, almost approving, before disappearing through a curtain behind the bar.

Damion leaned back and let it all sink in. The hum of conversation, the clink of silverware, the low rhythms of Spain itself.

He had no idea how much time passed before he heard the voice.

"Nice spot."

He turned slowly, already knowing who it was before he saw her.

Salina Maria Cabrera. Again.

But this time... different.

She was in a sundress the color of sunflowers, straps resting delicately on her shoulders, the hem dancing just above her knees as the breeze came through the window behind her. Hair pulled back, neat ponytail. Same confident posture. Same calm energy. But tonight, she looked less like a sailor and more like a woman who knew exactly who she was.

"You following me?" he asked, raising an eyebrow.

She smirked. "I was here first. You just didn't see me."

"Uh huh."

"Mind if I sit?"

He hesitated. "We're still in uniform, technically. *You do know how this looks?*"

"No one from the ship's here," she said, glancing around. "And if someone walks in, I'll just duck out the back. Easy."

Damion looked at her for a long second. Then nodded.

"Fine. But this isn't a date."

"Good," she replied, pulling out the chair opposite him. "Because I didn't bring flowers."

When the waitress returned with his food and beer, she gave Cabrera a quick once-over. "¿Y tú?"

"I'll have the same," Cabrera answered in clean, confident Spanish.

The waitress raised her brows slightly and nodded, vanishing again without a word.

"So," Cabrera began, "What did you guys get into after I left?"

"You mean, after you *broadsided* the Chief's Mess?" referring to a tactic used by old naval sailing ships. During combat, a ship would attempt a maneuver to bring the full weight of its side-mounted cannons to bear on an enemy vessel. Firing all these guns simultaneously from one side—a *broadside*—delivered maximum destructive power.

"Oh my God… *What did I do*?" Her voice was barely above a whisper, but the panic in it rang loud. "I thought I was being polite. I didn't mean to disrespect anyone."

Her hand shot to her mouth, fingers trembling as she gnawed nervously at a nail, eyes wide and unfocused. The room around her might as well have disappeared—she was somewhere else now, replaying the spontaneous meeting earlier in the day. The transformation was startling, thought Damion.

Just hours ago, she had radiated control, a force of nature wrapped in silk and certainty. Now, that same woman looked hollowed out, a shadow of herself, consumed by the creeping fear that she had unwittingly crossed some invisible line, committed some unspeakable social sin. She looked like a child caught in the act, lost and desperate to undo what had already been done.

After observing her reaction for a few seconds, Damion broke into her strained thoughts.

"Hey, don't beat yourself up. It wasn't you. Well, actually, *it was you*, but you didn't do anything wrong. You just showed up out of nowhere, looking like you came off a Vogue fashion model photo shoot, and approached a bunch of half-inebriated sailors who had no idea that you cleaned up so well. That's all it was, nothing more, nothing less."

Breathing a sigh of relief and relaxing a little, "Oh, thanks for that", she replied, with a look of sincerity on her face and in her voice. "I guess I had better stick to coveralls from now on."

"Hey, it's not your fault you knocked everybody's socks off."

Leaning to the side of the table and looking down at his feet, she replied with a smirk, "Looks like you still have yours on."

"I was standing the whole time," he answered with a half-smile.

Now that the ice had thawed, they began to talk about what they had done the rest of the day, right up until the waitress returned with their meals.

"Here you are — braised oxtail, cooked low and slow in red wine with a base of onion, garlic, peppers, and herbs. The meat is tender and comes with a sauce from the braising juices. On the side, you've got baked potatoes with onion, glazed carrots, and steamed green beans. Let me know if you'd like some bread or wine to go with it."

"Thank you very much", Damion replied.

Cabrera added, "Oh, this looks delicious. Thank you."

The waitress, smiling and feeling appreciated for her recommendation, moved off to tend to several local patrons who had just entered the cafe.

Over dinner, they talked casually - not about the ship, not about ranks or routines. They only spoke about the city. The food. The feeling of walking around without being watched or saluted. The freedom.

Cabrera told him about her home, Puerto Rico, her family, and how she had almost joined the Navy right after high school, but waited until her late twenties to take the leap. Damion shared stories of his younger brothers and how his mother still mailed handwritten letters like it was 1985.

The conversation wasn't forced, and the time passed by like a sailboat propelled by a light wind on a calm lake. No awkward pauses. No flirting, either—just respect. Curiosity. Maybe a little awe on both sides.

She wasn't at all what he expected. Not by a long shot.

And maybe, just maybe, he wasn't what she expected either.

When dessert came, it was simple—some type of tart with powdered sugar and citrus peel. Two small cups of coffee were placed on the table beside the dessert plate in front of them, while the *single* fork on the plate stared at them, daring to see who would take it first. When Damion tried to get the waitress's attention to ask for another, Cabrera took the fork, sliced a piece of the tart, and slowly ate it. She then gently placed the fork back on the other side of the plate, pointing it at Damion. When he looked up at her with one eyebrow raised, she said, "We can't just wait here all night for her to come back with another one." Shrugging and taking the fork, Damion dug into the tart. They split it without saying anything else, passing the fork back and forth as if it were just a thing people did.

The rest of the evening was spent in mutual silence as they sat quietly at the small table, the warm evening air caressing them. Throughout the cafe, the locals filled the space with laughter and animated conversation. The clink of cutlery and wine glasses blended with the scent of grilled seafood floating through the air. A soft guitar melody drifted from the nearby speaker, weaving through the night like a floating *guitarrista flamenco*. The atmosphere was lively, intimate, and unmistakably Spanish.

Eventually, Cabrera broke their reverie and glanced at the door. With a small sigh, "I guess it's about that time. I think its best that I should leave first. Just in case."

Damion stood as she did. "Probably smart."

She smiled - not the show-stopping kind from earlier. This one was smaller. Quieter. But somehow stronger.

"This was nice. Thanks for the *not*-date, Chief."

"Anytime, Ma'am," he answered while pretending to tip an imagined hat on his head.

Her head tilted slowly to the side as if trying to solve one last puzzle - "Salina."

Damion nodded, "Anytime...*Salina*."

And with that, she was gone.

A few minutes later, the waitress came back to check on them. She glanced at the empty chair, then at Damion.

"¿Volverá tu novia?" she asked. Will your girlfriend be coming back?

Damion took a sip of his coffee and smiled faintly.

"Ella no es mi novia." She's not my girlfriend.

The waitress paused, then said softly, "Qué lástima."

What a shame.

Damion didn't answer. He just leaned back and let the night settle in. With his eyes closed, he listened to the sounds of the city breathing as the memory of the fading, yellow sundress danced in his mind.

Chapter 3 – Haze Gray and Underway

The following two days slipped back into routine, the kind that sailors come to expect and oddly find comfort in. Regular workdays resumed onboard the ship, beginning with the piping of reveille and the ever-familiar buzz of shipboard life.

The smell of brewed coffee and recycled air mixed as the crew settled into their duty stations, checking equipment, standing watches, and preparing for whatever came next. The rust-colored sunrise bled over the horizon each morning like the start of a new painting, only to be followed by the scheduled clanging of tools, the thrum of shipboard machinery, and the occasional bark of a Petty Officer's orders to several junior sailors.

Liberty call continued at 1600 both days, and although Damion preferred solitude, he knew he couldn't avoid his crew forever—not after ghosting them that first night in Barcelona. So he threw on a clean T-shirt, his most trusted jeans, and joined the familiar chaos of bar stools, grilled octopus, and stories that grew more outrageous with each round of Estrella Galicia.

The nights on the town were exactly what they were supposed to be—loud, rowdy, and filled with laughter. Between greasy tapas, flirtations with waitresses who had no genuine interest, and the unavoidable "remember that one time in Naples?" tales, it was everything you'd expect from a group of sailors temporarily freed from the burden of discipline. No one asked where he had disappeared to that first night, and Damion offered no explanation.

He and Ensign Cabrera crossed paths several times during the day, often during duty changeovers or at the morning division muster. She was all business— uniform pressed, tone clipped, posture impeccable. There was no trace of sundresses or shared desserts in her eyes. Damion matched her professionalism, slipping effortlessly back into the rhythm of the chain of command. Whatever moment they had shared in that small, quiet café had been packed away, sealed, and stowed in both their mental sea bags.

If thoughts of that night still stirred in the recesses of Damion's mind, they were quickly suppressed by the steady beat of military life. Duty has a way of erasing the sentimental, at least temporarily.

To his great relief, the final two liberty days came and went without incident—no drunken sailors missing muster, no fights with locals, no one arrested for disorderly conduct. That meant no extra paperwork, no write-ups, and no all-hands butt-chewing from the CO. In Damion's job, that counted as a small miracle.

Then came the orders: the Daniel Shaw was headed back to sea to rendezvous with the Spanish warship *Cristóbal Colón (F105)* for scheduled MIO—Maritime Interdiction Operations.

After a short sea-and-anchor detail, the ship was back at sea. The Mediterranean stretched out like a restless silver-blue skin, rippling under the hull as the ship raced to meet the Spanish frigate at the designated coordinates. With flags snapping and radios crackling, the two ships aligned their formation to begin their joint mission.

A MIO operation is both delicate and decisive. It's not war, but it isn't a cruise either. The objective: stop and board vessels suspected of carrying contraband—drugs, weapons, trafficked persons, or anything flagged under international maritime law. Sailors suited up in full tactical gear, Kevlar and plate carriers hugging their frames as RHIBs—rigid-hull inflatable boats—were lowered into the water with practiced precision. Boarding teams carried sidearms, flashlights, and radio communications, as well as endless contact protocols, procedures, and safety precautions drilled into their heads like gospel.

The operations were methodical: hail, approach, board, secure, inspect. Three vessels were stopped over a 48-hour span—one fishing trawler flying a Liberian flag, a recreational yacht with falsified documents, and a rust-covered cargo boat from Algeria that couldn't account for several crates marked "machinery parts." All were compliant, if not entirely innocent, and all were logged, photographed, and released under watchful eyes.

By the time the mission ended, both crews had earned a break. But this was no ordinary wrap-up.

A makeshift competition had been quietly arranged between the two warships, utilizing water balloon artillery made from repurposed PVC pipes, elastic bands, and a great deal of creativity. Targets were hung from each ship's railings—one for each hit zone—and over a span of 30 minutes, laughter echoed across the waves as the sea became a battlefield of harmless, sloshing fun.

The Americans fired first—three direct hits, cheers erupting across the main deck. But the Spanish, armed with better aim and some kind of homemade compressed-air contraption, retaliated fiercely. When the final tally came in, it was 5-3 in favor of the *Cristóbal Colón*.

A chorus of good-natured jeers came over the open comms as the Spaniards radioed their victory, followed by a gracious salute and the promise of retribution from Daniel Shaw's commanding officer "next time." Damion chuckled to himself while watching the red, white, and gold flag of the Spanish ship shrink into the distance as they turned back toward port.

However, USS Daniel Shaw held her course, heading deeper into the endless sapphire of the Mediterranean, her hull slicing smoothly through a sea that promised more miles, more missions, and—if fate allowed — maybe a few more unexpected encounters waiting just over the horizon.

Over the following 6 days, the crew conducted routine patrols in the eastern Mediterranean Sea, north of Morocco, and just west of the Strait of Gibraltar.

Their primary mission was to identify all vessels transiting in and out of the strait. This was made much simpler with modern technology, such as AIS.

AIS (Automatic Identification System) is a maritime safety and navigation tool that broadcasts and receives information about a vessel's location, course, speed, and other details. This information is then displayed on a vessel's navigation system or shared with shore-based stations for tracking and monitoring. AIS helps improve situational awareness, aids in collision avoidance, and contributes to overall navigation safety.

For the Daniel Shaw crew, this meant less time visually identifying each ship as well as saving on fuel. The AIS information transmitted by the vessel of interest was picked up by receivers onboard the ship, then sent to the various shipboard systems, where specially trained operators review and compare the data with other sources to determine if the vessel warrants any additional observation or boarding for inspection.

In the last 72 hours, they had passed 150 commercial cargo containers and fuel tanker ships, all of which were equipped with Automatic Identification System technology. After each confirmed identification, Damion began to routinely hear his fellow shipmates quote an old Navy slogan that rang true: "Hurry up and wait."

As the ship cruised at a leisurely 12 knots, the crew went about their daily at-sea routines. Always ready to transit to battle stations in under 5 minutes, but feeling a little less stressed due to the lack of serious threats in the area.

Damion had finished preparing the paperwork for conducting a random urinalysis, which is routinely performed after a Navy ship leaves a port that openly promotes opportunities for sailors to engage in various types of illicit activity. Specifically, the use of controlled substances, which the Navy has deemed forbidden. In layman's terms – drugs.

Before submitting his recommendations up the chain of command, Damion decided to go topside to get some fresh air. Standing out on the flight deck with several other sailors, he looked out over the open sea.

Today, the flight deck offered a view that words could barely do justice. The Mediterranean Sea stretched out endlessly, its surface glinting like a polished jewel under the late-morning sun. The ship sliced through the water with a proud, effortless motion, the sounds of the crew working barely perceptible over the rhythmic crash of the sea against the hull. A salty breeze swirled in from the port side, wrapping around the sailors and playfully tugging at their clothes, carrying with it the unmistakable scent of the open ocean—clean, invigorating, and alive.

Sea-spray leapt from the waterline, catching the light and creating tiny rainbows that disappeared just as quickly as they appeared. The sea, with its rolling, glassy peaks, held the kind of calming authority only something ancient and powerful could possess. Then, just off the starboard quarter, a pod of porpoises appeared—sleek and agile, darting effortlessly through the waves like silver-tipped torpedoes. They swam in tight formation, dancing with the rhythm of the ship's wake, cutting in and out of view like they were putting on a show just for the crew.

Watching them, a memory surfaced, unshaken and vivid. Damion's mind was carried back to a simpler time, to the calm waters of the Chesapeake Bay, where just he and his father would set out on their small boat just after dawn. There was the same scent of the salt air, the cry of seabirds overhead, and the same sense of limitless freedom that came only when land faded into the horizon. He could almost feel the gentle creak of the wooden deck beneath them, hear his father's voice calling out a course adjustment, and see the churning wake behind the boat created by the 150hp Yamaha outboard engine.

Back to the present.

He remained still, one hand resting on the rail, the breeze flowing cool over his head, his eyes following the porpoises as they peeled away into the distance. Just for a moment, amidst the steel and technology of war, the sea had offered him a connection to something timeless. Something real. Something home.

The sound of a familiar laugh broke through his thoughts, and for the first time, he noticed Cabrera standing on the other side of the flight deck with two new junior officers. He did not know either of them but knew that it was only a matter of time before he ran into them on duty. As he looked on, Cabrera turned her head in his direction, acknowledged him with a nod and a smile, and then went back to her conversation.

Business as usual.

Damion had now gotten his fill of sunlight and fresh air. He turned to head back to his office when he noticed the sound of the engines slowing down, almost immediately followed by the excited voice of the Engineering Officer of the Watch (EOOW) on the 1MC:

"Engineering casualty – engineering casualty! Engineering casualty in GTM 2-Bravo!"

The high-pitched sound of the LM2500 gas turbine engines continued to dwindle as the ship reduced speed through the water.

"Another *fine Navy day*," thought Damion as he headed to the interior of the ship, back to the confines of his small office. Damion knew that it was just his imagination, but with the ship now moving more slowly through the water, time also seemed to drag by just a bit slower. He shook off the thought and continued to focus on his work.

It was just over an hour, and Damion was finishing up an inspection report for the Executive Officer, when three knocks sounded on the steel, watertight door, followed by the graceful entrance of Ensign Cabrera.

"Hey, Chief, you got a minute?"

"Of course, Ma'am. What can I do for you?"

"It looks like this engineering casualty will be sending us to Rota. The CO's going to put it out to the crew, but the CSO (Combat Systems Officer) wants force protection schedules. Like, yesterday."

"Of course he does," Damion smirked.

"So, can we hook up after lunch and brainstorm the plan together? I need the practice."

Seeing the opportunity to joke a little, he replied with a mock-serious face, "As long as you bring the flowers."

Not missing a beat, Cabrera half-smiled and replied as she reached for the door handle, *"Still not a date."*

Damion chuckled and said to himself as the door closed behind her. *"Cool, having a Div-O with a sense of humor."*

About a half-hour later, the ship's intercom crackled to life with the familiar tone of the Boatswain's whistle that silenced idle chatter and turned heads throughout the passageways and workspaces. From the bridge to the mess decks, even in the quiet confines of the berthing areas, sailors instinctively paused. The voice that followed was calm, firm, and unmistakably authoritative.

"Good morning, Daniel Shaw."

A momentary hush fell across the ship as everyone waited.

"We've experienced a mechanical issue with one of our main engines. The engineering team has done a fantastic job stabilizing the situation, and we're in no immediate danger. However, after reviewing the damage and weighing our options, I've decided to pull into Naval Station Rota for repairs."

There was a beat—enough time for the reality to settle in. A deviation from the underway schedule always had ripple effects, most of the time, unpleasant ones.

"I want to make it clear to everyone—this will be a *working port*. That means full, regular workdays. We've got a lot to get done while we're tied up, and your departments will be coordinating closely with port operations teams to make that happen."

He paused again, his tone softening just slightly.

"Now, I know some of you are looking forward to a little break - and you'll still get some. Liberty will be granted after working hours, assuming you're not on duty and your division's tasks are squared away. That said, no one leaves the ship until we've had our port brief. It will be held tomorrow morning on the mess decks. Attendance is mandatory for all hands."

The intercom clicked off, and with it came a low murmur rolling through the ship -sailors exchanging glances, some exhaling quietly, others already calculating how much time they might have onshore. It wasn't what they'd hoped for, but the Captain's tone left no room for negotiation. Sometimes, Murphy's Law went into effect regardless of the Navy's schedule.

As the ship changed course, heading towards Rota, Damion finished up his morning routine and then went to the Chief Petty Officer's Mess for lunch. The CPO Mess, or Chief's lounge, is the area of the ship reserved explicitly for senior enlisted personnel E-7 and above. This is where they ate meals, had CPO meetings, watched movies, or just hung out on or off duty.

After lunch was over, and the junior sailors had finished their cleaning assignments, Damion started preparing for his meeting with Ensign Cabrera. He didn't have to wait long before he heard the customary three knocks on the door. Ensign Cabrera came in, "Hi, Chief. Is this a good time?"

"Yes, Ma'am. All ready for you. Let's get this done."

Since he had previously trained her on his system for creating the security force watches, she easily kept up with the changes they needed to make before entering port. When they began, she had first sat opposite him at the small table, but then chose to sit next to him on the rather uncomfortable bench seat. Damion could feel the body heat radiating off of her, as well as smell the fresh, flowery scent of her deodorant, as she leaned in close while discussing the plans.

Naval Station Rota had its own security personnel both on land and in patrol boats, but there was still a possibility of additional threats. *"Every facet of force protection had to be accounted for, and it had to be airtight,"* Cabrera informed Damion of the CSO's comments.

"Airtight, huh? With all due respect, the CSO wouldn't know a solid force protection plan if it crawled up his butt with a chainsaw."

Cabrera didn't even try to hold back laughing while simultaneously covering her mouth, just as the door opened to usher in the arrival of QMC(SW)Valentino.

"Well, this looks cozy. What are you two plotting over there?" His matted hair, sweat-soaked CPO t-shirt, and workout shorts announced that he had just come from a treadmill run in one of the ship's three gyms.

Without stopping, he headed straight to the drinking fountain to fill up his water bottle.

Damion took the lead and answered, "The CSO has ordered us to create an airtight force protection plan for Rota. You know, Cas, something like he would have *written himself.*"

"Hah! The CSO wouldn't know force protection if it crawled up his butt with a chainsaw!" Then he added, *"With all due respect,* Ma'am."

Cabrera looked at Damion with a big smile, her head tilted in the same way she had on their "not-date."

"You guys have got a thing with chainsaws and butts," she mused.

Without looking up, Damion responded, "Chainsaws are serious business. No *buts* about it."

The sound of water flying out of QMC's mouth, followed by him trying to clear his throat while coughing, "Okay, you don't *ever* get to make fun of my jokes again." Shaking his head and chuckling, "I'm outta' here. Good luck with that."

They continued to work on the force protection plan, and surprisingly were not disturbed by any more of his fellow "khakis." When everything seemed in order and she was comfortable answering any questions that might come up about their work, she thanked Damion for helping her, then added, "So, what are your plans in Rota?"

Damion noticed that she didn't add "Chief" to her question.

"No plans in particular since this is an unscheduled visit. I might just do like I did in Barcelona. Go for a walk until I find someplace I like, and just chill for a bit."

"Hmm, that sounds nice. Maybe I'll see you out there."

Before he even knew he had said it, he answered, "I hope so."

Crap! Too late now.

Cabrera looked at him and smiled. *That* smile. Then she turned without saying another word and left the room, leaving Damion wishing that the ship's 25,000-pound anchor would fall on his head.

Chapter 4 – Shadows in Rota

The ship would be arriving early in the morning in Rota. So, after a short sea-and-anchor detail, they were back in Spain, tied alongside the pier.

Departmental musters were done and the crew shifted to inport mode. Now came the mandatory port brief.

Damion stood in the back of the cramped compartment, arms folded, posture relaxed, but eyes always working. One foot tapped slowly - a tick only those who knew him well would notice. The mess deck was full, and the sailors packed in as many personnel as possible to limit the number of required port briefings needed for a country they had already visited. Although it was another city, that didn't matter to the crew.

"If you've heard *one* Spanish port brief, then you've heard *all* the Spanish port briefs," joked one of the junior Petty Officers.

Damion had sat through this routine many times before as a junior sailor. A hundred ports, a thousand warnings. The script rarely changed. But Damion wasn't here for the script.

He was here for the players. Particularly, those who were deploying for the first time overseas, and also for the ones who had a track record of finding trouble wherever they went. The Captain had made it very clear that this was a working port, so Damion wasn't anticipating trouble from the crew, but you never know. *Sailors will be sailors.*

Unlike the port brief they received in Barcelona from the local Spanish liaison, today's brief would be conducted by Naval Station Rota Police personnel, since they were on a joint military installation. As he settled into his favorite spot, Damion anticipated that the briefing would be straightforward since it was coming from fellow military members. However, his mind did drift back to the Barcelona briefing conducted by the Spaniards.

The Spanish liaison had stood up front. Lean, professional, in a crisply pressed suit. Spit-shined military shoes, a face that looked like it had been carved from marble, and a mustache that must have been government-issued. His heavily accented English was pronounced and precise, just jagged enough to suggest he'd learned it for serious business, the kind probably done behind mirrored glass or in dark rooms.

"There are locations in Barcelona that are not... friendly," he began, accent sharp and deliberate. "El Raval. You may hear it referred to as the Red-Light District. Drugs. Prostitution. Trafficking. Gangs. Basically, it's a *very* bad place to be in."

He paused.

Damion appreciated the silence. Let the weight hang in the air a second.

"This area is off-limits to your crew. If you are found there, you can expect serious repercussions. Both locally and from your command."

A hand went up in the front row, of course. The voice was too clean, too upbeat, like Opie from the Andy Griffith Show.

"Sir, isn't liberty about trust?"

A collective turn - every seasoned sailor in the room shifted their gaze. Heads pivoting like gun turrets.

Damion didn't need to look. He knew the type. Fresh from A-school, maybe still writing letters home with hearts or emojis on the envelope. Liberty was still a postcard in that kid's head.

Somebody in the back muttered, "There's always one."

Another: "Bet he still calls his rack a bed." This comment garnered laughs around the room.

"Yeah, and his bug-juice, punch," followed by more laughs.

"Okay, knock it off," came an authoritative voice from the other side of the room.

The liaison blinked, uncertain if he'd missed the joke, but kept going. "You are not invisible here. Americans are easily recognized, and military members even more so. You are targets. High-value."

Damion had shifted, his weight rolling from one foot to the other, before he finally opted for the "parade-rest" position that balanced his stance. The Spanish liaison's comments weren't paranoia. They were facts. Threats did not always wear masks or look like the obvious villains in movies. Sometimes they wore perfume or expensive suits. Sometimes they smiled with perfect teeth and asked about your ship's schedule, or what type of weapons it carried. Whether by "honeypots" or "Casanovas", anyone could be a target.

Damion's mind returned to the current briefing, where the base police officer was now discussing embassy numbers, protocol, local customs, and curfews. But somehow, and for some unknown reason, his thoughts then shifted to Cabrera's laugh. Not the loud one, the small hand-covered giggle that only he heard at the café in the courtyard, and also in the CPO mess.

Refocusing on the military police officer finishing up his part of the briefing, Damion suddenly felt as if the room had gotten warmer. A gentle elbow in his side got his attention; Ensign Cabrera had slid in between the other Chiefs and was radiating him with her body heat once again.

"Penny for your thoughts, Chief."

"*Jeez*, Ma'am. What are you, part ninja?"

"It's a requirement to become an ATFP officer. It's on the final exam," she replied matter-of-factly.

"Wouldn't surprise me one bit," he replied.

"So, what faraway place had your attention so tied up just now?"

"I was wondering how much paperwork I am going to have to do if we stay here too long. This is a great crew, but they don't do so well if we are pierside in a foreign port for more than two weeks at a time."

"Well, hopefully the repairs won't take longer than that. I haven't heard anything about them in the wardroom yet."

"Well, the sooner, the better. By the way, was the CSO satisfied with the ATFP plan?"

"I *guess* so. He grunted and said it still needed some work, but he would clean it up because he didn't have time to explain to me all the corrections that needed to be done."

"Oh, okay. That just means that he liked it, will put his name on it, and send it directly to the XO. Looks like our job is done, Ma'am."

She looked at him with an incredulous look on her face, "*Seriously?*"

"Yup. It wouldn't look good on him if a solid plan came *directly* from the ATFP *junior officer*, and the

Chief responsible for training the security force. Don't worry, though. The XO knows the deal."

Cabrera was still staring at him as if he had just slapped her.

He then added, "Think of it this way, now he won't be hounding you for no reason, and you can relax a little the next time you go on liberty."

She stood there with her arms crossed and a faraway look on her face.

"You know, I've never been to Rota before. The town, I mean. Have you?"

"Yeah, more than my fair share of times."

"Cool. Do you know of any place that serves traditional braised oxtails? I heard that the Spanish were good at making them, and I would love to try them out while we are here."

Damion, aware of the packed room of sailors, knew that he had to be careful how he answered her little inquiry. Sailors were serious multitaskers trained to expertly do at least three different jobs on a ship, and although everyone was focusing on the briefing, their eyes and ears were still tuned into everything around them. This is what the military called SA, or situational awareness; a well-developed trait that could warn you of danger, or, with some juicy information, feed the always hungry rumor mill.

"I never would have taken you for someone who likes ox tails, but I think there is a spot on the other side of town. I will check with BMC and get back to you. He loves oxtails, so I'm sure he would know for certain."

"Okay, thanks," she replied, casually.

Finally, the police officers were finishing up their briefing, and the sailors were beginning to file out of the room. Damion saw BMC(SW) Stein and called him over.

"Hey Boats, what's the name of that place that has those oxtails you like so much?"

"*La Mama Casitas,*" he answered with a big grin on his face.

"You plan on heading over there? I'm ready when you are."

"Naw. Miss Cabrera here, was wondering where she could get some."

"Ma'am, you like oxtails? *Respect,*" he replied while nodding his head.

"Yeah. My pappi used to make them for me when I was a little girl in Puerto Rico. For some reason, I felt for them while here in Spain."

Damion wasn't sure if her story was true or if she was just messing with him and sending mixed signals. Either way, he decided that it was time for him to put some distance between himself and this conversation.

"Well, Ma'am," BMC continued, "It wouldn't be a date, but if you need some company finding those oxtails, you just let me know." Followed by a wink and the friendliest, innocent smile possible from a Chief Boatswain's Mate.

"Will do, Chief."

Damion decided that this was his chance.

"Well, there you go Ma'am. You're all set. Now, I had better get back to work. The ship's not going to police itself."

"Roger that, Chief. See you later."

Damion headed toward the watertight door, his mind racing, while Ensign Cabrera stayed to talk with the base police.

"Was she suggesting they meet up later, or was it just his imagination? He knew more than anyone not to assume anything. Men and women could say the exact same words, and have entirely opposite meanings. But she was not just a woman; she was a *sailor*, even if she was an officer.

Damion was lost in thought as he walked down the passageway. As he turned the corner, he walked right into Chief Valentino, who was chewing out one of his quartermasters.

"Sorry, Cas, didn't see you."

"No problem, boss. We are done here."

The young quartermaster raced off as QMC turned to Damion.

"You good, Brother? You look a little troubled."

"Yeah, Cas. I'm good. Just a lot going on."

"I hear you. I've got a lot on my plate, so I'm glad we made this stop. And, I'm definitely hitting the town tonight!"

"Well, just don't give me any extra paperwork to do tomorrow," Damion remarked, with a crooked smile as he continued down the passageway.

The rest of the workday passed without any fanfare. The mundane yet essential rhythm of ship life pulsed all around him. There was an unannounced inport firefighting drill scheduled for 1400, maintenance checks to be completed by COB, and a personnel inspection for the junior sailors on the fantail. Damion had grown so accustomed to this tempo that it was almost a song—familiar, repetitive, but necessary.

When the workday came to a close, and after most of the junior sailors ran off the ship into town, Damion changed into his civilian attire and left the ship.

The sun was beginning to drift lower in the sky, casting a golden hue over the quiet harbor town of Rota. Whitewashed buildings gleamed against the sky, their terra-cotta rooftops a familiar European motif.

Damion walked through the town with a quiet sense of appreciation. Rota wasn't as flashy as Barcelona, but it had its own laid-back charm. Kids played soccer in narrow alleys, their laughter echoing off the old stone walls. Small cafes bustled with locals sipping café con leche, and the occasional American sailor could be seen blending in awkwardly or loudly, depending on the amount of beer already consumed.

He stopped at a small bar near the plaza, drawn in by the live acoustic guitar playing from inside. The place was half full—locals chatting over tapas, a few sailors quietly dinking beers. Damion ordered a drink and took a seat near the window, letting the ambient warmth of the evening wrap around him.

His mind, however, was not so relaxed. It kept drifting back to Ensign Cabrera. Her voice, her words, the way she tilted her head just slightly when she spoke. Was it an invitation? Or simply a professional courtesy extended to a fellow service member?

As the sun sank below the horizon, casting long shadows across the plaza, Damion took a long sip of his drink and made a decision. He wasn't going to overthink it. He would enjoy this liberty, embrace the brief escape from the ship's steel corridors, and let whatever happened next unfold naturally. One thing was certain: this port visit was shaping up to be more than just a routine stop for repairs.

Chapter 5 – The Smuggler's Whisper

A thick, dense fog flowed in just before dawn on the portside edge of the aging Spanish cargo ship, El Perseguidor. The ship rarely left its moorings, but always seemed to have new crates being loaded or offloaded at odd hours. Hidden deep in the cargo hold, well below deck and concealed behind stacks of rusted shipping containers marked with the faded logos of long-gone shipping companies, lay a secret laboratory. Here, worked the Chemist," a man whose real name had been lost in years of false identities, dead-end travel records, and hastily burned documents.

The Chemist was a chemical engineer by training, but necessity, greed, and a multitude of bad life choices had turned him into an innovator of invisible threats. The laboratory was a strange hybrid, somewhere between a scientist's fever dream and a villain's hideout. Unlike the rest of the ship, this section had been transformed into a marvel of black-market engineering and modern scientific ambition.

Beyond a sliding steel door, rigged with biometric locks and a retina scanner salvaged from Eastern European arms dealers, the laboratory gleamed. What had once been a hollowed-out storage hold now resembled a hybrid between a private biotech startup and a clandestine research institute. Bright white light poured from LED ceiling panels. Every surface, from counters to cabinetry, was wrapped in seamless stainless steel, reflecting an obsessive commitment to cleanliness and control.

In the center of the lab, sealed behind sliding glass doors, was a state-of-the-art clean room, positive-pressure, climate-controlled, and maintained at a constant temperature and humidity. A wall of HEPA air filtration units lined the back, humming quietly but relentlessly, ensuring that not a single airborne particle or errant chemical fume could compromise his work. It was the kind of system most universities only dreamed about, installed with cash and no questions asked by a crew that knew how to keep their mouths shut.

Inside the clean room, rows of chemical-resistant lab benches housed an array of equipment. There were high-speed centrifuges, vacuum ovens, and precision balances accurate to a ten-thousandth of a gram. A pair of imported gloveboxes allowed him to handle the most sensitive compounds under a pure nitrogen atmosphere. Beyond that, a bank of analytical instruments: an LC-MS, a GC-MS, an FTIR spectrometer, even a compact scanning electron microscope - each one acquired from the shadowy gray zones between abandoned academic contracts and government surplus auctions.

A series of reinforced storage cabinets, all climate-controlled and electronically monitored, lined the wall. Each contained tightly inventoried vials of rare reagents—phosphorescent lanthanides, engineered polymer precursors, and proprietary cross-linkers - some so new that they hadn't even reached the legal market yet. Every chemical was labeled with industrial names in Cyrillic, Spanish, and English, barcoded, and tracked in a secure, encrypted database that the Chemist coded himself.

No corners were cut here. The Chemist wore a tailored, full-body Tyvek suit and custom-fit nitrile gloves. An intercom system allowed him to give orders or receive updates from the handful of trusted technicians and smugglers who came and went. Transparent whiteboards, flush-mounted on the walls, overflowed with his scrawled formulas, synthesis routes, and notes on test results. Each experiment was logged redundantly, both by voice command and by hand, into a server rack air-gapped from the outside world.

He had been perfecting a line of theoretical chemicals, "signature paints," he called them in his notes. Though in reality, they were a new breed of advanced polymers and gels. His latest obsession was an invisible polymer that could be mixed in both freshwater and saltwater, undetectable to the naked eye, and visible only when viewed through specially tuned optical filters. The science wasn't magic, just clever manipulation of fluorescence and refractive indexes.

First, he would synthesize a set of base polymers—polyacrylates, siloxanes, and polyethylene glycols—each tailored to behave differently depending on the environment. He used cross-linking agents in the presence of selected catalysts to control the viscosity and adhesiveness of the resulting gels. Next, he introduced trace amounts of rare earth elements—europium, terbium, and gadolinium—whose fluorescence could be tuned to respond to custom-designed wavelengths of light emitted by his own modified binoculars and night vision goggles.

Testing was everything. For each completed batch, he would start by simulating vehicle surfaces using plates cut from decommissioned trucks and jeeps, brushing on various mixtures, then subjecting them to cycles of temperature, humidity, and salt fog.

Next came testing in simulated saltwater and freshwater environments, using high-end climate chambers equipped with their own water quality sensors and circulation pumps. After exposure, each batch was analyzed under calibrated electronic viewers. For saltwater durability, he filled large drums with seawater pumped directly from the harbor, submerging test plates that had passed initial tests, for hours or days, then checking for any remaining fluorescent response with his handheld detectors. Any evidence of degradation was mapped, catalogued, and compared with theoretical predictions.

The failed test against the American warship had come as a surprise, but also as a challenge. The signature paint's fluorescence faded much too quickly in the saltwater. It had lit up beautifully for just under an hour, then faded and vanished. It was as if the salt in the seawater attacked the backbone of the polymer, severing its bonds. Or perhaps an ion exchange occurred that destabilized the rare earth complex. The Chemist pored over his notes, running new analyses, dissolving fragments of paint from recovered test plates, and preparing for the next round of adjustments.

He worked in silence, save for the soft hum of the HEPA units and the occasional electronic beep from his instruments. Outside the clean room, a secure refrigerator stored food, and a small cot stood ready for the rare nights he was able to sleep. The walls of the lab concealed additional security measures: sensors to detect even trace amounts of the signature paint, and biometric alarms to prevent theft.

Here, in this black-market sanctuary, the Chemist thrived. Everything gleamed, everything was measured, and every risk was accounted for, except, perhaps, the biggest one: what would happen if he failed? He worked alone most of the time, but always with the nagging feeling that he was being closely watched. The smugglers provided everything he needed: cash, raw chemicals, and protection, but little loyalty. They only cared about results. One of their Spanish contacts, a "liaison" in a naval uniform, was expected later that night for another test - this time with a new formulation that the Chemist hoped would resist saltwater longer. He had adjusted the polymer's hydrophobicity and tweaked the ligand shell on the europium complex, betting that it would endure the brine.

Every beaker, every stain, every whiff of solvent in the air reminded him that his work was both criminal and brilliant. He had dreamed of creating a breakthrough - something the world would remember his name for. But in reality, he knew that no one ever would. Still, as the fluorescent glow flickered on a new test plate beneath his specialized night-vision glasses, the Chemist allowed himself a thin smile. As long as the smugglers paid well, maybe that was enough for now.

Outside, the early morning fog began to lift, but to the Chemist, deep in the bowels of the ship, it was just another day.

Chapter 6 – Forbidden Streets

The late afternoon sun, warm and golden, sat low in the sky, casting long shadows along the cobblestone streets and bouncing glints of light off shop windows and polished railings. A soft breeze carried the occasional murmur of conversations in Spanish, laughter, and the distant cry of seagulls.

Salina Cabrera sat in a cozy corner spot at *La Mama Casitas*, which she had commandeered immediately after a young couple left the cafe. Alone now with her half-finished Estrella Galicia, streams of condensation trickling lazily down the sides of the brown glass bottle.

She absentmindedly traced them with a fingertip as her thoughts went elsewhere.

She had left the ship right after liberty call with the two new ensigns – Stephanie Cheng, a petite cybersecurity specialist from Pittsburgh who appeared to be of Asian-American descent, and Donna Reed, a tall, blond-haired, blue-eyed engineering graduate from Massachusetts. Both women were highly intelligent, easy to talk to, and with just enough awkwardness to remind her of her own early days in uniform. She smiled slightly, remembering their eagerness, their questions about watch rotations, how not to look too lost in combat systems meetings, and what to say when the Captain casually asks your opinion.

After about two hours, her two companions had been called back to the ship. Something about a mandatory briefing from the CSO. Now, she was free to continue exploring on her own.

Rota wasn't big, but its streets were charmingly unpredictable. Narrow alleys suddenly opened into flower-draped courtyards. Stone walls, chipped with age, stood proudly alongside freshly painted storefronts. She passed a bakery where warm loaves still cooled in the window, a scent that pulled her attention despite having no appetite.

A group of local teens kicked a worn soccer ball back and forth near a church plaza. An elderly woman, her gray hair pulled tightly into a bun, offered a gentle "Hola" and a knowing nod as Salina passed. At a small fruit stand, a middle-aged vendor greeted her with a smile, speaking rapidly in Spanish. Salina responded in turn with a smile and a modest "No, gracias," but the man didn't mind. He handed her a ripe fig anyway. When she grudgingly opened her bag, he quickly started waving away her attempt to pay, smiling and saying, *"Bella, bella."* She accepted it with a quiet "Gracias," appreciating the kindness.

She had strolled along the seawall next, watching the small fishing boats bobbing in the harbor. The golden light shimmered across the water, and children chased each other down the sandy beach below, their laughter echoing in the salty air. Her mind wandered as it often did in quiet moments.

Damion.

She hadn't seen him for most of the day, but his voice lingered in her head. Calm, low, and always steady, even when joking. There was something in the way he carried himself - confident, controlled, but never arrogant. The kind of presence that made people straighten up when he entered a room. He reminded her so much of her father, a man of few words and a solid moral compass. And yet, Damion had a sharp, dry humor that caught her off guard more than once and left her grinning like an idiot.

From the very beginning, when he had helped her find her footing after her first rough inspection, to the late-night laughs in his office, the wardroom, or the CPO mess, when both had been up for far too many hours. She tried to rationalize it as professional admiration, but that story was wearing thin in her own mind. Lately, it had been harder to resist the quiet pull. But the consequences were real, and she wasn't naive.

She knew the rules. Officers and enlisted personnel - no fraternization, no matter the rank, no matter the connection - it was off-limits. A personal, intimate relationship could end both of their careers in a heartbeat. She knew it, and she was sure that Damion knew it too. But knowing something and feeling something were often two very different things.

Still, there was *something* there.

She continued to trace the top of the bottle with her finger, her thoughts weaving through a labyrinth of possibilities, all of which unravelled like a thread, while the ocean breeze tousled through her long, dark hair. It was peaceful here - a perfect moment suspended in time.

"Nice spot," a familiar voice said behind her.

Her heart jumped.

She turned slowly, not surprised by the warm, knowing smile that met her eyes.

The quiet hum of the Spanish evening gave the outdoor café a kind of hushed sanctity, broken only by the occasional clink of glassware or a distant laugh from another table. Candlelight flickered lazily in the small glass jars set on each table, creating golden halos that danced on the faces of those seated close. One such candle cast its glow onto the features of Ensign Salina Cabrera, softening the sharp edges of her already striking beauty.

Damion leaned back in his chair for a moment, silently watching her. The light brushed her cheeks like a painter's final stroke on a portrait, her expression unreadable but undeniably captivating. Neither of them had said a word since he sat down, yet their smiles betrayed any attempt to feign surprise. This was no accident. Not even close. Cabrera traced the rim of her beer bottle with one finger, her body relaxed but eyes locked on his, testing him.

After what felt like a full minute had passed, she tilted her head slightly and spoke.

"Are you just going to sit there all googly-eyed, or are you going to get yourself a drink?"

Damion chuckled, leaning forward on his elbows, "It's been a long time since I had a reason to look *googly-eyed* at anyone."

Her eyebrow arched, but her smile softened, "You do realize that if someone sees us like this, it might actually look like a date?"

He met her gaze squarely. "You want me to leave?"

She didn't blink. "I think you already know the answer to that."

The small talk came easily. They leaned closer as the night grew darker, exchanging jokes and stories in quiet tones meant only for each other. The rest of the café melted into the background. Damion didn't know how long they'd been talking that way when a familiar, tightening chill crept into his chest. Something wasn't right.

He didn't move, didn't flinch. Just slowly swept his eyes around the surrounding tables without turning his head. No one seemed to notice them; there were no staring patrons, no obviously strange behaviors. Then he saw them.

A pair of eyes, distant and cold, stared directly at them. Lieutenant Bartholomew Baker, the ship's Combat Systems Officer. Approximately 100 yards out and closing slowly, flanked by the two fresh-faced Ensigns.

Damion slowly leaned back in his chair with the same smile still painted on his face. "Salina," he said evenly.

Her lips curled. "Yes?"

"Remember when we agreed that this could *possibly* look like a date if someone saw us?"

"Yes," she said, wariness creeping in.

"Well, it's time to put on your ATFP face. Don't react to what I'm about to say."

Nodding slightly, she sat up straighter, her training kicking in.

"The CSO is seventy-five yards out and heading straight for us. Now, he might just walk past. But more than likely, he'll stop and try to make a scene."

All of the color drained from Cabrera's face. Damion could see her knuckles turn white as she held the beer bottle tighter.

"Follow my lead," he said calmly. "Relax. Everything will be fine."

She gave a barely perceptible nod.

Damion launched into a fabricated story about onboard life - urinalysis percentages and sleep-deprived watch rotations - as if they were the most critical discussions of the night. Cabrera nodded at the correct intervals, forcing a neutral face.

Then came the interruption.

"*Ahem,*" a voice grumbled from behind Cabrera.

She jumped. Damion's eyes locked onto the CSO now looming above them like an angry storm cloud.

"Evening, CSO," Damion offered casually.

The CSO scowled. "Chief. *Ensign Cabrera.* What's going on here?"

"What do you mean, sir?" Damion asked, feigning confusion.

The CSO stepped closer. "I *mean,* an *Ensign* and a Chief sitting alone in a romantic little café drinking beer. *Someone* might think that you two are on a date," he answered, emphasizing every word.

Cabrera looked seconds from passing out.

Before either of them could respond, a loud voice boomed from behind the newly arrived group.

"You mean the *three of us,* don't you, sir? You know I can't let MAC go out on his own. You never know *what* kind of trouble he might get himself into."

The CSO, startled, turned to look directly into the grinning face of QMC(SW)Alvin *"Casanova"* Valentino, holding two cold beer bottles.

Cabrera blinked in disbelief. Damion blinked in salvation.

Brushing past the Combat Systems Officer, QMC *Casanova* looked directly at Damion while placing one of the beer bottles on the table.

"Here you go, Brother. Sorry, they didn't have that *toilet water* you usually drink, but this Estrella Galicia? Primo stuff."

He then turned to the CSO while smoothly taking the seat next to Salina.

"Anyway, Miss Cabrera here was telling us about how her Pops used to grill oxtails down there in Puerto Rico. He made his own sweet & sour sauce and everything." QMC added, the smile never leaving his face.

"Grilled oxtails?" came a shocked voice from Donna Reed, an engineering officer.

Still grinning, Chief Valentino continued, "Yeah, sounds pretty good, right?" Then added, "Hey, CSO, you and the newbies are welcome to join us. Make it a double date, or a triple date. I don't know. What do they call six sailors who hang out together and have a few beers?"

"They call them shipmates," Damion answered dryly.

The CSO frowned, clearly outmaneuvered.

"No thanks, *Chief.* We have another engagement to attend." And with that, he turned to leave, grudgingly followed by the two Ensigns, who waved goodbye, but looked as if they would rather have stayed at the café.

Not missing a beat, QMC Valentino spoke in a voice loud enough for the departing group to hear as they walked away, "Okay, Ma'am, why don't you finish telling us about your Pops and those oxtails!"

As they watched the group fade out of sight down the cobblestone street, Damion looked at Chief Valentino, who was silently staring in the opposite direction.

"*Thanks*, Cas. We owe you one."

"*You* owe me two. That beer wasn't free," he answered with a gentler smile.

He then stood and added, "You know I got your back, Brother. Just stay out of the CSO's target hairs, and don't get caught out here playing footsies, okay?"

Damion slowly nodded while lifting his beer towards the QMC in a mock toast.

Chief Valentino started walking away, but suddenly stopped. He slowly turned halfway around and looked over his shoulder at Damion.

"Hey, DJ, do us both a favor. Try and *stay out* of the Red-Light District, okay?"

Damion looked at him thoughtfully, then watched as he too faded away down the cobblestone streets.

Salina had been silent the entire time, not even daring to breathe. After Chief Valentino had left, she let out a long, loud sigh.

"Wow. I thought for sure we were royally screwed. If QMC hadn't shown up, it could have been *our* oxtails on the CO's grill!" she remarked jokingly.

Damion didn't answer, but sat silently and stared at the cold bottle in his hand. The chill, a subtle reminder of how dangerously close they had come to getting caught.

Cabrera was saying something, which snapped him out of his thoughts.

"What was QMC talking about when he said for you to stay out of the Red-Light District? I don't remember the port briefing saying anything about an RLD in Rota, only in Barcelona."

Damion thought for a few moments before answering, "Oh, there is *definitely* a Red-Light District in Rota now," he replied, taking a long sip of the cold beer and staring her straight in the eyes.

Cabrera looked at him curiously, not understanding what he meant. Her eyes then suddenly widened, and she sank back in the now uncomfortable chair as the realization set in.

"Oh, I understand," she whispered to herself in a low voice. *"I'm* the Red-Light District."

Chapter 7 – The Oath and the Flame

Damion woke early the next morning after a long, restless night. Returning to the ship after last night's near-miss with the CSO, he had tried his best to get some sleep, but every time he nodded off, her face, her eyes, her lips were there. Even her laugh echoed in his head without being invited in.

It was just past 04:30, a half-hour earlier than his normal time to get up, but Damion figured that he wasn't going to get any sleep anyway, so he might as well hop to it and get a jump on his day.

Sunrise was supposed to be around 05:30, and today he had planned to add two extra miles to his regular three-mile run. As the clock slowly ticked by, he prepared his running gear while waiting for some hint of light to appear in the early morning hours. Finally, Damion figured that he'd waited long enough and decided to head out and stretch on the pier before his run.

When he arrived on the quarterdeck, BMC(SW)Mike Stein was standing the watch as Officer of the Deck (OOD). His deep Texas drawl greeted Damion with a smile and a wink.

"Morning, DJ. You hangin' out with the Wardroom, huh? What are you guys, a couple now?"

Damion stood silent as the big Texan laughed and looked towards the pier.

"Are you *seriously* going to run with that numbnuts?"

Turning and looking down from the ship, Damion saw the CSO, the two new ensigns, and Salina Cabrera.

Damion let out a silent sigh of relief, realizing his little brush with Navy regulations had not made it back to the CPO Mess.

"Dude, the last thing I ever want is to be seen hanging out in public with that putz."

"I don't know D. He *does* keep good company," the BMC added, sarcastically. Obviously referring to the two new and attractive young Ensigns.

"Forced adulation and participation is my guess," countered Damion, followed by a grunt of agreement from the BMC.

As he headed down to the pier, he was greeted by what appeared to be a well-rested Salina Cabrera.

"Good morning, Chief."

"Good morning, Ma'am. CSO. Ensigns," he replied.

"*Good morning*, Chief," the two fresh-faced ensigns chimed in together, warm smiles on both faces.

The CSO simply replied, "Chief."

"You all heading out for a group run?"

"*I* am giving our two new *officers* a morning tour of Rota. Ensign Cabrera won't be joining us," the CSO stated, matter-of-factly.

"Well, Ma'am. I'm going to do my five miles today. You are welcome to tag along, if you think you can keep up."

"Oh, is that a *challenge*, Chief?"

"No, Ma'am. I would never want to embarrass my ATFP Officer in front of the newbies. You know, having to carry you back, and all," he added jokingly.

"Okay, then. *Challenge accepted.*"

The CSO looked on in irritation while the two ensigns watched the playful banter with big smiles on their faces.

After finishing their warm-up stretches, the two groups jogged off in separate directions.

The morning air was cool, not cold, with the kind of crispness that wrapped itself around your skin like a soft cotton sheet, fresh out of the dryer. A pale orange light stretched low across the base's perimeter road, casting long shadows that shifted gently with the movement of the trees lining the sidewalk.

They exited the gate onto Avenida de las Provincias Unidas. It was still quiet - no traffic, no buzz of scooters or chatter from town-goers. Just them, the sound of their breath, and the pulse of rubber soles against concrete. At the half-mile mark, the paved route curved slightly and led them through a stretch of coastal pine woodland still within the base's boundary. The pine needles overhead filtered the golden morning light like a lazy kaleidoscope. Dunes rose gently on their left, patches of sand smooth and undisturbed. Occasionally, the subtle rustle of branches would give away a tiny native chameleon, inching its way across the path or curling on a pine limb.

Just over a mile from the base, they crossed the main coastal road. The shift was immediate, from wooded stillness to open ocean breeze. The sea air greeted them like a familiar friend—sharp, salty, and full of stories. Cádiz Bay stretched out before them, shimmering with the promise of another warm day. The town's seafront promenade felt different underfoot—older stone, worn smooth by time and morning walkers.

"Smells like the sea and tostadas," Cabrera said, her voice even, as if her lungs weren't doing anything more than idle breathing.

Damion gave a thumbs-up.

They passed a row of beachfront cafés, still quiet but waking up, metal shutters sliding open, chairs being unstacked, the first hiss of espresso machines audible from inside.

Fishermen, already active, stood near their boats in the sand. Some were tying off lines; others rinsed down gear, chatting in that lyrical Spanish that rolled like surf.

Maintaining a steady pace, the promenade began to rise gently, lifting them to the base of the Faro de Rota. The lighthouse stood white and red, a sentinel of the Atlantic since 1910. Its paint gleamed in the light of the newly risen sun. The ramparts below were weathered, thick with stories, and the smell of sea spray hung in the air like an old song. The lighthouse cast a long shadow over the stone ramparts as the first full brushstroke of sunlight lit the Atlantic.

When they reached the turnaround point, about two and a half miles from the base, Damion and Cabrera stopped and stood side by side, hands on hips; their jog slowed to a thoughtful halt. Neither spoke for a long while; the only sound between them was the whisper of a gentle wind rolling in from the sea and the faint call of seagulls overhead.

The Atlantic Ocean was calm, but not completely still. Soft waves folded onto themselves. The sky above it was the kind of clear blue that only appeared first thing in the morning, and right before the heat of the day burned the moisture from the air.

Cabrera's eyes remained fixed on the water, watching the early glimmer of the day shimmer across Cádiz Bay. "You know," she started slowly, voice soft, "if the CSO and Valentino hadn't walked up last night…" She let the rest of the sentence hang like fog between them.

Damion didn't respond right away. He followed the arc of a small fishing boat moving across the horizon, then exhaled sharply through his nose. "Yeah. I know."

Cabrera turned to face him slightly, her expression open but guarded. "I kept thinking about it all night. After we left the café. Couldn't sleep."

He gave her a sidelong glance. "You too?"

She nodded, eyes returning to the sea. "There was just... something about that moment. Something that almost—" she hesitated, "...felt inevitable."

Damion chuckled under his breath, not out of humor, but to release the weight he'd been carrying since the night before. "I replayed it a hundred times in my head. The way you looked at me. What I was about to say. What I might've done if we hadn't been interrupted."

"The what ifs," she whispered. "They're brutal, aren't they?"

He gave a slow nod. "Worse than any midwatch or XO inspection I've ever had."

Another long silence stretched between them, but this time it wasn't awkward. It was shared, understood. They stood there, each lost in the same complex memories, the same missed possibilities.

Finally, Cabrera broke the silence, her voice barely louder than the breeze. "Wow… this *really* sucks. What are we going to do, now?"

Damion didn't look at her. Instead, he squinted into the sunlight and shook his head. "I have no idea." Then, with a bit of humor in his voice, he added, "Maybe we should just make out and get it over with."

She smiled faintly, the corner of her mouth curling up as she whispered, "I wish."

Their eyes met then, and neither looked away.

The moment felt timeless. Her hands, soft and sure, rested gently inside his as their eyes locked in silent conversation. Slowly, they leaned closer, pulled by a magnetic tension that had been building quietly between them for what seemed like an eternity. Inches apart now, they could feel the warmth of each other's breath, the space between them charged with anticipation.

Just as everything went silent and the world seemed to vanish around them, a piercing shriek shattered their intimate embrace, like a mirror smashed against a cement floor. A low-flying seagull streaked overhead, its wings slicing through the calm like a jet breaking the sound barrier.

Startled, they jerked their heads upward, eyes wide, watching the feathered intruder disappear into the morning sky. For a moment, both stood frozen in bewildered silence… then, as if on cue, erupted into laughter that echoed down the otherwise quiet path.

After catching their breath and regaining composure, they exchanged amused glances. No words needed. With another silent agreement and one last look toward the sky, they turned back the way they came, deciding it best to head out before another airborne surprise - or an unexpected pack of joggers - ruined the moment again.

The first mile jogging back to the ship was spent in silence as Damion and Salina maintained a slower pace. Each deep in thought, both worrisome and humorous. They had been alone at the lighthouse, no one within eyesight, just the two of them. The eye contact they had shared was a silent agreement to what would happen between them in the next thirty seconds.

Or so he had thought. Glancing over at Cabrera, he wondered if she was thinking the same thing that he was.

Another missed opportunity.

Damion and Cabrera continued their run back to the base, making small talk along the way. Nothing of note, just pointing out some of the sites they had passed previously. The early morning sun was rising fast, casting long shadows across the cobblestone streets of Rota, but the breeze rolling in off the nearby Bay of Cadiz kept the heat at bay, for now. They were making good time, falling into a steady rhythm, their steps syncing up naturally. Cabrera had a lightness to her stride, and Damion noted with some amusement how she managed to look graceful even when jogging.

As they turned a corner to enter the woodland path about a mile from the base, the terrain changed underfoot. The pavement gave way to dirt, gravel, and the occasional jutting root. The canopy of pine and eucalyptus trees filtered the sunlight, making it look like a flickering strobe of gold and green on the forest floor. Birds chirped overhead, and the distant sound of waves crashing on the coast had an oddly calming effect in the woods.

Then it happened.

A sudden crunch of shifting stone and a short yelp. Damion turned sharply just in time to see Cabrera tumble forward, her foot having landed awkwardly on a loose rock. She landed hard on one knee and caught herself with an outstretched arm, but not before her elbow made sharp contact with the ground.

"Salina!" Damion rushed over and knelt beside her. She winced but didn't cry out again. Her knee was already reddening, a small scrape forming, and her elbow had a nasty little gash that would probably swell up before long.

"I'm fine," she muttered, trying to sit up. But when she shifted her weight to stand, she winced again and reached for her ankle. That was not good. Her foot was already starting to swell.

"Nope, you're not walking on that," Damion said firmly. He then gently scooped her up to avoid putting any weight on the injured foot, and with both of her arms around his neck, he carried her to a weathered wooden bench tucked behind a small cluster of trees.

"Let's sit here," he said, lowering her onto the bench.

Cabrera didn't argue. Damion knelt in front of her and gently lifted her foot, placing it on his thigh. He loosened her shoe, then carefully peeled it off. Her ankle was already puffing up.

"Looks like a sprain," he said, more to himself than to her. He looked up, meeting her eyes. "I've seen worse, but you're not running on this."

She gave a soft laugh that was more breath than sound. "Guess I won't be beating your 5-mile time today."

Damion smirked and shook his head. "Guess not. But at least you still get points for style."

The woods around them seemed to pause for a moment, the sounds quieting just enough for the silence to stretch between them. Damion shifted, pulling a small, neatly folded cloth from his pocket—

a habit picked up from years at sea. He dabbed lightly at the blood on her elbow.

"We'll wait a bit," he said, not looking up this time. "Then I'll carry you back if I have to."

Cabrera leaned back slightly, watching him work. "You always this prepared, Chief?"

He gave a quiet chuckle. "Always."

Then, with a serious look on her face, she continued, "If I didn't know any better, I would think you planned this. Me, falling and getting injured. You, coming to my rescue. *Taking advantage of me while my emotions are down*. Isn't that what sailors do?"

"Actually," he replied without looking up, "that's what Army pukes do. Sailors are kind of like pirates – we just *take* what we want."

"Is that so?"

"Yep. And by the way, just to clarify...*your emotions are down*?"

"Could be," she answered wistfully.

As Damion finished wiping the blood from her elbow, and was placing the cloth back in his pocket, Cabrera lightly touched him on the shoulder.

"Do you mind looking at the back of my neck? I think I may have pulled something back there when I went down. Something just doesn't feel right."

"Sure, let me check."

Damion rose slowly from his kneeling position in front of Cabrera, his fingers brushing lightly against her ankle as he stood. A flicker of concern still lingered in his eyes as he leaned in slightly to get a better look at the back of her neck, where a strand of hair had stuck to her skin from sweat and the fall. Just as his head moved past hers, Cabrera turned unexpectedly, her face so close that Damion could feel the warmth of her breath.

Without a word, she leaned in further and pressed her lips against his - soft at first, then deepening with a sudden intensity that caught him completely off guard.

Their kiss burned with a quiet urgency, and when their lips gradually pulled away, a shared breath lingered in the stillness between them. With her hand lightly touching the side of his face, she quietly whispered in an unapologetic voice, *"This is me taking what I want."*

For the briefest of moments, his mind raced to catch up, stunned by the boldness and unexpectedness of the moment. But instinct and emotion overtook hesitation, and he responded in kind, wrapping one arm around her back and returning the kiss with equal fervor.

Time disappeared. The sounds of the woodland around them - birds chirping, leaves rustling in the breeze - faded into silence. There was no Navy, no mission, no crowd-filled courtyards. Just the two of them, suspended in a moment that felt both impossible and inevitable.

Neither of them could say how long the kiss lasted. Maybe seconds. Maybe hours. But when they finally pulled apart, breathless, their foreheads resting gently together, it felt like something had quietly shifted between them. Something neither of them was ready to name - yet neither could deny.

And in the soft light of the coming day, the two sat on that hidden bench just out of sight, wrapped in a moment that felt suspended in time - caught somewhere between the weight of duty and the pull of something less defined, but just as powerful.

Chapter 8 – Caught Between Duty and Desire

It was quiet beneath the protective canopy of the woodland trees, a hidden alcove of calm where the sunlight filtered in golden strands through the shifting leaves. The hush of the breeze rustling above them sounded like whispers, intimate and ancient. Somewhere in the trees above, birds carried on a soft conversation, adding to the slow rhythm of a moment that neither of them wanted to end.

They sat on the weathered wooden bench, the grain of it cool from the mottled shade. The forest floor was carpeted with a blend of pine needles and fallen leaves. Damion cradled Salina gently, her head nestled perfectly against the curve of his shoulder, her legs stretched effortlessly across his lap. One of his arms supported her while the other tenderly combed his fingers through the thick strands of her hair. His lips brushed her forehead, her temple, the tip of her nose - each kiss slower and more deliberate than the last.

Salina let out a soft hum of contentment, her eyes fluttering closed, her breath syncing with the steady rise and fall of his chest. A smile played at the corners of her lips, part amusement, part wonder - how had they stolen this moment, this little rebellion against duty and time? Every now and then, she tilted her face upward to meet his eyes and kissed him, soft and unhurried, with the quiet confidence of someone who knew this kind of peace was rare.

The world seemed to pause around them, holding its breath.

Eventually, Damion exhaled deeply, his hand slowing in her hair. "We're gonna be in trouble," he murmured, though his voice held no real urgency. "They're probably already checking the shore log for us."

Salina didn't move. She just smiled against his shoulder, nuzzling closer.

"It's only about a mile from the main gate of the naval station," he added, brushing a kiss just beneath her eye. "I can carry you the rest of the way. The gate guard should be able to call you a ride to the hospital. It makes no sense to go all the way back just to have Doc send you there anyway. Plus, we would never hear the end of it if everyone saw me carrying you back like a wounded bird."

She nodded against him, her voice barely more than a whisper. "Okay. Just... one more kiss."

And Damion gave it to her. A slow, deep kiss that made the forest around them blur into nothing. Then, with the care of someone handling something irreplaceable, he shifted her weight and stood. She curled her arms around his neck as he hoisted her onto his back. Her legs looped over his sides, her cheek resting between his shoulder blades. He adjusted his grip, steady and sure, and began the walk through the woods, back toward duty, consequences, and reality - but still carrying the memory of what they'd shared in the trees, as forbidden and perfect as it was fleeting.

Reaching the naval station's main gate, Damion didn't slow his pace. With Salina still on his back, he handed their ID cards to the young enlisted gate guard, who blinked once, did a double-take, and quickly masked his surprise with the kind of neutral expression that only the most disciplined E-3s could pull off. Still, Damion caught the faint trace of amusement twitching at the corner of the kid's mouth - after all, it wasn't every day you saw a Navy Chief carrying a Navy Officer piggyback-style.

The guard said nothing, as expected, but moved with crisp efficiency, radioing for a nearby security unit to transport Ensign Cabrera to the base hospital. Within minutes, a white-and-blue patrol vehicle pulled up to the curb. Salina was transferred gently into the backseat with the help of a Hospital Corpsman, the Navy's version of a certified nursing assistant. Her eyes found Damion's one last time before the car door closed. No words - just a look. He gave her a nod, then turned and took off at a jog.

By the time he reached the ship, the sun was quickly rising and removing any lingering shadows from the pier. As Damion climbed the brow, his sneakers had barely touched the non-skid before the Combat

Systems Officer stepped out onto the quarterdeck like a predator waiting at the edge of a kill zone. Arms crossed, jaw clenched, the CSO wore the expression of someone who'd been denied an easy target for far too long.

"Where is *Ensign Cabrera*?" he asked, his voice low but edged with authority.

"Hospital, sir," Damion answered evenly, standing tall. "She injured her foot during our run. Base police are transporting her now."

The CSO's eyes narrowed. "*Injured*?"

"Yes, sir," Damion continued. "She stepped on a loose stone and twisted her foot. Took a fall. Got a couple of nasty bruises, too. Nothing that looked too serious, though."

The CSO stared at him as if he were trying to ascertain whether Damion's story was true or if he was just attempting to cover for the missing Ensign Cabrera. There was a pause, brief, but just long enough for the tension to settle in.

The CSO grunted, gave a slow nod that could've meant anything, then turned without another word and disappeared back inside the skin of the ship, leaving Damion alone on the quarterdeck with only the echo of his own breath and the lingering trace of adrenaline still coursing through his veins from the woodland bench.

Damion decided to wait a minute to put some distance between himself and the CSO, and before leaving, he cast a quick glance across the open space at BMC(SW) Stein. The big Texan, always good for a laugh, subtly lifted one hand and gave the classic "L" for loser sign with a smirk, tipping his head in the direction the CSO had just stormed off. Damion couldn't help but chuckle under his breath, then turned and made his way inside the ship.

He hadn't made it to "Khaki Call" that morning, the daily pow-wow where officers and Chiefs were briefed on the day's agenda, updates, and other need-to-know information. That meant that before he could even think about grabbing a hot shower or changing into a clean uniform, he needed to check in with the ship's senior enlisted person, the Command Master Chief, or CMC.

Opening the anchor-crested door marking the entrance to the Chief Petty Officers' Mess, he was greeted by the familiar sounds of percolating coffee, the occasional laugh, and low-pitched conversations that only seasoned Chiefs could carry. The room buzzed with life, but before he could take another step, a thunderous voice bellowed from the back corner, "DJ, nice of you to finally join us."

There sat CMC(SW/AW) Beulah "Bucky" Buchanan. B.B. to the Chiefs – Master Chief to everyone else, gripping her old ceramic coffee mug like a royal scepter. A proud daughter of the Tennessee

Appalachians, B.B. always reminded Damion of one of those classical mountain women who hunted bears and taught her sons how to shave with a Bowie knife. Her face was weathered, her drawl unmistakable, and her presence filled a room like a shot of moonshine.

"Sorry I'm late, B.B.," Damion began, walking closer. "The ATFP Officer and I were out for a morning run. On the way back, she hit some loose gravel and went down hard. Twisted her foot pretty badly."

The CMC's eyes narrowed with concern, the mug pausing just short of her lips. "She okay?"

"Yeah, she's banged up a bit, a couple of bruises, but nothing too serious. I helped her back to the main gate. Base police transported her to the hospital from there. That's what held me up."

BB nodded, taking a long sip from her mug. "Alright then, go get yourself cleaned up."

As Damion headed toward the exit, a sly voice to his left slipped into the space like a knife between the ribs. *"Aww, did you break your little Ensign?"*

He turned slightly and locked eyes with EWC(SW) Sylvia Beechum, her piercing emerald stare framed by a smirk that could cut steel. Sylvia was the ship's electronic warfare guru, as tough as they came, and carried a known distaste for officers like some people carried allergies.

"Maybe you should have kissed her little boo-boo. *Make her feel better,*" she added, not even trying to hide her sarcasm.

Damion didn't bite. He returned her gaze with a straight face and replied, "Maybe I should have, Sylvia."

Without waiting for her comeback, he pushed the door open and stepped out into the corridor.

After taking a quick shower and returning to the now-empty Chief's mess, Damion grabbed an energy drink and returned to his office, where he snagged two meal bars from the "private stash" in his desk drawer.

His thoughts immediately shifted to Salina and how she was doing. Under the hidden canopy of trees, passions were set loose and unspoken secrets revealed. He desperately fought the urge to contact the hospital or the ship's Chief Hospital Corpsman for an update on her condition. Behaving like a frantic lover would not bode well for either of them. Besides, he already knew that she only had a sprained ankle and a few bruises. Salina had firmly insisted that he feel every part of her body for broken bones or anything that seemed out of place. *Just to be sure.*

After another minute or two of reminiscing, Damion snapped out of his daydream and focused on getting his work done.

The workday passed slowly, and when liberty call began for the crew, Damion decided to remain onboard, just in case he received a message from Salina.

None came.

The next morning, the officers and Chiefs gathered for Khaki Call. The Executive Officer discussed various information, including changes to the ship's schedule, the status of the engineering repairs, when they expected to be underway at sea again, and the only other information Damion was particularly interested in…Salina Cabrera.

The XO began, "As you all know, Ensign Cabrera injured her foot during morning PT (physical training) yesterday. The doctor at Rota hospital informed me that she has sustained a Grade II sprain - a partial ligament tear with swelling, bruising, moderate pain, and some joint instability, making weight-bearing difficult but not impossible. Recovery typically takes 3 to 6 weeks and will require her resting, possible immobilization, and physical therapy; rushing back too soon could lead to chronic issues or re-injury. With that said, Ensign Cabrera will *not* be joining us for the remainder of our MIO tasking. Her inability to maneuver safely throughout the ship while at sea would hinder her recovery and possibly cause additional injuries. Chief Jackson?"

"Sir?" Damion replied vigorously.

The XO continued, "The Captain has full confidence in your ability to lead the ATFP teams, so you will be taking point for the remainder of the MIO."

"Aye, Sir."

Damion felt as if a black hole had opened up in his stomach, and his body was being sucked through to some unknown dimension. Not because he was being put in charge of the ATFP teams - he was already leading them. The sinking feeling was due to the thought of not seeing Salina for the weeks that the ship would be out to sea.

Before they became intimate, Damion had already been impressed by her ability to quickly grasp hold of combat tactics, firearms proficiency, and her natural intelligence. When she first checked onboard the ship, Salina had been quickly assigned as the ATFP Division Officer, only because the CSO, who was also the Senior Watch Officer, wanted commissioned officers in charge of every facet of operational control. Damion was later thankful that his initial thoughts, as well as those of the CSO, he imagined, of her not being capable of doing the job, proved to be incorrect. And now that the Captain was putting Damion in command of the ATFP teams, if only temporarily, was sure to raise some additional hairs on the CSO's neck.

A win-win all around.

The XO finished up and dismissed everyone to go and relay the plan of the day to their respective divisions. When Damion turned to leave, the XO called him over.

"Chief, I need you to do me a favor. I know you got your hands full today, but can you take some documents over to the hospital to Ensign Cabrera?"

Damion's heart jumped up in his throat.

"I need her to finalize the recommendations she was submitting for the ATFP team operations."

"No problem, Sir. I'll head over there right after division quarters."

Damion then headed towards the flight deck to meet his division, but the only thoughts in his head were of Salina's voice and her smiling face.

Chapter 9 – Secrets Behind Closed Doors

The morning light slipped through the narrow window blinds in Room 214 of the Rota Naval Station Hospital. As the soft light cast angled shadows across the polished floor and the edge of the bed, Salina Cabrera blinked twice before fully waking, her dark lashes brushing against the pillow as she took in her surroundings. The room was clean and sterile, yet not cold. The walls, painted in a bright off-white, were lined with standard-issue hospital decor. A generic painting of a beach with a calm sea, a dull, gray cabinet for personal belongings, and a mounted flat-screen monitor still showing her name and patient status.

Her left foot, wrapped tightly in a beige bandage and propped up with crisp white pillows, rested in a padded elevation brace attached to the bed. The ache was still there, dull but manageable. Her left elbow and knee had also been wrapped in sterile bandages. Cabrera slowly adjusted her position, careful not to jostle her ankle, and let out a soft sigh. The sheets smelled faintly of fresh detergent and antiseptic, which surprised her as being strangely comforting.

She looked around, listening to the quiet hum of the ventilation system and the distant shuffle of footsteps outside. The staff, both Navy and civilian medical personnel, had been surprisingly kind. Not the rushed, short-patience kind of nice she had come to expect from some duty stations, but genuinely attentive. The nurse who brought her in had spoken to her like an old friend, and the corpsman had made sure she was settled comfortably before stepping out to get her a warm compress.

A soft knock on the door preceded the arrival of a breakfast tray. Scrambled eggs, two sausage links, a cup of fresh fruit, and a blueberry muffin - all sitting neatly on a plastic tray with a steaming cup of coffee. She smirked. Compared to the powdered eggs and reheated hash browns from the ship's galley, this felt like five-star dining. She took a small bite of the muffin, letting the sweetness briefly distract her from the thoughts pushing forward in her head.

Damion.

Her fingers tightened slightly around the coffee mug. She remembered every detail of the day before with unsettling clarity. The way he had touched her ankle, his calloused hands moving with a gentleness that contradicted his size and strength. The way he had looked at her, worry laced behind those hard-set eyes.

And then there was that moment - that pause in time where everything became real for both of them. It had seemed like an eternity that passed too quickly. Then, literally like her knight in shining armor, he had carried her to the base *on his back*. Cabrera remembered how safe she had felt as she wrapped her arms around his broad shoulders, her body pressed to his, feeling each shift of muscle beneath his sweat-soaked shirt as he carried her through the streets. The rhythm of his breath, the quiet grunts as he adjusted her weight, the scent of his sweat mixed with hers – forever burned into her memory.

She remembered wanting to kiss him one last time. Desperately. Just once more before the base police took over and helped her into the waiting vehicle. But there hadn't been a chance. Just a look, held for a second too long, filled with all the things they couldn't dare say out loud.

Now, lying alone in this quiet hospital room, Cabrera stared at the ceiling, her foot propped in place, but with a slight smile on her face. Her mind played back the scenes like a favorite movie until another soft knock at the door snapped her back to reality.

""Buenos días, mi rayito de sol."

Her heart skipped a beat as the smile on her face widened.

Damion.

"Good morning," came the soft, cheerful reply. "This is a nice surprise first thing in the morning." Then, with concern on her face, she lowered her voice, "Does anyone know you are here?"

Damion smiled, "Actually, it was the XO who asked me to come here and give you some paperwork. I guess he didn't want you to think that you were on leave. Plus, it saved me the trouble of figuring out how to come see you without it looking suspicious."

Damion picked up a chair sitting next to the entrance and placed it on the opposite side of the bed, facing the door. Cabrera looked at him curiously.

"This way, I have a clear view if someone starts coming down the corridor. A little early warning for me to let go of your hand."

"Oh," she replied, smiling and glancing down the hall. Seeing no one there, she let her right hand casually slide off the side of the bed as Damion gently caught it.

For a moment, they just looked at each other. Not a word was said, but everything was spoken in the silence between them. Then, as if on cue, they both spoke at the same time.

"I've been thinking about you since yesterday," they said in unison.

They both laughed softly, and Cabrera gave his hand a little squeeze. "You first," she said.

Damion shook his head with a grin. "Ladies first. Plus, you outrank me."

Cabrera rolled her eyes. "Fine. I just... I don't know. Yesterday felt good. *Too good.*" She paused, then continued, "This is a little embarrassing, but afterwards, I couldn't stop replaying everything in my head. You, checking me for any *extra injuries,* carrying me, even the way you were like, all protective over me after I fell."

Sitting up a little straighter and puffing his chest, "You *do* know that one of the main duties of a Chief is to take care of his J.O., right?" he replied.

She chuckled. "So I've heard. Well, you certainly took *good care* of me."

They continued talking about everything and nothing. Damion gently caressed her hand, running his thumb in slow circles over her skin. Cabrera talked about the hospital food, the kind nurse who smuggled in a decent coffee, and how the night-shift Hospital Corpsman brought her a stack of magazines from their lunchroom.

Their conversation was interrupted by three knocks before the door slowly opened, and in stepped a young Hospital Corpsman Third Class. She had soft features, blond hair, bright hazel eyes, and a confidence in her step that suggested she was used to taking control of situations. She glanced at Cabrera, then her gaze landed on Damion, who was now sitting with his hands folded on his lap. A smile flickered across her lips—more than just courteous. There was a brief flicker of interest.

"Chief," she said sweetly, giving a nod that was just shy of a playful wink.

"HM3," Damion replied, neutral and professional, but with just the tiniest hint of amusement in his voice.

She apologized for the intrusion, quickly checked Cabrera's chart and the elevation brace, then left with one final glance at the Chief.

As the door shut, Cabrera arched an eyebrow. "Well, well. Should I be worried about the competition? I don't think I can compete with regulation-length ponytails and freshly ironed scrubs."

Damion laughed. "Please. You've got nothing to worry about. Besides, I'm pretty sure her type is more... flex-and-flirt. I'm more boots-and-busted-knuckles."

They talked shop for a bit. Damion brought her up to speed on the ship's status, repairs, and the updated underway schedule. He handed her the slim folder marked ATFP.

She opened the folder, and the two of them reviewed every detail together. Their heads nearly touched as they leaned in. Occasionally, their hands would brush or their fingers would overlap. Each contact lingered just a second longer than needed.

Approximately fifteen minutes later, the door opened again. Same HM3. This time, she looked straight at Damion and smiled a bit wider. He returned the smile.

The Corpsman blushed, then quickly mumbled something about checking vitals before darting back out.

Cabrera waited two beats, then smacked Damion lightly on the leg. "You did that on purpose."

"Did what?" he asked innocently.

"You know what," she replied, trying not to laugh.

They sat in silence for a bit, content with the presence of one another, their hands gently touching. Eventually, Damion sighed.

"I had better get back to the ship. The XO might start wondering if I fell into a manhole."

He stood, lightly taking her hand. He looked down the hall—his security reflex still active. A nurse stood at the end, back turned, clipboard in hand.

Damion bent down slowly, eyes still on the hallway, and brought Cabrera's hand to his lips. He kissed it gently, just above her knuckles, lingering just long enough for her to feel the warmth of it.

"I'll be back," he whispered.

Cabrera watched him go, her heart thumping with a mix of affection and unspoken hope. She didn't need a goodbye kiss. That one on her hand said it all.

As Damion's footsteps faded down the corridor, Cabrera sat back against the propped pillows, feeling the warmth of his kiss still pressed into her skin. But before she could fully find comfort in her thoughts, a knock tapped on the doorframe.

A tall woman with round glasses stepped in wearing hospital-blue scrubs, a clipboard tucked under one arm, auburn hair pulled into a tight braid, and sharp blue eyes.

"Good morning, Ensign Cabrera. I'm Bethany Cobb. Civilian nurse, physical therapist," she said, politely. "You can call me Beth, if you like. I'll be conducting your physical therapy during your rehabilitation."

Cabrera gave a slight nod, quickly assessing the woman. There was a confidence and firmness beneath the calm, as if her presence alone could put even the most uncooperative patient in check. Bethany also didn't look like she believed in shortcuts or letting her patients quit.

Cabrera smiled, "Good morning, Beth. Please, call me Salina."

"Okay, Salina," she replied with a smile. "Well, the good news is that you don't have a Grade III sprain, which is a complete tear of your ligament. That means that we can start your physical therapy as soon as possible, and probably get you out of here and back to your crew in a minimum amount of time."

"Oh, that sounds great. So, what's the bad news?"

"We start now," Bethany replied flatly.

Bethany explained the Acute Phase and how, for the next five days, the focus would be on controlling inflammation and starting gentle mobility. She applied ice packs, wrapped Cabrera's ankle in compression, and elevated it with a folded towel under her calf.

"Ankle circles. Ten each way. Now," Bethany said flatly.

Cabrera gritted her teeth, forcing the swollen joint into slow, trembling rotations. Each motion pulled tension through her foot like piano wire with razors attached.

"Hurts?" Bethany asked.

Cabrera nodded.

"Good. That's not pain. It's progress."

That night, Cabrera lay awake, her foot still pulsing from the ice-numbed *progress*. But she didn't complain. Her thoughts were preoccupied, drifting elsewhere, back to an old wooden bench beneath a quiet canopy of trees, where time once paused just long enough to etch a memory she would never forget.

Each day followed a similar rhythm: compression, ice, elevation. Ankle circles and drawing the alphabet with her toes. The motions burned, especially the lowercase 'g' and the letter 'x' drawn as an hourglass symbol. Bethany watched with focused precision, correcting her form, offering neither sympathy nor softness.

"Do you want to climb ladders and board ships again, or do you want to feel good *now*?" she asked on day 3, when Cabrera paused in the middle of an exercise.

Cabrera didn't answer. She just continued to push through the burning pain, wondering if any of Beth's previous patients ever passed out from her routines.

By Day 5, she was tolerating brief walks to the bathroom with the help of a pair of crutches. A small victory, but to her, it felt like scaling a mountain.

Of course, she couldn't say anything to Beth, but she had some additional motivation to get her through the therapy.

Damion.

He had managed to visit her two more times during the week. Both times, he had carried the thin folder. Both times, the folder was empty. They were able to spend about thirty minutes together during each visit, and even dared a quick kiss before he left. The second time, she mused, they were almost caught when Ensign Reed and Ensign Cheng paid her an unexpected visit.

Instead of the customary three knocks and waiting a second before opening the door, the knock and door opening happened simultaneously. However, by the time the door had swung fully open, Damion had already moved to a "safe" distance from her and was handling the thin folder as if he had just finished reading the "documents" inside.

Casually looking up and greeting the two smiling Ensigns, Damion then relayed the 'get-well-soon' messages to Cabrera from her ATFP teams, wished her a speedy recovery, then excused himself. Cabrera had forced a happy smile as she spoke with her two new visitors, but her heart was sinking. She knew that this would be the last time she would see him before the ship departed on its mission.

During the next four weeks, Beth would mercilessly push Cabrera through the early, intermediate, and advanced rehabilitation phases, which she outlined while taping a resistance chart to the wall.

"We've covered range of motion first. Now, we will start with strength training." She then added, with conviction in her voice, "You are going to learn to hate me."

"Too late. I already hate you," the thought crept in, which Cabrera wisely kept to herself as Beth continued.

"That will be the right response. Anything else is unacceptable."

Then the towel stretches began. Beth looped a strap under Cabrera's foot, pulling until her calf screamed. Calf stretches followed, performed against the wall. Cabrera broke a sweat by the second rep.

Next came the isometric exercises.

"Push against me!" Beth would command, bracing Cabrera's foot with iron resistance. "Hold it. No cheating."

Cabrera was surprised at how deceptively brutal the isometric exercises were, but even more surprised that the balance drills were even worse. Tandem stance, single-leg with hand support. Cabrera's arms trembled with the strain, but she didn't fall.

Her nights were constantly restless. Her ankle and foot throbbed. Her pride did, too.

Yet in her quiet thoughts, she pictured Damion returning and finding her standing strong. And that image always seemed to get her through.

The transition to resistance band exercises felt like a betrayal of trust. The elastic bands looked harmless. They were not.

Inversion. Eversion. Dorsiflexion. Plantarflexion. Each angle tested Cabrera's nerves. The movements were robotic at first, then became sharper and more controlled.

Balance training ramped up. Standing on foam pads, Cabrera wobbled violently on the first day. Beth simply stared, arms crossed, offering no help unless she fell.

"You're fighting for your future self, not for me," she said, matter-of-factly. "Fight harder."

Functional drills kicked off with step-ups and mini-squats that made Cabrera's ankle burn and thighs quake. Without warning, Beth added a weight vest.

Cabrera nearly cursed at her, but refrained and regrouped. Instead, she nodded, lips pressed tight.

"It's not pain, it's progress. Fight for my future self. It's not pain, it's progress. Fight for my future self," she repeated over and over in a low, rhythmic mantra. Beth, standing in front of her and watching like a hawk, slowly nodded without saying a word, as a thin smile formed on her lips.

When it came time for the advanced phase, Beth added a new challenge to the workout routine. A "both sides utilized" or BOSU ball. The popular fitness tool sat in a corner of the gym like a mysterious relic - part alien pod, part torture device. Roughly two feet wide and unmistakably strange-looking, the BOSU ball looked like someone took a regular exercise ball, sawed it in half, and glued it to a dinner plate.

One side was a hard, flat platform made of durable plastic; the other side a rubbery dome that gave just enough under pressure to make your legs question their loyalty. Flip it dome-side up or down — it didn't matter. Either way, it turned every exercise into a tightrope act. Squats, push-ups, planks — simple moves suddenly demanded the focus of a gymnast and the core strength of a Navy diver. A gym staple for those who enjoyed the challenge of wobble-induced humility, or maybe just liked their workouts with a bit of adventure.

Balance drills with eyes closed were a cruel joke, followed by side shuffles, ladder drills, and jumping in place. The ankle throbbed with every hop, but it didn't buckle. Not anymore.

By Week 5, Cabrera was completing jog-walk intervals in short circuits on the treadmill. The first time she jogged twenty steps without pain, she stopped, as a tear ran down her cheek. Not from hurt, but because it finally felt real. She could see the finish line.

Beth, nodding her head and saying nothing, just handed her a towel.

The day finally came for Cabrera to conduct the functional test. She breezed through it without a hitch, as if she had never been injured.

"You're stable," Beth said, while finishing up her notes on the ever-present clipboard. "You are ready to return to your command."

Cabrera flexed her foot slowly, watching the smooth arc of movement. Pain-free. Strong.

"Thank you so much," she said, sincerely.

Beth didn't smile, but she did give a quick nod, "Don't thank me. You earned it."

Later that night, Cabrera sat by the window looking out at the serene surroundings of the hospital grounds. She was already packed, and her uniform was laid out. Tomorrow, she would visit the Personnel Support Detachment to check on orders for transport back to the ship. Hopefully, there would be a flight heading out soon, but she knew that she might have to wait a couple of days.

She would then head over to the Navy Gateway Inn & Suites. She wondered if the building's name had changed from the former "Bachelor Officer Quarters (BOQ)" so that it would sound more gender-neutral or family-friendly. She shrugged, thinking that it was probably more due to it sounding more luxurious than anything else. No matter. It would beat staying in the hospital any day.

Although sleep was far from her mind, Cabrera knew that it would be wise for her to try at least and get some rest. Her head sank quietly into the soft pillow, eyes drifting upward to the painted beach mural stretched across the hospital ceiling. For a moment, she let her thoughts drift to Damion, then suddenly, it was as if they were together again, walking hand in hand, the warmth of his hand curling around her fingers. She couldn't remember when she drifted away, only that somewhere between the peaceful stillness of the hospital room and the pull of wishful dreams, came distant sounds of crashing waves and the feel of white sand on her bare feet.

Sleep had finally found her.

Chapter 10 – Storm Over the Mediterranean

The sunlight had only just begun to warm the steel deck when Damion stepped out onto the starboard weather deck. The morning air smelled like sea salt and exhaust fumes from the ship's four LM2500 gas turbine engines.

The Mediterranean sun hung low over the horizon, casting a golden haze across the restless water as the USS Daniel Shaw cut through the rolling swells at a steady pace. A mild breeze kept the heat in check, while the sky, an endless canvas of blue interrupted only by the occasional wisps of cirrus clouds, offered the perfect backdrop for another long day at sea. The ship's crew had been busy for weeks, conducting maritime interdiction operations and running countless drills that seemed to blur one into the next.

The only pause in the ongoing operations came one mid-afternoon when the bridge received an all-ships broadcast over the general maritime radio frequency. The static-laced voice reported a disabled sailboat adrift somewhere southeast of the Balearic Islands. Its exact location was unknown, somewhere in open water. The message, relayed with the calm urgency of routine distress, asked all ships to be on the lookout for the vessel and its passengers.

As it happened, the Daniel Shaw was just fifty miles from the last known position - close enough to alter course and join the search without interfering with its deployment schedule. With engines humming and the sea foaming in her wake, the ship changed course, while the deck crew moved with the precise, unhurried choreography of seasoned sailors.

The call "Flight Quarters" rang out over the ship's announcing system. The familiar crackle of the 1MC echoed down steel passageways and across the open deck. The Boatswain's Mate's voice was steady, clear, and left no room for confusion:

"Flight Quarters, Flight Quarters! All hands man your flight quarters stations. Set material condition 'Yoke' throughout the ship. All unnecessary personnel, stand clear of the flight deck. Now, flight quarters."

With pre-flight checks complete, the ship's SH-60B Seahawk helicopter roared to life. Painted in weathered haze-gray, the bird's block "NAVY" letters and black tail numbers stood out against its sun-faded skin. Compact yet muscular, the Seahawk's nose jutted forward with an array of sensors and radomes, cockpit windows wrapped around in a sleek, tinted shield. Its four-bladed rotor slashed the air in a heavy rhythm, while the splayed landing gear looked ready for whatever the deck or sea might throw its way. Long, narrow tail boom ending in a spinning rotor, rescue hoist mounted, and sliding doors revealing a utilitarian, cable-lined bay. The Seahawk, callsign "Bay Raider 616," was all business, a familiar and reliable workhorse in the fleet.

Fifteen minutes after lifting off, the helicopter crew spotted a stark white sailboat bobbing awkwardly in the swells, looking more out of place than ever. Through binoculars, it was easy to see that the boat was not being managed by anyone with even a passing familiarity with the sea. The sail furled awkwardly, lines tangled, and the expensive hull drifted at the whim of the wind. The two well-dressed young men and four scantily clad females on board, their hair tousled more by confusion than by the breeze, waved their arms in frantic relief as the Navy helicopter circled overhead.

The truth was visibly clear: these were no hardened mariners, but a pair of wealthy, twenty-something yuppies who saw the sailboat as less than a vessel and more as a floating status symbol. The engine had failed, and with it, any illusion that they were masters of the sea. One of them, the owner's son by the look of his nervous hands and monogrammed shirt, at least had the sense to pull out his phone and call his father—a decision that likely saved them hours, if not worse.

By the time the Daniel Shaw arrived on the scene, the sun was beginning its descent, casting long, shimmering trails across the water. Two of the ship's engineers, toolkits slung over their shoulders and faces set with quiet professionalism, climbed aboard the errant boat. They made quick work of the engine trouble, the sound of ratchets and quiet curses drifting across the waves. Within the hour, the sailboat's engine coughed, then roared to life, and the grateful passengers, now a little less sure of their place in the world, were sent on their way towards land with a new "sea story" to tell whoever would listen about their perilous adventure at sea.

As the day progressed, Damion was vaguely aware of the ship setting flight quarters multiple times. Deep into his own work, he simply chalked it up to the flight crew getting airtime for their monthly flight pay. He knew that they were required to fly a certain number of hours each month in order to receive the additional incentivized pay for the aircrew. Shortly after Bay Raider 616 landed back onboard and the ship secured from flight quarters, Damion' office phone rang.

"MAC Jackson."

"MAC, XO. Can you come to my cabin?"

"Aye, Sir. On my way."

After making sure all loose items were properly secured – no one liked picking up and reorganizing their paperwork due to the ship making a high-speed turn and everything being thrown all over the place – Damion locked his office door and headed to the Executive Officer's cabin.

After three knocks, Damion heard the XO's familiar *"Enter"* from behind the door.

Entering the cabin, Damion noted that the XO was standing instead of sitting at his desk, with a faded blue folder held firmly in his hands. The folder had a plastic CONFIDENTIAL seal wrapped around it.

"Chief, close the door and have a seat." The XO began directly. "What I'm about to tell you is strictly need-to-know. Only the CO, you, and I are privy to this information. No one else in the crew can know about this."

Damion, noting the seriousness of the XO's words and tone, nodded, "Understood, Sir." Then, after a moment, added, "Not even the Command Master Chief?"

Leaning against his desk in thought, the XO added, "I will see if I can get B.B. read in on this, but that won't be our concern."

The XO then approached Damion and handed him the sealed folder. On the cover stood the words in bold letters:

*Naval Criminal Investigative Service, Special Agent Maya Torres – Authorized by Commanding Officer, USS Daniel Shaw (DDG-148)

Damion's heart skipped half a beat.

He hadn't seen Maya Torres in over a decade, since Bahrain, when they were wearing the same rank and chasing down black-market smugglers who had more tattoos than common sense. Damion remembered those nights as if they'd been stamped in bold print on the insides of his eyelids. The dull glow of worn-out headlights bouncing off wet concrete, the air heavy with diesel fumes, and the smell of shisha tobacco laced with something far less legal.

The smugglers back then were a ragtag patchwork of bad decisions and quick money, sporting cheap ink that crawled down their arms and necks in sharp, angry patterns. Their tattoos looked less like art and more like a criminal résumé—each symbol, skull, or dagger a silent boast about jobs pulled off and debts left unpaid. They moved in small packs, skulking through the labyrinthine alleys near the port, whispering to dock workers, slipping packages beneath pallets of fruit or inside crates marked for diplomatic delivery.

Maya always seemed to spot them first. She had an uncanny knack for picking out the real threat from the noise, like a bloodhound stalking its prey. There was one night in particular, humid and restless, when she'd yanked Damion down behind a rusted generator just as a group of smugglers sauntered by, their conversation edged with something sharp and sinister.

They'd been carrying Navy duffel bags stuffed with everything from counterfeit electronics to fake gold watches and cartons of American cigarettes. All sorts of contraband with price tags that could make a junior sailor's head spin and their wallets empty. He still remembers the tone of Maya's voice in his ear, low and certain, "On my mark. Don't let the tall one double back." The operation had been swift and ugly. All of the smugglers had been captured, except for the ring leader and one of his crew. The joint American and Bahraini Public Security Force (PSF) sustained only one casualty, so all in all, it was a good bust.

Now, Torres was a certified, badge-wielding bulldog with a security clearance that outstripped most of the ship's senior officers.

Not daring to open the folder too quickly, Damion looked up at the XO, hoping for a quick explanation as to why she was involved in whatever this was.

The XO began slowly. "NCIS has received some anonymous information that one of our officers may have been targeted and/or compromised by a foreign intelligence gathering agency. And, they have asked for you specifically to assist in the investigation."

Damion, slightly relieved that this was not about him and Cabrera, but with concern in his voice, replied, "Of course, sir. I will assist them in any way I can, but isn't this a little unorthodox? NCIS reading in a Chief Master-at-Arms into one of their investigations, especially when it involves a Navy officer?

"Well, Special Agent Torres feels that your previous work with her makes you a trustworthy and valuable asset to the investigation. You know, that's not exactly a bad bullet point to have in your record during the promotion board for Senior Chief, or if you ever decide to convert to Warrant Officer. Plus, your position on the ship gives you a valid excuse for snooping around." The XO continued with a half-smile on his face, "Besides, the CO already guaranteed NCIS that you would assist in the investigation. Just don't open the folder until you meet with Torres."

"Understood, sir. So, will I be receiving additional info from Torres via secure comms, or do I need to contact her when we pull into port?"

"Neither. She's already onboard and waiting for you in the Wardroom. This investigation is time sensitive, so Bay Raider diverted to Rota earlier today and picked her up."

Taking a deep breath, Damion stood, "Well then, I guess I had better not keep her waiting."

The XO, coming closer to Damion, spoke in a low voice. "Look here, Chief. I know that I don't have to tell you to make sure that you and Torres cross all the 'T's' and dot all the 'i's since we don't know how this investigation will pan out. The anonymous information could be valid, or this whole thing could just be a misunderstanding. Either way, keep in mind that a Navy officer's career is at stake and can be seriously impacted if this thing is mishandled or if rumors get out about them being under investigation. Not to mention the effect it would have on the rest of the crew."

Damion nodded in agreement while tapping the folder in his hands. "I understand the implications, sir. I promise you, everything will be handled by the book, and with the utmost secrecy." He then turned to leave, but the XO stopped him.

"There's just one more thing, Chief," the XO added. The officer being investigated is Ensign Cabrera.

A cold chill ran down Damion's back as he left the XO's cabin and headed down the tight corridor. The recycled air flowing through the ship's ventilation system seemed unusually stale, and the background sounds of sailors' hushed voices made him feel as if he were walking through a prison where everyone already knew what was happening.

As promised, he found NCIS Special Agent Maya Torres in the Wardroom, seated at the far end of the large table with her long legs crossed like she owned the entire ship. The room was empty. Just the two of them. She stood up when he entered.

"Hello, DJ," she said, smiling thinly. "You got older."

"And apparently, you got dangerous," he replied.

"Always was. You just weren't paying attention."

She continued with the small talk. "I always thought that the officers got the best of everything. This coffee...is not it. Can I pour you a cup?"

"I'm good," he answered while taking a seat. "So, what's this investigation all about?"

Torres glanced at the closed door, then back at him, her voice lowering into that careful tone that preceded every classified conversation everywhere.

"I need your help, Damion." Then, nodding towards the sealed folder, "You can open that now."

Breaking the seal on the folder, Damion could barely maintain his poker face at what he saw. Photos. Screenshots. Intelligence summaries. Time-stamped frames from Barcelona and Rota. One wide-angle from across a street. Two zoomed close enough to make out the condensation on his beer glass. And in every one, Cabrera was visible.

"What am I looking at?" he asked carefully.

Torres tapped a photo. "Three days ago, this man," she pointed to a background figure behind Cabrera in one of the images, "was flagged by Spanish intelligence. He is a known associate of a Moroccan-based intelligence broker suspected of selling NATO ship movement data. He was within thirty feet of your Division Officer."

"That's not a crime," Damion said flatly.

"No, it's not. But as you can see, he is curiously present in a majority of the photos. And here's an interesting little fact: Ensign Cabrera's credit card was used that same evening at a shop that we now know is a front for several illicit activities. Possibly an accidental exposure. Possibly not," Torres replied smugly.

"She didn't," he started, then caught himself. "She's clean."

Torres' eyes softened a fraction. "I'm not saying that she's dirty. But someone thinks that she may be a mark. We're not investigating her, yet. But we are investigating the possibility that she's being targeted."

Damion exhaled through his nose, long and slow. "Do you think she is compromised?"

"Possibly, more like watched. Followed. Maybe tested. But you," she paused, "are our best chance to find out if she is, or what she might not even know she gave up."

He straightened his shoulders. "So what do you want from me?"

"Stay close. Don't spook her. See if she brings up anything that might sound suspicious or out of the ordinary. Watch who she talks to. If anything – anything - feels off, you contact me."

Damion didn't respond right away. Then, "You know what this could look like? Me sniffing around my Div-O like a jealous sailor. Some folks on this ship is already half-convinced that we've got a thing going on."

"You do," Torres said bluntly. "Emotional involvement's why I picked you. She trusts you. Use that." She then took a long breath and slid a thin manila folder across the table towards him. He opened it. The cold chill that previously ran down his spine had returned.

The folder contained only two photos. Timestamped. The first one was a wide-angle, full-body shot showing Damion and Cabrera facing each other with the Rota lighthouse in the background. The second was a close-up of them standing close together, locked in each other's eyes and holding hands, just before the shrieking airborne alarm flew overhead.

Damion's head swirled as he thought of what to do next.

"Nothing happened between us at the lighthouse," he finally managed to say.

"I know," she replied. "No additional pictures. However, it does look like *something* was about to happen, and you understand how perceptions are to the Navy. You know, I actually lost you guys on your run back, and thought you might have stopped to finish what *didn't happen*, but then I saw you carrying Cabrera back to the base all bruised up."

Tossing the photos onto the table, he stared at her. "You're using me."

"No. I'm protecting you. Both of you. And possibly the mission."

A long pause stretched between them. Finally, he nodded in submission. During the next thirty minutes, Torres briefed him on the information provided by the Spanish government regarding the criminal organization and the man sitting in the background, whose finger was pointed directly at Cabrera.

When Damion left the Wardroom with the briefing folder tucked under his arm, his expression was unreadable, his thoughts 500 nautical miles away in the Province of Cádiz, Andalusia, in a small seaside town named Rota.

Chapter 11 – The Price of Silence

The morning sun was still low, painting the base in soft amber tones as Cabrera stepped out of Naval Station Rota Hospital (Building 1802). The air had a clean, salty hint of the nearby ocean, mixed with the scent of freshly cut grass from the base groundskeepers. Cabrera adjusted her lightweight Navy-issue jacket, the fabric rustling quietly as she began walking south along the main paved route.

The base was already awake. A group of sailors jogged past in their PT gear, their rhythmic footfalls fading behind her. She passed the Human Resources building, its dull, beige walls catching streaks of golden light, and then the administrative offices, where a few civilian personnel were busy unlocking doors. The distant hum of a forklift echoed from the supply depot somewhere beyond her line of sight.

As she neared the central hub, the familiar sight of the Quarterdeck came into view. Building 1, standing like a stern sentinel at the heart of base activity. Sailors moved briskly in and out, some with clipboards in hand, others talking quietly as they passed through security. PSD, as she had been told, was just off to the side.

Inside, the cool, conditioned air contrasted with the warming morning outside. The sailor at the counter, a stocky Petty Officer with sharp eyes but a polite tone, apologized before she even asked.

"Ma'am, the civilian who processes permanent transfer orders is out today - personal errand. Should be back first thing tomorrow."

Cabrera's lips pressed together, hiding her disappointment. Before she could ask what that meant for her, he continued. "I can issue you temporary orders so that you can check into the Navy Gateway Inn & Suites until tomorrow, if you'd like. We haven't had many transits come through this week, so they should already have a room available."

She thanked him with a smile and a polite nod, then waited while he quickly printed out the papers. She was in and out of PSD in less than 10 minutes. That had to be some kind of record, she thought to herself while heading out the door.

The Navy Gateway Inn & Suites room was modest but clean, with a faint scent of industrial laundry soap. After setting her small duffel bag on the neatly made bed, she changed quickly from her uniform into civilian clothes. Fitted jeans, a loose white blouse, and simple sandals. Her reflection in the mirror looked... different. Less like a patient recovering from a month in the hospital and more like herself again.

She stepped outside, breathing in deeply as if she could pull freedom itself into her lungs. The sky was a brilliant blue, streaked with wisps of clouds, and the warmth of the sun on her skin felt like a luxury after so many days trapped under fluorescent hospital lights.

Cabrera walked without a destination, letting her feet choose the path. The base faded behind her, replaced by narrow sidewalks lined with flowering shrubs and the distant murmur of traffic from the town beyond the gates. She strolled past small cafés and shops, catching snippets of conversations in Spanish, the smells of baking bread and brewing coffee teasing her senses.

At some point, without consciously deciding it, her steps slowed as her heart caught in her chest when she recognized where she was.

Their tree-lined tunnel.

The canopy of interwoven branches above filtered sunlight into dancing patches on the ground, just as it had before. The smell of earth and leaves hung in the air. Her gaze fell ahead, and there it was, the weathered old bench where so much had changed between her and Damion.

She approached slowly, almost reverently, running her fingers along the scarred wood. The carvings of initials and crude symbols seemed like silent witnesses to countless untold stories. She sat, her body sinking into the familiar grooves of the bench, and memories swept over her. The warmth of Damion beside her, the feel of his hand tracing the outline of her face, the soft laughter they had shared when they realized how foolish they both felt for waiting so long to admit their true feelings.

Her eyes shifted to the dirt path in front of her, fixing on a broken stone lying in the middle. She tilted her head.

"No way. Could that be the same one?" she murmured under her breath.

She bent down, picking it up. The stone was jagged, one side pointed. Then, a mischievous thought sparked in her mind, curling her lips into a sly smile.

Glancing around to make sure no one was looking, Cabrera turned back to the bench and pressed the sharp edge to the wood. Slowly, carefully, she carved each letter, her heart thumping harder than it should have for such a small act of rebellion.

When she finished, she looked at her work - simple, discreet, but hers. Running her fingers over the fresh grooves, she felt an odd sense of connection, as if she had just left a secret message for Damion, even though he would never see it.

Feeling slightly guilty, she looked down at the stone still in her hand.

"Can't leave this where someone else might slip on it," she said quietly, almost like she was justifying her next action to the universe.

She then tossed the stone into the bushes, brushing her hands off as if that absolved her of any wrongdoing. With a satisfied grin spread across her face and her mood lighter than it had been in weeks, Cabrera stood up and gave the bench one last glance as she slowly exited the tunnel.

The sun hung high in the Catalonian sky, making the narrow streets shimmer with heat and late-morning energy. Cabrera wandered through winding alleys and sun-bleached squares of the old quarter, a faint hint of guilt trailing behind her like a persistent shadow. It was an odd feeling, having so much free time while the rest of the crew was back out at sea, but there was nothing she could do about it - orders were orders. The breeze was warm but not oppressive, teasing her hair as she ducked into pockets of shade offered by ornate wrought-iron balconies and bougainvillea vines climbing up brick façades.

As noon crept up, Cabrera's body and conscience both told her it was time for a break. She found herself drawn to a little café just off the bustling main avenue, its outdoor tables shaded by wide, faded umbrellas. She picked a spot near the corner, settling in with the gentle hum of voices and distant guitar music from a nearby street performer. The waitress, prompt and smiling, brought a small menu with penciled-in specials. Cabrera ordered the catch of the day: a steaming plate of grilled dorada, nestled atop herbed potatoes, flecks of parsley, and a wedge of lemon, all glistening with olive oil. She added a chilled bottle of sparkling water, the condensation trickling down its green glass.

As she waited, Cabrera let her eyes wander. Tourists photographing every crumb, locals lost in animated conversations, and a little girl sharing ice cream with an older gentleman, whom Cabrera assumed was her father. She barely noticed the tall, striking woman seated across the patio, watching her with an unreadable expression. When Cabrera finally met the woman's gaze, she offered a polite half-smile then looked away, trying not to invite any unwanted conversation.

She'd just begun to relax when a shadow fell across her table. "Can I join you?" The voice was soft, but there was a firmness beneath the words that made Cabrera's shoulders stiffen.

Startled, Cabrera turned to see the woman up close. She stood a little over six feet, framed by a cascade of jet-black hair that fluttered in the gentle breeze and filtered the sunlight above. In one hand, she held a bottle of a local fruit drink, condensation beading on the glass. Her dark brown eyes, intense and sharp, studied Cabrera with the ease of someone accustomed to being in control.

Cabrera scrambled for the right words, not looking to encourage a conversation, as well as trying to avoid offending the imposing stranger. However, before she could answer, the woman set the bottle on the table and flashed a practiced smile. "Don't worry, Ensign Cabrera. I'm not going to ask you on a date."

Cabrera's surprise must have been obvious, but she recovered quickly, narrowing her eyes. "How do you know who I am?"

The woman, never breaking eye contact, slipped a wallet from her jacket. With practiced subtlety, she flashed a badge and an ID card: Special Agent Maya Torres, NCIS. She took a seat without waiting for an invitation, her posture relaxed but vigilant. Cabrera hesitated, then nodded, still unsure of what to expect.

Torres wasted no time. She opened with a few casual questions about Cabrera's recovery - how the rehab had gone, whether she was truly fit for duty, and so on. Cabrera responded politely, sensing that Torres was testing her. The conversation further drifted to praise for the hospital staff. Then, just as Cabrera was about to let her guard down, Torres' tone changed.

"We have a situation, Ensign," Torres said, lowering her voice. "NCIS has reason to believe that someone on your ship has been leaking MIO tactics to a foreign intelligence service." She outlined how a coded message intercepted by counterintelligence sources, along with corroboration from a confidential informant, pointed directly to information which only a select group aboard the ship would know. Details flowed -dates, specifics, all delivered with the calm precision of someone who had rehearsed the lines a dozen times.

Cabrera bristled while listening to Torres' detailed monologue. "My MIO teams are hand-picked, Agent. Every single one of them is a hundred percent gung-ho and reliable. There's no way—"

Torres raised a hand, silencing her. "The leak came from someone with advanced training - someone in a senior position." She let the accusation hang in the air, thickening with each passing moment.

There was a long pause, the only sound the distant clatter of plates from inside the café. Torres finally leaned in, voice dropping to a whisper. "How well do you know Chief Jackson?"

Cabrera kept her face still, heart pounding beneath the surface. "Chief Jackson is one of the best CPOs on the ship. He's an outstanding leader - respected, sharp, and he trains his teams to be the same."

Torres listened, eyes unreadable, then offered a faint smile. "That's good to hear. But there are… inconsistencies in his background. I need you to get close to him. See if anything seems off when you're back on the ship."

Visibly startled, Cabrera took a moment to answer. "I'm not comfortable spying on my Chief," she replied, voice barely above a whisper. "No thanks. Get someone else."

Torres, eyeing her closely, let the silence stretch, then asked, almost casually, "When was the last time you spoke to your sister, Christina?"

That caught Cabrera off-guard. "I haven't seen her in years. Why are you asking?"

Torres regarded her, then leaned back, hands folded. "Your sister's under investigation in Florida. She's suspected of helping to re-found the Fuerzas Armadas de Liberación Nacional. You know, the FALN. She has already been complicit in several protests organized by the new group. Some violent, one with an injured bystander."

Panic fluttered in Cabrera's chest, causing her to become speechless at the direction this conversation was heading. Fortunately, the waitress arrived with her plate of grilled dorada and a basket of warm, crusty bread. As the waitress expertly placed the meal in a pre-arranged setting, Cabrera became acutely aware of how the environment had shifted. The café's cheerful chatter seemed to recede, muffled behind a sudden wall of pressure, as if a storm were gathering out at sea, invisible but close. The sun, moments before warm and golden, now pressed down with a heavy, stagnant heat that felt thick against her skin. Even the breeze, which had danced so playfully with the café umbrellas, seemed to vanish, leaving the air unnaturally still, suffocating.

Across the plaza, the sharp colors of tourist shirts and vendor stands blurred at the edges of her vision, as if she were peering through rain-specked glass. Laughter from a nearby table drifted past her like the echo of a memory, almost foreign, almost mocking. In that moment, Cabrera felt stranded - alone on a beach as a tidal wave rose behind her, or a swimmer caught far from shore, the water darkening beneath her feet, no lifeline in sight. There was no way out that didn't lead directly into deeper, unknown waters.

Her hands, suddenly cold despite the heat, gripped the edge of the table. The food before her might as well have been on another planet. The world she knew - her rules, her loyalties - now seemed fragile, all certainty sucked away by the low, relentless pull of something vast and dangerous just beyond the horizon. The sky, so blue just moments ago, now felt like an endless void.

And across from her, Special Agent Torres waited, patient and silent, as if she had all the time in the world.

After asking if she or her "friend" needed anything else, the waitress left them to attend to the other customers. Cabrera clenched her hands under the table. "Wait a minute. What does my sister have to do with any of this – with Chief Jackson?"

Torres answered without hesitation. "Leverage. Help us, and your career won't be touched by your sister's activities. Refuse, and I can't make any promises."

Cabrera stared at the untouched food, her appetite gone, and the warmth of the day suddenly feeling even heavier and oppressive. *"You're blackmailing me to go after my Chief?"*

Torres shrugged, "Think of it as helping us to clear his name. If he's clean, no one ever needs to know you were involved. If not," she stood, eyes softening just a fraction of a fraction. "I'll be in touch. And, Ensign, this conversation stays between us. Enjoy your lunch."

As Torres disappeared into the noonday crowd, Cabrera was left alone, her lunch untouched. Watching the sunlight glint off of her water bottle, she imagined feeling the world tilt beneath her feet, like a roller coaster car just before the big drop. The afternoon sunlight filtered lazily through the café's awning, dappling the table in front of Cabrera with uneven patches of gold. She sat there, motionless, for what felt like hours, lost deep in a heavy fog of her own making. The lively noises around her - bursts of laughter, the distant clang of a tram - might as well have been a world away. When Cabrera finally blinked herself back to reality, razor-sharp clarity snapped into place with the force of a hard slap.

Enough was enough.

She straightened in her seat, squared her shoulders, and drew a deep breath that was half resolve, half defiance. *"Who are you?"* she heard her mother's voice deep in her subconscious. *'I am the Anti-Terrorism Force Protection Officer aboard one of the U.S. Navy's deadliest warships!'* And if Damion is right, and he usually is, she was a damn good tactician, too. Time to start acting like it. She wasn't going to let this

Torres character knock her off balance, no matter what agency she was supposedly whispering for.

Cabrera shook her head once, sharp and precise, as if to physically dislodge the doubts that Torres had managed to plant. She knew Damion - knew him as well as anyone aboard the Daniel Shaw. Solid. Dependable. There was no chance that he was wrapped up in whatever shadowy business Torres hinted at. Or was there? For a flickering second, that seed of doubt tried to sprout, watered by suspicion and just enough fear. But her gut, and she admitted, her heart, told her otherwise. Still, Torres had rattled her, and she hated that almost as much as the suspicion itself.

"Pull it together, Salina," she muttered, her voice barely audible above the shuffle of the busy cafe. "Treat it like a mission. Trust your instincts. Keep your eyes open. Move if you have to, but don't jump at shadows." She repeated the mantra twice, then gave herself a small nod, finding some comfort in the routine of preparation.

Huracán Torres had blown through and left her a little battered, but not broken. As the last swirl of doubt faded, she reached for her lunch, now a cold dish she'd neglected for far too long, and attacked it with the grim determination of a sailor about to head into the unknown. Plans would need to be made, contingencies outlined, and she'd have to stay sharp. No matter which way this thing ended up going, one thing was for certain - she would not be caught flat-footed.

A sudden breeze kicked up, ruffling napkins and causing the ends of the tablecloth to curl. Cabrera narrowed her eyes, scanning the busy street with renewed focus. One more deep breath, and she was ready. Whatever storm was coming, she was in the fight now.

Finishing her lunch, Cabrera decided she would walk the scenic route back to the base while collecting her thoughts. Her encounter with Torres had left her on alert, and she had the uneasy sense that she was being watched. It was possibly just paranoia. Then she had a thought, as a smile crept onto her face. Just to be on the safe side, now would be a perfect opportunity to practice conducting an SDR, or surveillance detection route.

Leaving the shaded comfort of the café at Av. de la Diputación, 18, Cabrera stepped out into the golden afternoon glare that pressed down on the narrow street like a warm hand. She casually slid her sunglasses over her eyes, taking a slow look left and right, letting her gaze linger just long enough to appear normal. She started down the avenue, her pace deliberately unhurried, the soles of her sneakers silent against the sun-warmed tiles. Cars moved lazily past, their windows reflecting strips of sky and the shapes of strangers. Cabrera let her eyes drift to the storefronts - a bakery with fresh churros and pestiños, a faded blue door - each window briefly becoming a makeshift mirror. In the shimmer of a display case, she caught sight of a silver sedan idling two cars back, its driver pretending to study a map. She tucked the image away, noting the color and the license plate. Nothing too unusual, but her instinct prodded her forward.

At the next intersection, she took an unexpected right turn onto Calle Santiago Guillén Moreno, forcing herself not to look over her shoulder. Instead, she studied the glassy reflection in the door of a pharmacy. The sedan didn't follow. Cabrera paused to tie her shoe, using the chance to scan the faces behind her. A group of teenagers passed by, lost in their own world. No threat, nothing out of place, so far.

She continued, weaving through side streets lined with orange trees whose fruit lay half-smashed on the pavement. She made another sharp left, doubling back toward the main avenue, then crossed diagonally through a small plaza, stopping by a stone fountain to check her phone, but really to let the pedestrian traffic flow around her. In the polished chrome of a parked motorcycle, she spotted a man leaning against a lamppost: medium build, dark slacks, and a fedora angled low over his face. Cabrera almost laughed at the melodrama of it, but the knot in her stomach tightened anyway. She watched him out of the corner of her eye as she resumed walking. He glanced her way, then exaggeratedly raised a newspaper to his face, the very image of a spy movie cliché. She slipped into a small beauty shop, pretending to browse, and watched through the smudged glass as he drifted away, heading in the opposite direction. Just a local with a flair for old-fashioned style, it seemed.

With the sun dipping lower, painting the sky with ribbons of orange and violet, Cabrera resumed her winding path. She walked parallel to the main boulevard, ducking through alleys and pausing at a bus stop where she blended into the small crowd. Every few minutes, she checked the mirrored windows of parked cars, catching nothing but her own reflection and the blurred forms of passing strangers. No sign of the sedan. No shadowy figure in a hat. Her pulse eased, but she remained vigilant.

At the last stretch, Cabrera skirted the edge of the city park, slowing her pace, one last pause beneath the thick boughs of an olive tree to let any remaining tail slip past. The air felt cooler here, heavy with the scent of grass and old stone. The gates of the base shimmered up ahead in the late light. Not far now. She took a final look behind her - nothing but the usual traffic, an old man with a dog, two kids kicking a soccer ball. A sudden rustle in the thick, tangled bushes beside her broke the stillness and sent a quick shiver up Cabrera's spine. She stopped mid-step, rooted to the cobblestone path, eyes locked on the patch of green that now quivered just inches away. For a heartbeat, nothing else existed - just the quiet, her own sharply drawn breath, and the uncertain motion in the shadows.

Then, from beneath the glossy leaves, a pointed nose emerged, followed by a wary set of brown eyes and, finally, the scrappy frame of a stray dog. Its fur was mottled, patches of caramel and dirt, tail wagging with cautious hope. Cabrera let out a laugh, the kind that bubbles up from embarrassment, and felt the tension drain from her shoulders. She shook her head, chiding herself under her breath, then continued towards the base.

After presenting her ID card to the broad-shouldered guard whose granite stare and rigid posture made it clear that he was not someone to be trifled with, Cabrera slipped through the gate, exhaling a breath she hadn't realized she'd been holding. No incidents and no followers, the city faded behind her as she walked across the base. Just another sailor returning at the end of the day, her nerves settling with each step.

Chapter 12 - The Weight of Uniforms

Cabrera returned to PSD the next morning, already anticipating the usual shuffle of paperwork and clipped conversations. As she stepped up to the front desk, the civilian clerk who had been missing the day before didn't even look up when she informed Cabrera, flatly, that travel orders would not be issued. "The ship's coming back in two days. You'll be on temporary orders to base security until then." No explanation, no apology, just another turn in the routine. Cabrera nodded, pretending this wasn't exactly what she'd expected. Two days of walking in circles, most likely. Base security meant little more than signing a few logs, walking around the same corridors, and listening to the occasional radio check. The only upside was that nobody would probably bother her, which would give her all the time she needed to focus on what really mattered - her plans for handling the new situation with Damion. Two days. She would be ready.

The next forty-eight hours unraveled exactly as she had expected, with all the excitement of a watch-stander's graveyard shift. No urgent calls, no drills, not even an invitation for a ride-along with one of the base's security police. With nothing pressing for her to do, Cabrera filled the hours the way she always did - with purpose. Even if that purpose was self-assigned. She had sketched out several new boarding tactics for her MIO teams, just enough to drop on the CSO's desk to show that she hadn't been lying around doing nothing for the last month. However, her mind kept returning to the woman she now only thought of as *Huracán Torres*. She turned that name over and over, as if it might break apart and reveal its secrets if she concentrated hard enough.

Now, two days later, she was standing at the pier, gear slung over her shoulder, watching as the Daniel Shaw was nudged closer to the concrete piers by a pair of tugboats. She let her eyes wander across the decks, searching, until she found Damion, exactly where she knew he'd be. He was leaning casually just aft of the midships ladder, one hand on the lifeline, the other shielding his eyes. Their eyes met. A silent exchange, barely a flicker, but enough for Cabrera to feel a quick jolt - like someone had grabbed her arms and given them a quick shake. She was grateful that no one seemed to notice.

After the ship was made fast, Cabrera stowed her bag in her stateroom. She then made sure that she checked in with the XO to give him a quick update on her operational status. Afterwards, she made her way below to track down Damion, armed with a folder full of MIO updates. She rehearsed her lines in her head, already knowing she'd have to balance the official with the personal while in the presence of the crew. As she walked through the passageways, she was met with nods, genuine welcomes, a few jokes about how the place wasn't the same without her. She felt it - the sense of being missed.

She reached the Chiefs' Mess, pausing for the perfunctory three knocks before stepping inside. The room was alive with movement. Around one table, several departmental Chiefs had staked out their territory - some leaning over stacks of administrative reports and repair logs, others in tight clusters debating personnel issues, and the usual back-and-forth about liberty schedules just beginning to bubble up. There was the low, constant hum of voices: discussions about missed maintenance windows, someone lamenting about a busted AC unit in berthing, as well as two Chiefs in the corner quietly planning out which beer and tapas bar they'd hit first once liberty call sounded. Amid the swirl of khaki uniforms, Damion stood at the coffee machine, deep in conversation with another Chief. He caught sight of her, paused, and waved her over.

"Welcome back, Ma'am," Damion said, flashing the easy grin she remembered. "How'd the rehab go?"

She shrugged. "It went. At least I can walk a straight line now without the corpsman following me with a crash cart."

They both laughed, slipping easily into the old rhythm. He handed her a cup of coffee, gestured for her to sit, and they traded the usual updates - how she'd been, what she missed, who'd filled in on her teams. Damion launched into the rundown: MIOs completed, a wild story about a disabled sailboat, a couple of near misses, and the endless reports that came with each one. Cabrera pulled out her folder. "I drafted some new boarding tactics while I was out. Thought we could go over them - maybe in your office? Little quieter."

Damion nodded, collecting his stack of paperwork. They made their way out, navigating the maze of passageways and sailors, and slipped into his office, closing the door behind them. For a beat, they just stood there, the silence stretching between them, each unsure of what the other might say or do next. Then, without another word, they closed the distance, arms wrapping around each other, mouths finding and locking in a kiss that had been waiting for weeks. The world fell away, reduced to the steady thrum of hearts and the familiar, reassuring grip of each other's embrace.

They finally broke apart, breathless, sharing the same words at the same moment. "Missed you." It was enough to make them both laugh, hands still tracing lazy patterns on arms and backs, reluctant to let go. A sharp three knocks on the door broke the spell. Damion stepped away, opening it just enough to accept a sheaf of paperwork from a wide-eyed young sailor, who quickly retreated.

As soon as the door closed, Damion turned back, a wry smile on his face. They settled into talking, low and close, about everything they'd missed.

Everything, that is, except their contact with Maya Torres. That was a subject, each secretly hoped, would not need to be brought up. Ever.

Eventually, Damion broke the news. "Just so you know, there's a base function tonight. All khakis not on duty are required to attend. Spanish military liaison's hosting off-base. Khaki uniforms are mandatory."

Cabrera rolled her eyes but nodded, already ticking off the next uniform inspection in her mind. They lingered a little longer, stealing a few more moments, a few more kisses, before Cabrera finally pulled away. "Not that I want to leave, but I should probably make my rounds," she said, voice soft. "We'll have time later. I promise."

After one more quick kiss, she left the office, the echo of their reunion lingering in the air, a promise reserved for the end of the day.

Evening settled in with a mild breeze, warm enough to hint at the city's sunbaked afternoons, but cooled now by dusk's approach. The Spanish villa, painted in sun-bleached terracotta and accented with tiles of cobalt blue and goldenrod yellow, came alive with the sounds of laughter and spirited conversation. The iron gates stood open, inviting guests onto a courtyard tiled in swirling patterns, lanterns flickering above in every shade from pomegranate to tangerine.

Inside, long tables had been set out beneath the open sky, thick linen cloths stretched over their surfaces, edged with bold, red embroidery. The smell of fresh bread and olive oil mingled with the tang of garlic, sweet tomatoes, and slow-cooked meats wafting from platters as local servers—wearing pressed white shirts and crimson sashes at their waists—circulated among the guests. Plates of tapas were everywhere: tortilla Española, marinated olives, slices of jamón ibérico arranged in careful curls, shrimp in smoky paprika oil, tiny stuffed peppers, and piles of crispy patatas bravas. Jugs of sangria, bobbing with chopped fruit and ice, lined the tables beside bottles of Rioja and frosty Estrella Galicia beer.

Above the din, a trio of guitarists and a lone violinist filled the night with quick, joyful chords and swirling flamenco rhythms, their fingers moving in a blur. A few locals, bold and barefoot, tapped out the syncopated steps of a Sevillana dance near the fountain, drawing a crowd of curious sailors and Chiefs who clapped along, some even daring a spin or two themselves. Overlapping voices, a jumble of English and Spanish, spilled through the rooms and out onto the verandas—jokes, stories, and toasts mixing together in a cheerful haze.

Damion drifted through the crowd with a glass of beer in hand, the condensation cool against his palm. He spotted Cabrera on a wide veranda, surrounded by a cluster of uniformed figures. She stood out - not just for her posture or the curve of her jaw when she laughed, but for how she seemed fully present, at ease in the celebration, yet always just a little apart, as if saving part of herself for something private.

The CSO, his frame blocking most of Cabrera from view, leaned in to say something. Damion grinned, taking his time. He eased up behind them, letting the music fill the silence between his steps. Just as he got close enough, he delivered his line - "So, what's going on here? I'm not sure if you two should be standing that close. Looks a little cozy," then took a long, lazy sip of his beer, eyes glinting over the rim.

The CSO spun around, face set like someone who's already decided he won't laugh, not even a little. "Haha, very funny, Chief." Cabrera's hand darted up to her mouth, muffling a giggle, her eyes wide with the danger and delight of it. Damion, not missing a beat, shrugged. "Just kidding, sir. This is one heck of a party, right?"

A pause. Then, the CSO let out a grudging, "Yes, it is," before disappearing into the flow of guests, leaving Damion and Cabrera staring at the back of his head, blank-faced and alone on the veranda.

"I can't believe you just said that!" Cabrera whispered, scandalized and thrilled all at once, as the lantern light danced wildly in her eyes.

"Serves him right. Besides, what's he gonna' do, fire me?" Damion said, smirking and raising his beer in a mock salute before taking another pull. The music, the laughter, and the feel of genuine camaraderie all wrapped around them like a warm, golden cocoon.

They leaned against the cool stone rail, side by side, quietly taking in the surrounding fiesta. They talked about the evening - the savory tastes of the food, the open-hearted welcome of the locals, the feeling of being somewhere far from home but at ease, together. They both agreed there was something in the air - something different that made the ordinary seem a little more magical, a little more alive.

Eventually, reality, along with the subtle glances and half-smiles from several of their peers, nudged them back into the crowd in separate directions. They made the rounds, talking with the hosts and locals, expressing appreciation to the caterers and servers for doing a fantastic job, and just offering smiles and small talk. "You are the Navy's ambassadors," echoed the CO's preparatory speech in the back of his head. Whenever he and Cabrera accidentally crossed paths, they were cautious not to linger together too long, but always kept each other in sight. The party mellowed as midnight drew near, senior officers bidding goodnight, and the last few guests trading stories over half-empty glasses.

As the villa emptied, groups of Officers and Chiefs, accompanied by several newly acquainted local friends, peeled off into the city's narrow streets, laughter echoing into the night. Damion caught Cabrera's eyes across the courtyard - just for a second, a promise flickering between them - before their friends and the night carried them away in separate directions.

After leaving the fiesta, Damion stuck close with his group of fellow Chiefs, their laughter rolling down the street as they meandered through the heart of Old Town. Up ahead, he spotted a handful of young sailors, faces pink with cheap beer and bravado, clustered around three striking Spanish women. The girls stood poised, amused, while the sailors leaned in, trying to be charming but looking more like puppies begging for scraps.

Damion watched, the familiar coil of responsibility settling into his gut. He could tell by the glaze in their eyes that the sailors couldn't have spotted trouble if it had bit them in the forehead, which he could easily see happening tonight, in their current condition. He started to cross the street, planning to step in with a cautious word or two - nothing heavy-handed, just a nudge back to safer ground - when the women, almost as if on cue, lost all interest. Their expressions changed, eyes darting down the block, and without another word, they vanished into the crowd. Damion barely had time to wonder before he saw the reason: a pair of local Policía Nacional in crisp uniforms, walking a slow beat down the street. Whatever intentions those girls had, they wanted nothing to do with the law.

The moment passed, crisis averted, and Damion caught up with his buddies. They found an empty table at a nearby café and dropped into their seats with the easy, unspoken camaraderie that Chiefs carried everywhere. The conversation wound through all the familiar territory — Navy gripes, home-cooked food, old port stories - each man letting the day's stress dissolve into good company.

A sudden voice called out, "Hey, Sailor!" followed by a fit of laughter that broke through the din. Every Chief at the table snapped his head around, just in time to see Donna Reed, Stephanie Cheng, and Salina Cabrera grinning ear-to-ear at them from the curb. Stephanie, cheeks flushed and hair a little wild, laughed again and gave a sloppy salute. "I've always wanted to say that," she slurred, giggling at her own boldness.

BMC Mike Stein didn't miss a beat, grinning as wide as a barn door. "In Texas, we don't count heads, we just add plates!" he said, his voice stretching out every syllable with pride. The three women blinked, uncertain, until QMC Valentino leaned forward, all charm. "What he means is, the more the merrier! Pull up some chairs, ladies. We're not Officers, but we *are* gentlemen."

The waitress appeared like magic, balancing a tray of cold beers, and the group settled in, women and men sliding into the rhythm of good shipmates and new stories. They drank and laughed, the night spinning out in good cheer, until Donna and Stephanie - energy undimmed - announced a plan to find another pub. Cabrera shook her head, a tired smile playing on her lips. "I think I've seen enough of Rota for the last month. I need to get back to the ship and sleep. The Captain may have given the crew three days' liberty, but I plan to use at least two of them to catch up."

She started to fish for her phone, checking for taxi numbers. Damion caught her eye, already making up his mind. "I'll sit with you while you wait. If you can't get a cab, I'll walk you back. Wouldn't be right, or safe, to let you go alone." Cabrera just nodded in agreement.

After several rounds of "see you tomorrow" and light-hearted "don't get into trouble," the group dissolved in twos and threes down the block, voices carrying in the air. Damion and Cabrera drifted away from the café and found a bench nearby, sharing the easy quiet that comes from being too tired to talk, but not ready to say goodnight.

He nudged her, a teasing smile on his lips. "Did you plan this? Sneaking away for some alone time?"

She snorted. "I wish. I didn't plan to hang out with Donna and Stephanie either. But you try saying no to those two after a month stuck on the ship. And Stephanie, what a lush. She only had three beers before we showed up, and they turned her into *that*."

Shaking his head, Damion commented, "Yeah, she seems like a real party animal."

"I would say so. *And, I think she has a crush on you.*"

Damion turned and looked her in the eyes, "Are you nuts? No way."

"Yep. Didn't you see the way she kept checking you out all night? That was *definitely* crush-worthy. Plus, when we're alone, she always finds a way to bring you up in our conversations. I *think* I'm starting to get a little jealous."

Damion turns halfway towards her with a serious expression on his face, "Well, you shouldn't be. She and I could never be together. The Navy has rules about officers and enlisted personnel fraternizing, and I don't need double-trouble."

Cabrera bursts out laughing, covers her face with her hands, then peeks out between her fingers at him.

"You did *not* just say that!"

They talked a little longer - about everything and nothing - letting the time stretch out as far as they could. Eventually, when the wait for a taxi grew too long to bother with, they shrugged in unison and decided to walk back together. At least they had this time, just the two of them, and if they happened to find a quiet, shadowed corner along the way, well - sometimes a proper goodnight could make even the longest day worth it.

It was well past midnight, and the city had long settled into a slower, quieter rhythm. Street lamps glowed against the darkness, their pools of amber light stretching in uneven patches across the old cobblestones. The deep blue of night pressed in from every side, lending a hush to the air, broken only by the occasional distant laugh or the muffled sound of footsteps on stone. The air carried the salty tang from the nearby bay, and somewhere in the distance, a radio played a slow, mournful Spanish ballad. Damion and Cabrera walked side by side, slow and unhurried, their footsteps barely echoing off the old stone walls. There weren't many people out now, only the occasional shadowy figure slipping through the winding alleys.

They walked close enough to feel the warmth from each other's arms, yet careful to resist the urge to hold hands. Never quite touching, not in any way that a casual passerby could mistake as a couple walking together. But every so often, as if choreographed, the backs of their hands would brush, an accidental spark of something private, something just between them.

The street ahead curved and narrowed, funneling between two aging stucco buildings. That's when Damion noticed the cluster of five men standing directly in their path. German, most likely tourists by the sound of their boisterous laughter and guttural jokes, and unmistakably drunk, their faces flushed and voices loud enough to ricochet off the shuttered windows above. They blocked the street, shoulder to shoulder, beer bottles clutched loosely in their hands.

Damion and Cabrera exchanged a glance - a wordless understanding passing between them - but kept walking. As they drew closer, Damion nodded politely, voice steady but firm. "Excuse me, gentlemen. Mind if we get through?"

All five turned at once, movements lazy and uncoordinated, like a pack of bored wolves. Their eyes lingered on Damion for half a second before sliding past him, fixing on Cabrera with an unmistakable hunger. The largest of them, a bearded man with massive shoulders, easily six and a half feet tall, peeled away from the group and sauntered forward, a sneer crawling across his lips. His friends barked laughter behind him, egging him on.

He approached them with a cocky swagger, leering at Cabrera as he slurred out something obscene in half-broken English. The others guffawed, repeating the line with even less class. A giant, compared to Cabrera, he closed the distance to within arm's reach, then, without warning, the big man reached out and planted a thick hand on Cabrera's shoulder, fingers digging in just enough to cross a line.

Cabrera didn't hesitate. Her right fist shot up in a tight, perfect arc, an uppercut that landed square under his jaw with a sharp, satisfying crack. The man's head snapped back, mouth slamming shut and teeth cutting through his lip as he stumbled backwards, nearly losing his footing. For a second, the only sound was the clatter of his beer bottle hitting the stones and breaking into a hundred pieces. He shook his head, hand rubbing the bottom of his jaw. Smirking through the blood trickling from his split lip, he grunted, "Not bad for a girl," then he bared his bloody teeth in something that wasn't quite a smile. With a guttural growl, he lunged at Cabrera, arms outstretched and hands opened wide.

For a split second, Cabrera froze, caught off guard by the man's speed and raw aggression. Damion, however, reacted before she could think to get out of the charging bull's way. He slid in between them, arm sweeping Cabrera behind him as his left foot caught the charging man's ankle in a sharp trip. The giant crashed down hard, stone scraping against skin and bone.

The rest of the group quickly circled in, red-faced and furious, each one spitting curses in German. The leader rolled to his feet, eyes wild, and spat blood. "I'm gonna' rip you apart, schwachling, and then your little girlfriend's next," he barked, face twisted in rage. The others tightened the circle around Damion, five pairs of fists clenched and ready.

Damion stood his ground in the narrow, amber-lit street, the smell of brine and dust thick in the cool evening air. For a moment, time seemed to slow as the wolves circled with drunken bravado and a dangerous glint in their eyes. The leader barked something in German - whether a command or a curse, it didn't matter. What mattered was the sudden shift in the air, tension snapping taut like piano wire.

The first man lunged with a clumsy swing. Damion sidestepped, grabbing the man's arm and driving his own elbow hard into the soft tissue above his ribs. The man folded instantly, collapsing to his knees with a strangled groan. Almost before he hit the ground, the next two came at Damion from opposite sides. A quick pivot - Damion ducked under a wild punch, catching one by the shirt collar and slamming him into the wall. Plaster crumbled, dust blooming, and the man dropped in a heap.

The third swung a bottle, but Damion met him with a snap kick to the knee, the joint buckling at an ugly angle. He twisted away, letting the man crumple to the stones. The fourth and fifth hesitated, eyes wide with uncertainty, but then rushed him together. Damion grabbed one by the wrist, yanked him off balance, and drove a quick, sharp knee into his gut. The last man, the leader, charged in blindly, all brawn and bluster, but Damion caught him with a sweeping low kick, sending him sprawling across the cobblestones for a second time.

It was over in seconds. Five bodies lay scattered around Damion, their groans echoing off the close walls. Cabrera stood frozen behind him in disbelief. The blood had drained from her now pale face in the half-light, and her hands were clenched tightly by her sides.

He had held back, using only enough force to knock them off balance, never following through with a finishing blow. He did not want to have to explain to the Captain, or worse, to B.B., why he had caused an international incident for the unnecessary use of force on a bunch of drunk civilians while walking down a dark side street with his Divo. No, that was a conversation he *absolutely* did not want to have.

However, the men were obviously slow learners.

Stung more by pride than pain, three of the attackers struggled upright, faces twisted with humiliation and rage. The leader spat on the ground, eyes blazing, and reached into his jacket. The others followed, each producing a gleaming switchblade with a practiced, menacing flick of the wrist. Metal glinted in the lamplight. The street suddenly felt colder, and the threat just became real.

The big man's voice was a low growl, thick with contempt. "Now, American, let's see how tough you are."

Damion's eyes narrowed as something ice-cold settled in his gut. The kid gloves were now off.

The first knife-wielder lunged. Damion sidestepped, trapping the man's wrist and slamming a bone-crushing elbow into the attacker's jaw, disarming him with a twist that sent the blade clattering to the street and the unconscious attacker into the wall. The second attack came from behind. Damion spun, heel driving into the man's knee, dropping him with a guttural yell. A fist flew wildly at his head, but Damion ducked, drove a knee into the man's ribs, then finished him with a knife-hand strike to the throat.

The big man came last, charging like a ravenous bull, arms swinging and hands open like giant meat-claws. Damion met him head-on, catching him with a multi-combination offensive attack: first, countering the aggressor with a low block, then snapping a quick jab to the man's nose. In the same fluid motion, his left elbow arced sharply upward, crashing into the man's chin with jarring force. Without pausing, Damion finished the combo with a devastating roundhouse kick that sent the man sprawling across the narrow street for the third and final time.

Within seconds, all five men lay scattered on the cobblestones, groaning or unconscious. Alive, but no longer a threat.

Cabrera stood motionless, eyes wide in shock, chest rising and falling with adrenaline. She stared at Damion, and then at the pile of "not so cocky now" men. Somewhere, a window slammed shut.

Damion grabbed her by the arm, voice low and urgent. "We need to go. Now. Before the police show up." Without waiting for a reply, he led her quickly down the street, their footsteps muffled by the ancient stones, disappearing in the darkness and the winding alleys of the old town. Behind them, the night returned to silence, broken only by the distant sound of an approaching siren.

Chapter 13 - An Impossible Choice

A rare cold front from the West had moved in over Rota during the night, causing the morning temperature to drop several degrees below what was usual for a Spanish autumn day. The skies were a dull slate gray, heavy clouds rolling low and fast as if chasing the wind that swept across the bay. USS Daniel Shaw sat moored quietly at the pier, her steel hull streaked with condensation that glistened faintly in the early light. The cold breeze carried a briny smell from the Atlantic, mixing with the faint scent of diesel and wet rope from the pier's bollards. The water slapped lazily against the concrete pilings, sending soft echoes across the otherwise still waterfront.

The pier itself was nearly empty, save for a lone forklift parked near a stack of wooden pallets. A few seagulls perched along the railing as if standing a military watch, their feathers ruffling in the biting wind. A Spanish harbor patrol boat cruised slowly by in the distance, its engine humming low against the morning quiet.

Damion had slept very little after the previous night's encounter with the drunken Germans. Lying awake in his rack, he'd replayed the entire confrontation over and over, dissecting every move, every word, trying to decide what he could have done differently to avoid it. But, in the end, all of the mental debating he was doing always would end in the same conclusion, the moment the big drunk had grabbed Salina.

He smiled faintly now as he tugged on his t-shirt, shorts, and sneakers. Salina's reaction had been as unexpected as it was impressive. That uppercut had stunned the German as much as it had surprised Damion. "Not bad," the man had admitted with that crooked grin before everything went sideways.

Since he was already awake, Damion figured he might as well make use of the cool morning air.

Moving through the quiet passageways, the usual hum of shipboard life was absent. The crew had two more days off, and the silence felt almost unnatural.

Exiting the watertight door onto the starboard weather deck, Damion showed his ID card to the quarterdeck watch and informed them he was going for a run on the base. After a quick nod and salute from the young Petty Officer, he made his way down the brow onto the pier. He stretched for five minutes, loosening his legs and shoulders, then began jogging at a comfortable pace.

The cold air bit at his skin, his breath forming faint clouds as he settled into his stride. His thoughts drifted to Salina again. She had been shaken right after the fight, and he'd practically dragged her away at first. By the time they had reached the main gate, she was almost back to her usual self, but there had still been worry in her eyes. He decided to check on her later, once the ship was fully awake and personnel began moving around. Otherwise, it might look strange going to her stateroom at this time of the morning.

From the pier, Damion turned right, heading past a small supply warehouse. The warehouse doors were closed, but the faint smell of machine oil lingered in the air. Running along the edge of the pier road, he passed stacks of shipping containers painted in dull blues and grays, some marked with U.S. Navy stencils, others with Spanish base designations. He veered left onto the main road that ran parallel to the water, jogging past the large maintenance hangar where a few Spanish sailors were already working early on a patrol craft. The rhythmic clang of metal echoed inside the open bay, briefly breaking the otherwise quiet morning.

Crossing the small bridge over a drainage canal, he followed the road toward the housing area. A row of eucalyptus trees lined the roadside, their tall, pale trunks swaying slightly in the breeze. The scent of their leaves mixed with the salty air, a clean, crisp contrast to the industrial smell of the pier. He cut past the base chapel, its simple white stucco walls and modest bell tower standing out against the gray sky. A few early risers were seen near the small park across from it, walking dogs or pushing strollers.

Continuing on, Damion looped around the perimeter road that ran along the edge of the airfield. The distant rumble of aircraft engines broke the stillness as a Spanish Navy C-295 transport plane taxied slowly along the runway. He kept his pace steady, passing the chain-link fence that separated the running trail from the airfield. Beyond the fence, seagulls scattered as the ground crew moved about.

As he approached the recreational area near the base gym and pool, a handful of Marines were already doing PT, their cadence chants faint but distinct in the crisp air. Damion gave a quick nod to a pair of Chiefs jogging in the opposite direction.

Finally, he cut back toward the waterfront, following the road that wound past the old stone seawall. The view opened to the bay, where fishing boats bobbed gently in the water. The cold front had turned the sea a deep, steel blue, the choppy surface reflecting the heavy clouds. Damion sped up slightly as he neared the pier, finishing his run by sprinting the last quarter-mile back to the ship.

Back at the pier, Damion spent fifteen minutes stretching. First hamstrings, then quads, then deep lunges to loosen his hips. He rolled his shoulders, then dropped into push-up holds to stretch his chest and arms. The cold air stung his skin as sweat cooled against his back.

Finished, he climbed back aboard the ship, exchanging a quick word with the quarterdeck watch before heading below. A hot shower followed, the steam cutting through the chill still lingering in his muscles.

By the time he entered the Chiefs' Mess, the smell of scrambled eggs, bacon, pancakes, and fresh coffee filled the air. A few Chiefs were already seated, laughing over some inside joke. Damion grabbed a tray, ready for breakfast and whatever the day might bring.

After breakfast, the ship began to come alive. Voices echoed off the steel bulkheads, hatches opening and closing, and the distant whir of equipment powering up somewhere below decks.

As he walked, his mind drifted back to Salina. He could still see her face from last night, the way her expression shifted from anger to worry in those tense moments after the fight. He wondered how she was feeling this morning, if she'd shaken off the lingering unease or if it was still eating at her.

Maybe I should've checked on her earlier, he thought, running a hand along the cool bulkhead as he turned down another narrow passageway. No, that wouldn't have been smart. After all, she wasn't some helpless damsel in distress. The lady could take care of herself.

He had just started up the metal steps of a midships ladder when he saw movement coming from above.

Salina.

She was descending the ladder, one hand gripping the rail, the other holding a folder tucked neatly against her chest. Her hair, pulled back in a loose bun, still carried that reddish-brown hue that caught the light in just the right way, even in the dull glow of the ship's overheads. She was dressed casually, in civvies like before, though today she wore a dark navy hoodie and fitted jeans.

The moment she looked down and saw him, her lips curved into a small, knowing smile.

"Chief Jackson," she said, her voice carrying a teasing edge as she slowed her steps. "Fancy meeting you here."

Damion stopped at the bottom of the ladder, one hand resting on the rail. He allowed himself a faint grin. "Figured I'd come find you before you got yourself into any more bar fights."

That earned him a quiet laugh, and she shook her head as she descended the last few steps.

"I think you handled that pretty well without me," she replied, stopping just a step above him. "But for the record, I had that guy."

"Yeah," Damion said, tilting his head slightly, his grin widening. "I saw. You damn near broke his jaw."

Her smile softened at that, but her eyes held something else—something unspoken, a flicker of the tension from last night that still lingered beneath her usual confidence.

"Not quite. I hit that guy with everything I had, and he still didn't go down."

"Are you serious? Dude was a beast. He even *growled* at you. I'd wager that if it had been one of his flunkies you punched like that, they would have been crying for their mama."

Cabrera laughed, then paused for a beat, studying his face, then gave a slight nod. "I'm fine. Really. It's just... I wasn't expecting to spend my night dodging fists, that's all."

Damion nodded slowly, letting the moment hang between them.

Breaking the silence, she began, "Well, I had better get going and get caught up on the work I missed during my rehab." Then, lowering her voice, she added, "Maybe we can meet up later after I'm done?"

"I'll be in my office all day," he replied.

"Good, then I'll see you later. And, you can tell me how you did what you did. That obviously wasn't the first time you used whatever that was."

Damion watched her disappear down the passageway, while thoughts about his own past slowly crept their way into the forefront of his brain. Turning and continuing up the ladderwell with his destination now unclear, he started wondering if he should ever tell her about his life before the Daniel Shaw, and if so, *how much* of it he should reveal to her. The need to be honest with Salina pulled at him constantly, given their newly formed relationship. Of course, they could never be seen together publicly while they were both on active duty. One of the strictest taboos, the Navy frowned rather badly upon fraternization between Officers and Enlisted personnel. Even so, here they were, and he felt that it was important to tell her at least a little about his background. And, just as equally important, what *not* to say to her about his background. Some dead dogs needed to stay buried. And then, there was this investigation that had him secretly spying on her. Every time he thought about it, he felt a little nauseous as a knot the size of a golf ball formed in his gut. Shaking his head as he reached the top of the ladder and headed out the watertight door, Damion thought to himself that being between a rock and a hard place would be more comfortable right now than the situation he was in.

Standing on the weather deck, Damion noted that the cool morning had already succumbed to the rapidly rising sun, which painted streaks of gold and soft orange across the choppy water. Damion stood alone, leaning casually against the railing, his arms folded as he vacantly scanned the harbor. To anyone passing by, he looked relaxed, just another Chief enjoying the rare stillness of a liberty morning. His eyes appeared to be scanning the harbor with the same quiet vigilance he used when at sea, following the slow bobbing of moored buoys and the rhythmic sway of several small boats, but his mind was far away. The soft crunch of boots on the nonskid deck plating broke his concentration. QMC(SW) Valentino approached cautiously, his expression unreadable but his tone carrying a hint of curiosity.

"Morning, DJ," Valentino started, keeping his voice low as he glanced toward the pier. "What's going on?"

Damion turned his head slightly, "Morning, Cas. Not too much, just catching a bit of air."

Valentino paused for a moment, then continued, "No, I mean, *what is going on?*"

Damion turned and looked directly at Valentino, his brow furrowing. "What do you mean, what's going on?"

Valentino shifted his weight, clearly debating whether to press the issue. "The same female NCIS agent who flew onboard when we were out at sea... she came aboard again this morning. I didn't know who she was at the time, but I was on the quarterdeck when she signed in. Maya Torres, NCIS."

For a half-second, Damion felt a flicker of surprise, but he kept his expression locked down tight, the way years of training had taught him. He shrugged, his face a perfect mask of disinterest. "No idea. I haven't heard anything."

Valentino studied him for a moment, searching for a tell, then finally gave a short nod. "Alright, Boss," he said before heading back toward the superstructure "Give me a head's up if you hear of some type of crap heading our way, okay?"

"You know it," DJ replied, hoping the only crap would be Torres stepping in it for bringing this here. Only when Valentino disappeared from sight did Damion allow his mind to race. Why was Torres back on the ship? His gut tightened, and a low buzz of unease ran through him. Whatever the reason, knowing Torres, it probably wasn't good.

The soft crunch of approaching footsteps pulled him out of his thoughts. A young Seaman – the Messenger of the Watch - stood stiffly in front of him, her hands clasped behind her back.

"Good morning, Chief. The XO requests you in his stateroom when you have time," she said formally. Then she added, as if by rehearsed instruction, "He didn't want to pass the word over the 1MC, so as not to disturb the crew still sleeping off liberty."

Damion almost smirked at that. Good one, XO, he thought. Making the *request* sound like it was not a big deal, so as not to encourage any rumors by the junior sailors. Everyone knew that on a ship, rumors moved faster than air through the recirculated ventilation system. So, when the XO "requested" you, it meant now, not "when you had time."

"Thanks, shipmate," Damion said simply, and continued leaning on the railing. He waited well until she had disappeared around the corner on her way back to the quarterdeck, before he headed back inside the ship to the XO's stateroom. The air felt heavier as he stepped into Officers' Country, the silence of the ship filling the narrow passageways. The XO was already standing outside his stateroom, arms crossed, and without a word, motioned for Damion to follow. They walked briskly to the CO's cabin, and after a short knock, the XO opened the door.

Inside, the Captain sat behind his desk, his face neutral but his posture saying plenty. Across from him sat Special Agent Maya Torres, her dark hair pulled back neatly, her NCIS badge clipped at her side.

"Good morning, Chief," Torres said, her tone a forced politeness, but all business. "Sorry to interrupt your liberty."

"Morning," Damion replied, keeping his voice even, giving her nothing.

Torres exchanged a glance with the CO before turning back to Damion. "I've already briefed the Captain and XO, but you need to be brought up to speed."

She leaned forward slightly, her eyes sharp. "One of the suspect boats your ship boarded during that earlier MIO, that the Daniel Shaw inspected and released, was also intercepted by the Spanish frigate *Cristóbal Colón* two days later, before they pulled into port. A large quantity of contraband was discovered on board. The Spaniards are saying that there's no way a trained boarding team could have missed it."

Damion didn't move, didn't blink. *The Spaniards are saying?* He thought to himself.

Torres continued. "They're suggesting that someone might have been providing information to the smugglers - someone with knowledge of ship movements and patrol areas. That kind of information is limited to a very select group."

Damion caught the word choice. *Someone.* Singular. Not perpetrators.

Torres added quickly, "No one is being implicated. Yet."

But Damion knew better. If the evidence started leaning the wrong way, it could easily point to Cabrera. Or him. Or any of the senior boarding personnel.

She continued, detailing how the Spanish authorities delayed informing their American counterparts because they were conducting their own investigation. They had received an *anonymous* tip, which eventually led to a dock worker at the naval station. That worker had been *encouraged* to provide any information he knew of, which resulted in the location of a warehouse used to store contraband.

Torres straightened, her tone shifting. "We're going to raid the warehouse. I want you to be there. Strictly as an observer, of course."

Damion looked at her carefully, "Of course."

Chapter 14 - When Honor Trembles

The warehouse was actually an old auto repair shop that sat on the edge of town, its faded paint peeling in long strips, and the air heavy with the smell of rust and oil. Inside, dust motes floated in the shafts of sunlight cutting through broken windows. The Spanish Guardia Civil moved methodically through the space, cataloguing evidence as their boots crunched over the aging cement floor. Piles of contraband sat in one corner: designer handbags wrapped in clear plastic, stacks of name-brand sneakers, counterfeit luxury watches glittering under the dull light, and boxes of expensive liquor. Some of the bottles still had seals with tax stamps from other countries on them.

Damion walked slowly through the warehouse, careful not to touch anything, his eyes scanning every detail. He turned at the sound of an animated discussion, where one of the Spanish police officers was holding a gold chain necklace up to the light, discussing it with his comrade. Damion could not see it up close, but he could see the gold cross pendant covered with dust from the warehouse. Maybe someone who worked at the auto shop, a visitor, or even one of the smugglers had dropped it. Regardless, it was now evidence. As he continued walking around, something about the place felt wrong. Everything looked old, used, or corroded with time. Everything, except for the fuel drums stacked neatly in a shadowed corner. They were dusty, yes, but not as aged as the rest of the equipment in this place. He slowly approached the first drum, tapping the side with his knuckles. Full. Curious, he put on the gloves

Torres had graciously loaned him and pried the lid open with a crowbar. A thick, oily liquid coated the inside. It moved sluggishly, like motor oil, but there was no odor. He moved to the next drum, and then to a third. Same thing. Some type of substance that only a lab would be used to identify it, if Torres thought it might be relevant to the investigation. When he opened the fourth drum, his body froze mid-motion.

Inside, arranged with disturbing precision, were the butt-ends of a large quantity of Russian Kalashnikov assault rifles, their brown, wooden stocks pressed tightly in a circular formation. The rifle barrels, having been removed to make room, were secured together with metal strapping bands and stood separately in the center of the drum. Three double rows of rifle stocks formed a perfect spiral, and from a quick glance, Damion counted at least 40 on the top layer alone. Judging by the depth, there were likely three complete rows packed into the container. Damion stepped back, then snapped his fingers twice – short and sharp. Torres appeared almost instantly, flanked by the Spanish lieutenant and his assistant. All three stared into the drum, their faces hardening as the reality sank in. Across the warehouse, several Spanish officers shouted to one another as they too uncovered more drums under a dusty old tarp. Fifteen in total.

A Guardia Civil officer approached them at a hurried pace, carrying a weathered ledger. He handed it to his lieutenant, who flipped through it, frowning deeply before passing it to Torres.

The Spanish officer glanced at Damion, his voice carrying an edge of suspicion. "According to this, that shipment was delivered the day before your ship returned to Rota. Almost as if someone was planning to pick it up after you arrived."

Damion kept his face impassive, but inside his mind was spinning like a radar locked in continuous sweep mode. *The day before the Daniel Shaw returned to Rota...* The Spanish lieutenant's words echoed in his head, heavy with accusation.

Ignoring the lieutenant's comments while resting one hand on the edge of the fuel drum, he stared at the neat spiral of rifle butts. His eyes swept over the precision of the packing job. Whoever did this wasn't just some low-level smuggler tossing gear into barrels; this was deliberate, organized, and very professional.

"Fifteen drums," Torres murmured beside him, more to herself than anyone else.

Damion didn't look up at her. Instead, he crouched down and studied the floor beneath the drum, noticing faint drag marks in the dust. Confirmation that these drums hadn't been sitting here for years like the rest of the junk. They'd been moved recently, maybe even staged.

Suddenly, the cross pendant flashed in his mind, uninvited but sharp, like a photograph burned into memory. Salina. The way she had twirled the necklace absently at Mama Casita's, the sunlight catching on the unique carvings. His jaw tightened. The necklace that the officer had held up to the light. It had looked vaguely familiar, but it couldn't be hers. After all, this was Spain. There had to be ten million of those types of necklaces here. He didn't want to connect her to this, but even so, the possibility gnawed at him like a dog with its favorite bone.

His thoughts were interrupted by two Guardia Civil officers speaking in rapid Spanish, their voices tense but controlled. One of them glanced at him briefly with just a flicker of suspicion before looking away. They're already building their narrative, Damion thought grimly. An American ship arrives, contraband is conveniently intercepted, and now weapons show up the day before we pull in. Too neat. Too damn convenient.

Torres was eyeing him now, her arms folded, expression unreadable. "Something on your mind, Chief?" she asked casually, but he could hear the layer beneath her tone – probing and calculating.

He gave her the same shrug he had given Valentino earlier that morning. "Just thinking how lucky we are that you got that tip about this warehouse. Could've been missed completely."

Her eyes narrowed slightly, just for a second, before she looked back down at the ledger. She knew he was holding something back.

The Spanish lieutenant stepped forward, his voice calm but deliberate. "Señor Jackson, does your team ever operate close to Rota? Perhaps with 10-12 miles during previous boardings?"

Damion met his gaze squarely. "No, Lieutenant. Our MIO ops are conducted *at sea*, not in another country's territorial waters. Especially, not our allies. Which means that this warehouse isn't exactly in my area of responsibility."

The lieutenant's lips pressed into a tight, thin line, unconvinced but unable to push further without evidence.

Torres flipped through the ledger, her brow furrowing deeper. "This delivery... the timing is precise. Whoever arranged this shipment knew exactly when the Daniel Shaw was scheduled to return. And that's information not everyone has access to."

Damion stayed silent, but his mind replayed the chain of events, checking every possible weak link in the ship's operational security. Only a handful of people knew the Daniel Shaw's schedule in advance. So, who's feeding them, and how?

One of the Spanish officers called out from across the warehouse, holding up a small handheld radio wrapped in a plastic evidence bag. Torres and the lieutenant moved toward him, leaving Damion standing by the open drums.

He looked back down into the drum. The black rifle stocks stared up at him like dead eyes. For just a fleeting moment, he imagined Salina twirling that gold cross in one hand, while shooting one of the AK rifles with the other.

He exhaled slowly. If that necklace is hers... she's involved in this somehow. And if she's involved, this whole thing just got personal.

Damion straightened, his expression hardening into the same steel calm he wore during boarding operations. Whatever this was, someone had set the stage perfectly, and whether they realized it or not, they had just pulled him into the center of it.

And Damion Jackson wasn't about to be anyone's pawn.

Long shadows stretched across the cracked pavement outside of the warehouse as the Guardia Civil officer secured the evidence for transport. Damion stayed back, leaning casually against the side of one of their trucks, watching Torres give her closing notes to the Spanish lieutenant. To anyone looking, he was just another Chief waiting for orders, unbothered, unhurried.

But inside, his thoughts stayed locked on one thing - the necklace.

The gold cross with its delicate, hand-carved etchings wasn't just some generic trinket picked up at a tourist shop. Clearer now, he could picture it perfectly against Salina's skin, the way she absentmindedly spun it between her fingers while laughing at something he had said at Mama Casita's. That moment had felt innocent then, but now... now it carried weight.

When Torres finally stepped away from the lieutenant and started back toward him, Damion pushed himself off the truck, his face the picture of calm professionalism.

"We're done here," Torres said, adjusting the strap of her evidence bag. "Spanish authorities will catalog the rest. NCIS will get copies of everything by tomorrow."

"Got it," Damion replied with a nod. "You need me for anything else?"

"Not today." She gave him a long look, as if trying to read him, then finally turned to talk to one of the police officers.

Good. That was precisely what he wanted.

As soon as she had moved out of earshot, Damion stepped toward one of the Guardia Civil officers still loading evidence crates. The man looked up, slightly wary at first, but relaxed when Damion gave a polite nod.

"Perdón, Jefe," Damion began, slipping into the bit of Spanish he'd picked up from his travels. "The necklace you found earlier - the gold one with the cross. Do you still have it?"

The officer frowned slightly. "Está con los otros objetos. With the other items," he said, pointing to a sealed evidence container.

Damion nodded thoughtfully, keeping his tone casual. "I thought I saw one like it before. Just curious."

The officer shrugged, uninterested, and went back to securing the evidence. Perfect. No suspicion.

When Torres called for him to head back to the transport van, Damion fell in step beside her, saying nothing. But his mind was already working on the problem.

If that necklace was Salina's, and NCIS figured it out first, the chain of suspicion could turn ugly fast. She could claim that it wasn't hers, but if there were fingerprints or DNA evidence, then it would be over for her. He needed to confirm it before anyone else connected the dots. No time for a night on the town, he needed to get back to the ship.

The sun had long set by the time Damion stepped back onto the Daniel Shaw. The harbor lights shimmered off the still water, their reflections stretching like thin fingers across the surface. From somewhere beyond the pier, the faint hum of distant music and laughter floated on the night air, while liberty call had pulled most of the crew into town. The ship itself felt quiet, almost hollow, with only the watchstanders moving about.

Damion crossed the brow with the same unhurried stride he always used—never rushing, never giving anyone a reason to look twice. At the quarterdeck, he exchanged a brief nod with the duty Chief before disappearing into the ship's interior.

Once inside the CPO berthing, he sat on the edge of his rack, pulling out his phone. He didn't bother scrolling through messages - there hadn't been any from her, and he hadn't expected any. They hadn't had the opportunity to speak since he ghosted her due to the unexpected warehouse raid. Both of them were playing it carefully. He assumed that she knew that if he hadn't met her, then something very important must have come up. He opened his phone and went straight to the photos, thumbing through the shots he'd taken at Mama Casita's. There she was, smiling, leaning forward across the table, sunlight catching the gold cross she wore. The same unique carvings stared back at him from the zoomed-in image, etched into his memory as clearly as if he were holding it in his hand.

He leaned back against the cool steel bulkhead, staring at the picture for a long moment. If that necklace from the warehouse was hers, this was bad—worse than bad. But he couldn't accuse her, couldn't even let on that he suspected anything. Not yet.

Now, he just needed to find a way to confirm it without Torres or NCIS catching wind of what he was doing. The second they knew he was digging on his own, he'd go from "helpful Chief" to "person of interest" faster than the ship could change course.

He slid the phone back into his pocket, his jaw tightening for the third time that day.

Salina wasn't going anywhere. She was here, within arm's reach, every day. And if she was guilty, or worse, if she was innocent but caught in something she didn't understand, then he had to find out before someone else decided it for her. If she was involved, even accidentally, NCIS would eat her alive.

And Damion wasn't going to let that happen.

A sudden grumble from his stomach reminded him that he had missed dinner while out playing observer with Torres, so he decided to go to the Chiefs' Mess and raid the snack reserves, which all the Chiefs donated funds to. As he started to enter the mess, a familiar voice called out.

"Hey, Chief. You got a minute?"

Turning and looking down the passageway, he saw Cabrera, dressed in a turquoise sundress and matching sandals, casually coming towards him. Her hair was let down except for a single, long braid lining the left side of her face. A lone sign of rebellion against the rest of her perfect ensemble. Damion observed that she wasn't wearing her necklace.

"Always," he said, catching his breath and trying to sound normal. "I missed dinner earlier, so I'm just gonna' grab something from the Mess."

They both stepped inside, allowing the door to close automatically behind them. Seeing that the room was empty, Damion turned to her and spoke first.

"Wow, you look great. You got a date or something?"

"I thought I did," she said matter-of-factly.

"Oh yeah, sorry about earlier today. I got called away by the XO to take care of something he wanted done asap."

Looking disappointed, but understanding how things worked in the military, she answered, "No problem. Duty calls." Declining a soft drink offered by Damion, she sat down at one of the tables before continuing.

"They pulled me into an intel briefing today. Real vague. Something about foreign surveillance in the port."

Damion raised an eyebrow, carefully neutral. "Really?"

"Yeah. Said not to worry. That it was probably nothing. But the way they said it? Sounded more like, *'You are being watched.'*" She crossed her arms, leaning back against the cushioned bench. "Have you heard anything?"

He hesitated. Then lied. "No, I haven't."

She studied him for a moment. "Something feels off. You ever get that? You can't explain it, but you know it's there?"

She feels it. Whether someone had spoken to her directly or not, Salina knew she was under scrutiny.

"All the time," he replied.

"I just…" She cut herself off, glanced at the table, then back up and looked him straight in the eyes. "You'd tell me, right? If something was wrong?"

Damion swallowed. The weight of Torres's words echoed in his head. *Don't spook her. Watch who she talks to.*

He nodded slowly. "Of course. You'd do the same for me." A firm statement, not a question.

She smiled, tight, but genuine. "Good. Thanks." Then, tilting her head with a twinkle in her eyes, *"Do you think we have time to…?"*

Damion paused in mid-bite of the power bar he was eating and looked at her with a smirk, "If we walk together *anywhere* at this time of the night with you dressed like that…"

She laughed softly, "Can't blame a girl for trying, right? Well, I guess I will see you tomorrow then. Goodnight."

When the door closed behind her, Damion leaned forward with both elbows on the table and his hands on his head.

He was in too deep, and the tide was rising.

Chapter 15 – Every Single Glance

The next morning, the air aboard the ship felt different. Even before Damion had his first cup of coffee, he could sense it in the way people moved through the passageways: quieter, more deliberate, as if everyone was trying not to draw attention to themselves. The hum of conversation that usually floated through the mess decks was gone, replaced by low murmurs and quick glances toward anyone wearing a khaki uniform.

Before the passing of *Morning Colors* (a naval tradition of raising the American flag conducted every morning at precisely 8 a.m. and sunset), Torres and two additional NCIS agents had come aboard and were making their presence known. Rumors had initially begun to spread about several drunken "khaki" *bad boys* involved in a fight in town, leaving several tourists in the hospital. The junior personnel thought that it must have been some of the Chiefs, because the Officers were not exactly known to be the "old salty" types who enjoyed getting into fistfights. Of course, this old myth about Navy Chiefs was utterly false. Although the average modern-day Navy Chief Petty Officer was highly trained, they were also very professional and able to do much more damage with their words and a pen than their predecessors would have ever thought possible. However, there *were* times when a couple of collars still needed to be roughed up a little.

Damion leaned casually against the bulkhead outside of the Chiefs' Mess, watching as two NCIS agents walked past with one of the ship's Petty Officers trailing behind them. The kid looked nervous, his eyes darting around like he wanted to melt into the deck. They disappeared into the Operations office, the watertight door shutting firmly behind them.

Across the passageway, QMC Valentino caught Damion's eye as he passed by, his face tight. "They're pulling people in one by one," he muttered under his breath. "Boarding team personnel only, so far."

Damion gave the smallest of nods, masking the unease curling in his gut. "Figures."

Valentino didn't stop, just kept walking, but the look he gave Damion spoke volumes. *Be careful. They're looking for someone to blame something on.*

Torres had tried to be smart. She hadn't ordered an all-hands or departmental muster, nor focused on any one specific division. Instead, they came on board early and were working quietly, surgically, appearing to pull random sailors aside for "informal conversations." But word was spreading anyway, just like Damion knew it would.

He decided to go to his office and start on some work while he had the chance, his mind already racing through the possibilities of these interrogations. If Torres and her team were focusing on the boarding crew, it meant that they were trying to narrow the list of people with operational knowledge. It also meant that if they had even the slightest suspicion pointing toward Salina, or him, they'd move fast.

And Salina, tough as she was, wasn't built for this kind of pressure. Damion had seen hardened sailors crack under far less scrutiny. If Torres cornered her with the right questions, she might stumble into saying something that looked guilty, even if she was innocent.

He pushed away from the bulkhead and began walking, his steps measured and deliberate.

As he moved through the passageway, he passed Torres, acknowledging her with a nod and a simple, *"Morning"*. She gave him a polite nod, her expression neutral, but her eyes followed him for a moment too long before she turned back and continued to join her fellow agents.

"She's looking at me also now," he thought.

By the time Damion reached his office, he'd already made up his mind. Waiting to see how this played out wasn't an option. If Torres was determined to make a scapegoat out of someone and targeted Salina first, it could all spiral out of control.

He needed to confirm the truth about that necklace, and he needed to do it soon. And if it *was* hers, he had to find out why it ended up in that warehouse before NCIS connected the dots for themselves.

Entering his office, Damion decided to leave the watertight door open, his mind already forming a plan. *No more hiding. No more waiting.*

If he was going to clear her and his team, or confirm what he feared, he had to move fast, and he had to do it before Torres tightened the noose around both of their necks.

It didn't take long.

Barely an hour after Damion sat down at his desk, a dark shadow fell over the entrance, followed by two sharp knocks on the door. Not the courtesy three knocks of a shipmate stopping by.

"Enter," Damion replied, not looking up and maintaining a nonchalant tone.

Special Agent Maya Torres stepped inside, followed by one of her fellow NCIS agents carrying a slim folder tucked under his arm. Torres's expression was polite, almost pleasant, but her eyes were sharp, studying him the way a hawk studies a mouse.

"Chief Jackson," she said evenly. "Do you have a few minutes?"

Damion gave a slight shrug, leaning back in his chair like he had nothing better to do. "Sure. What's up?"

Torres nodded, stepping inside and shutting the door behind her and her partner. She didn't ask if she could sit; she just pulled out the chair across from him and sat down, resting her hands lightly on his desk. The other agent stayed standing by the door, his eyes passing between Damion and Torres.

"We're just doing some follow-ups," Torres began, her tone casual, conversational. "You know how it is with these kinds of investigations, lots of little pieces to keep track of."

Damion gave her the faintest of smiles. "Sounds like a lot of paperwork."

"It is," she agreed, smiling back briefly before her expression settled into something more sinister. "But some of those pieces... well, they involve your team. And you were in charge of those boarding operations."

Damion didn't flinch. "That's correct."

Torres studied him for a moment, letting the silence stretch just long enough to feel intentional. "The Spanish authorities are still insisting that the contraband discovered on that smuggler's boat would've been hard to miss. Very hard, actually."

He kept his face relaxed, relaxing even more in his chair and interlacing his fingers. "I can't speak for what the Spaniards found after the fact. I can only speak to what we saw when we boarded. And we followed SOP to the letter."

"Of course," Torres said, nodding as if she agreed with him. But she didn't look away. "Still... whoever helped these smugglers clearly had access to information that they shouldn't have had. Movement schedules. Patrol patterns. That narrows things down considerably."

Her assistant finally stepped forward, opening the slim folder and sliding two photographs across the table. Damion glanced down at them briefly. One was a picture of the warehouse from the previous day with the drums of weapons in the background. The second was of all the guns removed from the drums and organized in rows on the floor of what appeared to be another unknown warehouse.

Torres didn't say anything at first, just watched his reaction.

Damion gave the photos a single, casual look, then slid them back towards her. "Hell of a haul. Someone's going to miss those rifles, and I suppose your bosses are going to be thrilled that you found them."

The corner of Torres's mouth twitched. "You're not surprised."

"I may have been surprised when I opened the first drum. Not so much now. I've been doing this a long time," Damion said calmly. "Weapons caches generally don't shock me anymore. People will smuggle anything if there's enough money in it."

Torres tapped the folder lightly, her gaze never leaving him. "True. However, the timing of this shipment, which was delivered the day before your ship returned to Rota, makes it... interesting."

Damion shrugged, his face giving away nothing. "Could also be a coincidence. Do you *really* think that someone on *my* team is involved?"

"I think someone with access to sensitive information is involved," Torres said evenly. "And the list of people who have that access is pretty short."

For the first time since she entered, Damion leaned forward slightly, resting his forearms on the desk. His tone stayed even, but his eyes locked onto hers.

"If you're asking whether anyone on my team leaked anything, I'll tell you what I've already told my Captain...no. We followed procedures. We did our jobs. Period. And if someone else wants to blame my team in order to cover their own mistakes, then they are going to have a serious fight on their hands."

Torres studied him for a long moment, her eyes narrowing slightly, but she didn't push further. Instead, she gave a slight nod, almost like she was filing away his reaction for later.

"We're just asking questions, Chief," she said, standing smoothly. "But I appreciate your time."

She turned to leave while the other agent gathered the photos in the folder, then followed her out.

As soon as the door closed behind them, Damion sat back in his chair, exhaling slowly. His face was calm, but his mind was anything but.

They're closing in, and she doesn't believe me. Not yet, anyway.

He rubbed a hand over his jaw, his eyes narrowing. *Strange that she didn't ask any questions about Salina or even if I had an update on whether I had learned anything new.*

His mind drifted, not because he wanted it to, but because some memories had a way of clawing their way to the surface whether you wanted them to or not.

And there it was. Bahrain. That night on the docks. Every detail coming back with unsettling clarity.

The humid night air had been hot and heavy with the smell of exhaust fumes from the dilapidated fishing dhows moored to the pier. The boat crews and regular workers had gone home for the day, and the docks were empty except for the joint forces security team and the unsuspecting criminals running an illegal operation, which Damion and company had come to shut down. The raid had been fast and methodical – a standard operation for what was supposed to be a low-risk smuggling bust. Electronics, fake passports, contraband alcohol, nothing they hadn't seen before.

He remembered Torres beside him, moving with the same calm efficiency she had always carried, even back then. She had been his partner for that operation, and for most of the night, they worked seamlessly together. She covered angles, he cleared containers, both of them communicating in quick, clipped whispers.

But then things had gone bad.

One of the smugglers broke cover, bolting from behind a shipping crate. Damion and Torres chased, their boots pounding against the cement deck of the pier. The man was desperate, cornered, and when a Bahraini PSF policeman moved to intercept him, the smuggler spun and drove a blade into the officer's side.

Damion remembered the shock and terror on the officer's face as the smuggler wrenched the blade free and then turned and charged straight at him.

Everything after that happened in seconds.

Damion stepped forward, intercepting him before Torres had a clean shot. He grabbed the smuggler's wrist, twisting hard, his other hand striking him square in the chest to drive him back. It worked - too well.

The smuggler stumbled, his heels catching on a mooring line, and he went down hard. The back of his head struck a metal cleat with a sickening *crack* that Damion could still hear in his sleep. He had just stood there and watched the limp body.

Torres had been the first to kneel beside him, checking for a pulse. She looked up at Damion and shook her head once. No words, just that look.

The investigation that followed was quick and thorough. Multiple witnesses, including Torres, had testified that Damion acted in self-defense. The smuggler had been armed and had already stabbed a police officer. The death was ruled accidental.

The incident was documented in the task force's after-action report, but at Torres's insistence, it never made it into his permanent service record. "You don't deserve to have that black mark follow you forever," she had told him quietly after the debrief, her voice low so no one else would hear.

Case closed. The operation ended. Everyone moved on.

Everyone except Damion.

He tried again to push the memory back down, to lock it away permanently, but Torres's presence here had brought it all rushing back like a tidal wave. It was as if the memory had a life of its own, making him re-live the incident over and over again as if trying to show him something. She hadn't said a word about Bahrain since she arrived, but the way she had watched him during their earlier conversations made him wonder if she was thinking about it too.

And there it was again. The memory would not stop forming in his mind. Taking a deep breath, Damion closed his eyes and focused on the steady background sounds of the ship's equipment and AC system. After several minutes of deep concentration, tuning out everything else around him, he revisited that night once more.

He could see Torres moving with precision through the maze of shipping containers, her sidearm drawn, her voice calm and steady as she directed the security team. They had worked side by side, clearing crates and calling out positions, until the chaos began.

Damion's eyes suddenly opened. *That was when they got separated.*

The smuggler he ended up killing - the desperate one who stabbed the Bahraini security policeman - hadn't been the leader. The leader had slipped away in the confusion, and Torres had gone after him.

He remembered it clearly now. Torres breaking off, sprinting down a narrow row of stacked containers after the man. She hadn't waited for backup, hadn't called out a location over comms, just... disappeared into the dark.

While Damion was taking down the smuggler who charged him, Torres was not *actually* present. It was only after the man lay dead, his head cracked open against that metal cleat, that Torres reappeared, breathless but composed. She'd told him the leader had gotten away. At the time, he hadn't questioned it. Things moved fast in operations like that. People sometimes escaped, even when the exits were covered. But now... now, the details didn't sit right. Every exit *had* been covered. The security team had locked the piers down tight, every checkpoint manned, and they'd been tactically positioned to prevent any boats from slipping away. And yet, Torres had insisted that the leader managed to vanish.

And, there was the contraband. At the time, it had been considered a substantial bust - electronics, counterfeit IDs, and illegal liquor. But the more Damion thought about it, the more something felt wrong. The illegal gang they had been chasing was not suspected of ties to weapons smuggling, and none were recovered. However, sitting in his office aboard the Daniel Shaw, these new, confusing thoughts only amplified the unease that had begun earlier, now twisting angrily in his gut.

What did happen that night? And why didn't he remember these new memories until now?

Torres had been the only one with eyes on the leader. The only one who knew what direction he ran, and the only one who had chased him. She had been gone just long enough for the chaos to settle before she reappeared, claiming he had slipped away.

At the time, he'd trusted her completely. She had been his partner that night, the one who had backed him up when the smuggler died. The one who had quietly made sure the after-action report didn't haunt his service record.

But now?

Now, the more he replayed that night, the more Torres herself was starting to look suspicious.

If someone back then had been helping the smugglers, just as someone clearly was now, could it have all started in Bahrain?

And worse... had Torres been involved all along?

Chapter 16 – Storm on the Horizon

NCIS interviews had been running nonstop all day, and the ship felt like a pressure cooker ready to blow. Damion kept his face passive, his hands busy, his routine steady, as if nothing about the investigation concerned him. But his mind betrayed him. Every time he caught sight of Special Agent Torres speaking quietly with her partners or taking notes with that sharp, calculating look in her eyes, he felt the noose tighten. She was building something solid.

For hours, he'd been lost in his own head, sifting through memories, dragging up everything he could recall from the time he worked with Torres in Bahrain. Late reports she brushed off. Absences, she explained, with vague excuses. Coincidences that didn't feel like coincidences now that he was looking back at them. His gut told him there was a connection, something he had missed back then that might matter now.

A growl from his stomach snapped him out of his thoughts. Glancing at the time, he realized he'd worked straight through lunch. Shaking his head, he made his way to the galley.

"Hey, shipmate," he said to the young Third Class Culinary Specialist (CS3) behind the counter. "Think you could fix me up something with whatever's left? Doesn't have to be fancy."

"Of course, Chief," she said with a bright smile. "I'll bring it to the Chief's Mess."

"Appreciate it," Damion replied, already moving toward the Mess.

Just as he reached the door, Cabrera appeared like she'd been waiting for him. Folder in hand with a determined look in her eyes. "Chief Jackson, I've got the updated security force training schedule. Can we go over it now?"

"Yeah, let's look at it," he said, motioning toward the door. "Come on in."

Inside, Command Master Chief B.B. Buchanan was seated at one of the tables.

"Ensign Cabrera," B.B. greeted her with a nod. "Welcome back. How was your rehab?"

"Cabrera smiled, "Thanks, Master Chief. Glad to be back. It was more like a month of torture, but it got me fit to fight again."

"Dat a girl, Ma'am," replied B.B., her Tennessee accent emphasizing the "*dat*." Getting up from the table, she added, "Good to have you back, especially with all the crap that's flying around here right now."

"Thanks," Cabrera replied with a solemn nod.

As B.B. headed for the door, she gave Damion a look that lingered just long enough to say *I know what's going on*. He didn't return it, didn't even twitch—just gave a slight nod that could've meant anything.

Once the door shut, Cabrera took a seat across from Damion and slid the folder over. But she didn't open it.

"You've been quiet," she said, voice measured. "Even for you."

"Just busy. A lot going on," Damion replied, already flipping the folder open.

"Busy," she repeated, as if testing the word. She didn't look at the paper. "Yeah. There is. But you're acting like it's not just NCIS that's got your hackles in a knot."

He paused, barely, then kept reading. "I don't rattle that easily. You should know that by now."

"Hmm," she murmured, "Yes, I *do* know." Her eyes didn't leave his face. "You think I can't see when someone's chewing on something tough in their head?" she continued, voice low now, direct. "You're off balance and your timing's slow. That's not you. Your head's not in the fight."

He gave her a look that might've been a warning or might've been nothing at all. Damion exhaled slowly. His jaw tightened. "What are you fishing for, Salina?"

"I'm not fishing," she said. "I'm watching. And you're slipping."

That landed harder than he expected. He stayed quiet, but the throbbing veins in his neck told him that she had gotten to him.

She leaned in slightly. "Torres?"

He didn't answer, but his silence spoke enough. Cabrera glanced at the open folder and leaned back again.

Before she could press, the young Petty Officer from the galley came in with a plate of steaming food that made Damion's stomach growl before he could see what it was.

"Here you go, Chief," she chirped. "This is something we'll be serving when the local dignitaries come aboard. We're testing the recipe now, so you get to be our guinea pig."

"Oink-oink," Damion said with a smirk that didn't quite reach his eyes.

The CS3 giggled, then turned to Cabrera. "Ma'am, want to try some too? Wouldn't hurt to get a second opinion."

Cabrera tilted her head, still watching Damion. "Sure. Why not?"

The Petty Officer hurried out and returned less than a minute later with a second plate.

"Not bad, shipmate, not bad at all," Damion said after taking a bite.

"Agreed," Cabrera added, but her gaze stayed on him. "Compliments to the chef."

The young Culinary Specialist beamed, thanked them both, and hurried back into the galley, leaving Damion and Cabrera alone with their plates and the growing tension between them.

Cabrera decided to break the silence, placing her fork down slowly on her plate.

"I didn't think I'd have to remind you," she said, "but if there's something I should know, something that affects this crew, you'd better start figuring out how to talk to me about it."

Damion looked down at his plate, then back at her. The mask was still on, but now, it had a crack in it.

"You can trust me," she said softly, almost as if she were trying to convince herself.

After a few more moments of silence, "Well," she said resignedly, tapping the folder, "can we at least talk about the schedule? Unless there's something else you want to get off your chest first?"

Damion didn't answer right away, chewing deliberately, his face giving away nothing.

The tension that had built up between them was thick enough to cut with a knife, and he knew that there was an urgent need to diffuse the situation before he lost any chance of finding out if she was hiding something. Damion takes several quiet, deep breaths and forces himself to lower his guard. Feigning a satisfied smile from half of the food he had just eaten, he let out a long sigh of relief.

"Okay, that feels much better. Last time I'm skipping lunch," he added with a chuckle. Then, "Sorry about that. It's been a long day." Cabrera says nothing, but continues to eat quietly.

He lets a few moments of silence pass, just long enough, he hopes, for her to relax a little. He knows that he has to play this next part carefully, because if she thinks that he is testing her or probing for information, then all bets are off that she will ever trust him again. Even if she is innocent, and he is only trying to help her.

While looking at the folder, he says in a low voice, "Hey...you were looking pretty awesome yesterday. You really know how to make a sundress look good."

A slight smile from Cabrera, "Thanks."

Damion continued in a playful tone, "Yeah, you were *almost perfect*. The only thing missing was some jewelry, like your gold chain with the cross pendant. Now *that* would have topped off the whole outfit. You still wearing that cross you always have on? The one you were playing with half the night at Mama Casita's?"

Her fork paused mid-motion. Just for a second, but he caught it. She looked up, eyebrows raised slightly. "What are you now, my fashion consultant? And uh... yes, I still have it. Why?"

He gave a slight shrug, keeping his expression neutral, unconcerned. "No reason. I just noticed that you used to twirl it all the time when we were out in town. Haven't seen you wearing it lately, that's all."

Salina hesitated, then gave a little laugh, shaking her head. "Oh, I still have it. I just... don't wear it much when I'm on duty. Don't want to catch it on anything."

"Fair enough," he replied. "It just looked like it meant a lot to you. Family heirloom or something?"

Another pause. Shorter this time, but there. "It was a gift," she said finally, her tone casual, but her eyes didn't quite match the ease in her voice.

Damion nodded, like he accepted the answer, like he was just making small talk. But his mind was already working, cataloging every flicker of hesitation, every shift in her body language.

If she really did still have it, then either the one in the warehouse wasn't hers, or she had another explanation ready, one she didn't want to share yet.

Either way, Damion knew one thing for certain: Salina was nervous. And nervous people made mistakes.

"Good to know," he said, finishing the final pieces of food on his plate.

"Now that the meal is done, maybe we should finally look at these training schedules?"

He smiled and gave her a slight nod before turning his focus on the papers, his face as calm and unreadable as ever. But inside, his thoughts were already shaping into a plan.

If she still had that necklace, he needed to see it with his own eyes. If she didn't... then he had a problem that he wasn't quite ready to deal with yet.

The workday had ended, and Damion headed into town. He needed some time to himself, away from everyone. Alone. He walked aimlessly, hands tucked loosely in his pockets, his mind far removed from the bustling streets around him. His thoughts replayed the events of the past week like a film he couldn't switch off. His first meeting with Torres, that subtle tension that lingered between them, and, more recently, the uncomfortable exchange with Salina in the Chief's Mess. Her distant, guarded answer when he had asked about the necklace still gnawed at him, increasing the suspicion that she was hiding something from him.

He barely registered the laughter of tourists passing on the street or the busy interactions of the local vendors at their shops. He was adrift in his head until something unexpected caught his attention.

A balloon.

A single, bright red balloon bobbed lazily in the air about ten yards ahead, tethered to the small hand of a young boy walking beside his mother. The glossy rubber surface reflected the sunlight as it swayed gently back and forth in the breeze, dancing as if teasing the boy who clutched it. For some reason, Damion's gaze locked onto it, following its hypnotic movement as if the world had narrowed to that single red dot swaying against a pale-blue sky.

The boy's mother, wearing a light summer dress that fluttered in the breeze, looked down at him and said something in Spanish that made the child smile brightly and nod. They stopped at a small shaved-ice stand, its colorful bottles of syrup glistening in the sun. The vendor put on a show, swirling vivid streaks of blue, red, and green flavoring onto a mound of ice, and the boy clapped his hands with excitement, his balloon bouncing wildly with the motion.

Then, it slipped.

The boy gasped as the balloon tugged free of his grip, floating upward with each gust of wind. Without hesitation, he darted after it, his small feet slapping against the stone sidewalk.

That was when Damion saw it - the danger unfolding in seconds.

The boy was running directly toward a narrow gap between two parked cars, oblivious to the busy street beyond. From Damion's vantage point, he caught sight of a compact sedan approaching, its tires humming on the cobblestones. The driver, distracted and with his view blocked by the parked vehicles, had no idea the boy was about to dash into the street.

Damion's body was moving before his mind had finished processing the situation. He calculated distance, speed, and angles instinctively, just as he did during security operations. His voice cut through the noise of the street, sharp and commanding. "¡Alto!" he yelled, hoping the boy, or at least the mother, would hear and understand.

The mother spun around just in time to see her son disappear between the parked cars. Her panicked cry echoed off the walls of the narrow street.

Damion ran faster now, his sneakers pounding against the uneven stones as he sprinted full force toward the gap. The approaching car's horn blared, the driver angrily waving him off, not yet seeing the danger. Damion ignored him, his focus locked solely on the boy.

The child emerged from between the parked cars, eyes locked on the floating balloon, completely unaware of the danger until the sharp screech of brakes tore through the air. The car skidded, its tires squealing against the slick, uneven stones of the old street.

Damion launched himself forward.

With a surge of adrenaline, he scooped the boy into his arms just as the car bore down on them. Jumping and twisting in midair, he shifted his weight, cradling the boy against his chest. His back slammed onto the hood of the car, the impact jolting through his spine as the vehicle finally screeched to a stop.

For a moment, there was silence except for the ticking of the car's engine and the faint rustling of awnings overhead.

The driver sat frozen, his wide eyes reflecting shock and terror. The mother was already running, her sandals slapping against the stones as she reached them. She snatched her son from Damion's arms, sobbing as she peppered his cheeks with frantic kisses, asking rapid-fire questions in Spanish to make sure he was unharmed. The boy, still clutching Damion's shirt with one small hand, nodded, his face buried in his mother's neck.

Damion rolled off the hood and crouched in front of the car, momentarily winded, his chest rising and falling as he caught his breath. A few bystanders rushed over, their voices a mix of Spanish and English, checking if he was okay.

He pushed himself upright slowly, rolling his shoulders to work out the shock from the impact. The mother turned back to him, tears streaming down her face, and in a sudden burst of emotion, she hugged him tightly, kissing him on the cheek as she whispered, "Gracias, gracias, gracias..." over and over.

Then she pulled back, fumbling at her neck. She unclasped her necklace - a delicate gold chain with a small cross pendant etched with intricate, swirling carvings. She held it out insistently, her hands trembling as she pressed it toward him.

Damion raised a hand in protest. "No, señora... It's not necessary."

But she insisted, her voice firm even through her tears.

Reluctantly, not wanting to offend her gratitude, Damion accepted it. As the gold caught the fading sunlight, he stared at the pendant more closely. Its ornate patterns, almost floral in design, were strangely familiar.

Then it hit him.

The carving was an exact match to the necklace Salina wore. The same one he thought she had been evasive about when he'd asked her. The gift.

Damion's heart skipped a beat as he looked back at the mother, his mind racing.

"*Gracias*, señora. *Gracias*."

Chapter 17 - A Fragile Light in the Darkness

Damion opened his eyes slowly, the bright lights above him painfully coming into view as a blur. His head was pounding, and he felt the dull throb of pain behind his eyes. He tried to move but quickly realized he was lying on his back on what felt like a gurney. Two unfamiliar faces hovered over him, both dressed in dark blue uniforms with medical patches on their shoulders - Spanish paramedics. And somehow, he was now in the back of an ambulance.

He opened his mouth to speak, and one of them gave him a nod, then began speaking gently in accented English. "Señor, can you hear me?"

Damion gave a faint nod, wincing slightly from the pain.

"What...?"

"Everything is okay. You are in an ambulance, and we are taking care of you. Witnesses say that you were walking away from the accident when you passed out about an hour ago. You most likely have a concussion from hitting the car. We've bandaged your head, but we need to ask you some questions, okay?"

"Yeah," Damion muttered. His voice was hoarse.

"What is your name?"

"Damion Jackson, US Navy."

"Do you know where you are?"

"Rota old town. Near the port."

"Do you remember what happened?"

Damion blinked a few times, then nodded. "A little boy was about to be hit by a car. I pulled him out of the way and cushioned him from the impact with my body."

The paramedic gave a short smile, nodding and looking at his partner, who continued checking Damion's blood pressure. "Good, good. Everything looks stable, but we strongly recommend that you go to the hospital as soon as possible for a full examination. You could have internal swelling or delayed symptoms. We can take you there now, or drive you back to the base if you prefer."

Damion ignored the offer for a moment. "The little boy... is he alright?"

"Sí, he's fine. Not a scratch on him. Thanks to you."

The second paramedic chimed in, this time more animated. "You are a hero, my friend. That boy surely would have died if you hadn't pulled him out of the way."

Damion exhaled, letting the words settle in his mind. He didn't feel like a hero. His head hurt like hell, although something much deeper was bothering him; something beyond the near-death experience with the car.

Finishing up their preliminary examination, the two paramedics stepped out of the ambulance while Damion remained lying on the gurney. After a few minutes, he heard one of the paramedics speaking rapidly in Spanish to someone just outside of his view. The tone was warm and familiar. A few seconds passed, then there was a pause in the conversation, and the paramedic stepped to the side. Standing just beyond the open door, framed by the soft shadows of the late day, was the mother and the little boy. The boy clutched her hand tightly, half-hiding behind her leg. His eyes were wide, uncertain, scanning the interior of the ambulance until they settled on Damion. Seeing the frightened little face, Damion forced a half-smile, raised one hand, and gave the boy a thumbs-up. The boy's expression changed immediately. His mouth curled into a big grin, and he leaned out from behind his mother, giving a timid wave. The mother placed her hand gently over her heart, then brought it up to her lips and blew him a kiss. Damion smiled and nodded to the mom as the paramedic slowly pulled the door closed. The latch clicked softly into place, and the ambulance began to move.

As they slowly rolled along the streets toward the naval base, Damion sat propped up in the back, cradling his head with one hand. His thoughts were spinning faster than the wheels beneath him.

Maya Torres.

Every detail from Bahrain up to now started falling into place like pieces of a puzzle he hadn't realized he'd been assembling. The reports. The missed busts. The strange inconsistencies. His gut was telling him what his brain had tried to ignore for far too long: Torres was somehow tied to the smuggling ring. And if that were true, he'd need more than gut suspicion. He needed proof.

His thoughts then shifted to Cabrera. That tense conversation they had, the edge in her voice, her guarded posture. Damion had always trusted his instincts, and right now, they told him that she was innocent, and he was going to need her help if he wanted to unravel this. He would have to open up to her. Trust her. And hope like hell she wasn't in on it.

The ambulance pulled up to the main gate, and after an ID check and explanation for the transport, they were allowed to proceed onto the base. When the ambulance reached the ship, Damion stepped out slowly with the help of the paramedics. His legs felt a little unsteady at first, but he quickly regained his composure. He made his way up the brow and reported to the Officer of the Deck, briefly explaining about the accident and that he would be going to the hospital for a follow-up.

"But first," he added, "I need to check on something."

Using the quarterdeck telephone, he called Cabrera's stateroom. Her voice answered quickly.

"Ensign Cabrera."

Seeing the concerned looks from the Petty Officer of the Watch and the Messenger of the Watch, he gave them a thumbs-up and silently mouthed *"I'm okay,"* before continuing his call.

"Hello, Ma'am, It's Chief Jackson. I need to talk to you if you have time. Can you meet me in my office in about ten minutes?"

"I'll be right there," Cabrera replied without hesitation.

When she arrived, she stopped short in the doorway. Her eyes widened at the sight of the bandage on his head, the stiffness in his movements.

"What happened to you?" She gasped, closing the door behind her.

"I had a little head-butting contest with a SEAT Ibiza, and I lost. I'll explain later," he said. "We need to talk privately... when I get back from the hospital. And before Torres starts her next round of interrogations." She nodded slowly, her expression hard to read, but the concern in her eyes for him was genuine and unmistakable. He reached over and lightly brushed a stray hair from in front of her eyes, then gently stroked the side of her face. Cabrera placed her hand softly on top of his, then stepped in close and kissed him softly on the lips. They stood there for a few moments, holding each other without saying a word. Damion slowly stepped back and said that he needed to get to the quarterdeck before the OOD sent the Messenger to make sure he hadn't passed out somewhere.

"Once today is enough," he said with a chuckle, which only made Cabrera look at him with even more concern.

Heading up to the quarterdeck, Damion saw that the duty driver and the duty Hospital Corpsman were already on the pier, waiting next to the ship's vehicle. Damion slowly made his way down the brow, climbed in, and closed his eyes as the car pulled away. He sat in the back seat, his head leaning against the window, eyes half-open but unfocused. The duty driver kept his eyes on the road, while the duty Corpsman, a Second Class Petty Officer with a calm voice and quick hands, sat beside him with his medical record.

Damion didn't say much. He answered a few questions in short bursts, mostly about how he felt and if he could still see straight. The Corpsman noted his vitals and mentioned they'd run more tests at the hospital.

Before they'd even cleared the last stretch of road outside the base perimeter, Damion's body gave in. His eyes fluttered closed, and his head slumped forward slightly. The Corpsman leaned over, gently shaking his shoulder, but Damion didn't respond.

"He's out," she said to the driver. "Keep going. We'll let the doc take it from here."

At the hospital, Damion woke up in a dimly lit examination room, feeling as if his head was packed with wool. The doctor, a Navy lieutenant with sleeves rolled up and a clipboard in hand, stood at the foot of the exam table reviewing notes on a tablet.

"You've got a concussion, Chief," he said matter-of-factly. "And a handful of nasty bruises from what was reported as the hood of a moving car. But no broken bones, no internal bleeding, and your scans look good."

Damion nodded slowly. "So, I'm not dying?"

The doctor gave a slight smirk. "Not today, anyway. But you will be feeling it for a while."

He walked over, tapped a few notes into the tablet. "Vitals are strong. Blood pressure's a little elevated, nothing alarming or unexpected considering the cause. I'm putting you on light duty for the next two weeks. I'll write up the chit and pass it to your Corpsman."

He handed him a prescription slip. "800 milligrams of Motrin as needed. Hydrate, rest, and avoid strenuous activity. You'll likely deal with headaches, some fogginess, maybe even mood swings. Sleep as much as you can. And if anything feels worse than it did today, come back immediately."

Damion nodded again, slower this time.

The ride back to the ship was quiet. The Corpsman looked over at him a couple of times but didn't say much. Damion drifted off again somewhere around the halfway mark, the hum of the road beneath the tires enough to lull him into a deep, exhausted sleep. Back at the pier, the Corpsman gently shook him awake. Damion stirred, groaned, and sat up like every muscle had gone stiff.

"You need to sleep in sickbay tonight, Chief," she said, already climbing out of the vehicle. "I need to keep an eye on you."

Damion opened his mouth to protest, then thought better of it. He followed her onboard with slow, deliberate steps, made his way to sickbay, and climbed onto the bed with all the energy of a man twice his age.

The Corpsman was still speaking softly, giving some final piece of medical instruction. "Just try and get some sleep, Chief. Wake me if..."

But he was already out. Asleep before she had finished the sentence.

The next day, Damion awoke to the sound of muffled voices coming from outside the closed-off section of sickbay where he had spent the night. He couldn't make out the conversation, but he knew that it was bordering on becoming a tense exchange. Finally, he heard the outer door open and close, shortly followed by a soft knock on the door.

"I'm awake," Damion said, with his hand covering his eyes. The door opened, and in came the Hospital

Corpsman who had escorted him to the hospital the night before.

"Good morning, Chief. How are you feeling?" her voice soft and eyes tired, but full of concern and professionalism.

"Like I got hit by a car, but I'm alive."

This elicited a slight smile, but didn't make the concern in her eyes go away.

"Well, you were in and out of consciousness all night. You even had a slight fever, but it appears to be gone now."

"Sorry about that, HM2. I didn't mean to keep you up all night."

"No worries, Chief. Just part of the job," she replied with a slightly wider smile. "You had a few visitors this morning. The CO, XO, Master Chief, and several of the other Chiefs. And also, Ensign Cabrera." Then, glancing at the door, she looked back at Damion and added, "I think Ms. Cabrera was more worried than any of them." And with that, she got up and started heading for the central section of sickbay.

After a few steps, Damion called to her, "Who was that you were talking to just now?"

"That was the female NCIS agent. She wanted to come in and talk to you. She said she had some questions that only you could answer."

"And what did you tell her?"

"I told her that the Captain said to make sure that no one disturbed you unless the ship was on fire, so she would have to wait until you were up and about."

"And how did she take that?"

"She wasn't too happy, I suppose. She tried to intimidate me with her badge, but I told her that I had direct orders from the CO, and she would need to get permission from him before I let her in. She backed off after that."

"HM2, I think you just became my favorite shipmate."

She let out a soft giggle, then left, closing the door behind her. Damion was starting to feel the full aftereffects of the accident. There were parts of his body starting to hurt that he was sure didn't come in contact with the car. Good thing this wasn't his first time getting banged up a little. He knew what to expect and figured he would be almost back to himself in about three days. Hopefully. As he was doing a mental check of the pains in his body, he heard the outer door to sickbay open and close, followed shortly by a soft knock on the door.

"I'm decent," he answered. The door opened, and in came the Senior Chief Hospital Corpsman, HMCS(SW)Diana (Doc) Jones.

"Jeez, DJ, you look like crap," she said with a smile and some concern on her face.

"Good morning to you, too, Doc," he shot back.

Pulling up a folding chair next to the bed, she asked, "What were you thinking about, Brother? You couldn't get out of the street fast enough?"

"If I had done that, the mother of a little boy chasing a balloon would be making funeral arrangements today. Now, she won't have to."

Her eyes locked onto him, and for a moment she said nothing. Then, nodding her head slowly, she extended her hand towards him in a fist. *"Represent, Brother."* Damion nodded once, acknowledging the show of respect and returning the fist-bump. He then related the full story of the accident while she conducted her post-examination of him. Without him realizing it, she also included questions to test his short-term and long-term memory, which, afterwards, she was confident had not been affected.

As she finished the exam, she suggested that he eat some food, since it was almost lunchtime. Damion was shocked to learn that he had slept for most of the morning, so he started to get up. HMCS stopped him and said that her HM2 would get him lunch, and he could eat it there in sickbay, where it was much quieter. The throbbing still in his head was all the convincing that he needed. Since he was on bed rest for right now, his body may as well do just that. His brain, on the other hand, had already returned to solving a long-overdue problem slowly creeping up in the back of his mind.

As the rest of the morning shot by, Damion tried to focus on the multitude of problems that seemed to pop up all at once, but he was having no luck in finding solutions to them. It was proving extra difficult to remain focused on anything when visitors "authorized" by his new, favorite shipmate kept stopping by to check on him. Mostly it was his fellow Chiefs, but the XO did call down to check on his condition.

It was around mid-afternoon when the HM2 poked her head in the open door to let him know that he had another visitor. The smile on her face told him that it wasn't NCIS Special Agent Torres. As she disappeared from view, Cabrera slowly stepped around the edge of the door frame and entered the small room.

"Hi, Chief," she started. "It's nice to see you awake. How are you feeling?"

With a thoughtful look on his face, he said, "The words pain and stiff come to mind, but it could have been much worse."

She took a step closer, raising her voice slightly so that the *ever-observant* HM2 sitting in the next room could hear without leaning towards the door.

"I'm glad that it wasn't. The ship and the team need you." Then she silently mouthed the words, "*We need to talk.*"

Damion nodded in agreement and motioned for her to sit on the folding chair. He whispered that they could talk in his office later. He was sure that the Corpsman wouldn't object to him leaving to take a hot shower and get a change of clothes. He then raised his voice a little higher and told her of the previous day's events. Cabrera sat, listening intently as Damion recounted the story of the accident, ending with the boy's mother taking off her cross and giving it to him as a thank you.

"Now, we have a matching set of jewelry," he said while pulling out the cross from beneath his shirt and watching for changes in her expression. Cabrera takes the cross in her hands, looking at it closely.

"Almost," she replies. "Mine has a bit of amber near the top, and this one is all gold." She then reaches into her shirt, pulls out her necklace with the cross pendant, and leans closer, placing the two side-by-side.

"See?" she replied without looking up.

The adrenaline spreading through Damion seemed to knock down the throbbing in his head as he let out a sigh of relief while staring at her. Cabrera looked up at him with a half-smile, and curiosity etched across her face. Snapping out of his trance, Damion looked down at the two pendants, nodding slowly.

"Looks like you are right. They look identical at first glance, but I guess you have to have a good eye to spot the subtleties in them," he replied, breathing lighter now.

Cabrera continued, "I know I said that I don't usually wear it in uniform, but with everything that's happening, and especially with what's happened to you, I thought it might be wise to keep it on."

He just nodded and was about to reply when he was interrupted by the sound of a soft throat-clearing coming from the young Corpsman standing at the door, looking embarrassed that she might have interrupted something she wasn't supposed to see.

Damion and Cabrera slowly sat up straight as he said, "Don't worry, HM2, we're just comparing jewelry, nothing more. I promise."

Now, feeling even more embarrassed, she stuttered, "I'm sorry, Chief, I didn't mean anything like..."

Damion raised his hand, "You've been taking real good care of me, shipmate, so you can think whatever you want. But, *there's nothing to see here*," he replied in a lyrical tone.

Giggling and relaxing a bit, she replied, "Well, Senior Chief is off the ship, and I have to go on a supply run. Will you be okay for about an hour while I'm gone?"

"Sure. And I promise not to raid the medicine locker."

Smiling, she headed toward the door, then suddenly stopped and turned back to him.

"Oh, by the way, just so that you know, if you leave sickbay, the door will automatically lock behind you, and you won't be able to get back in until Senior Chief or I come back."

Damion nodded, "Got it. I'll stay put."

The moment she stepped out and the outer door had closed, Cabrera threw her arms around his neck and kissed him with a passion that swept away the last echoes of pain pulsing in his head.

Chapter 18 - The Consequences of Touch

It was nice being able to spend a little time alone together in private, behind a locked door, without worrying about someone sneaking up on them unexpectedly. Cabrera stayed with him for only 15 minutes after the Corpsman had left, to avoid drawing any attention or having to explain to any other visitors why she was alone with Damion in sickbay for so long. They would make time later, after the ship was relatively empty and most of the crew were on liberty. Damion, now feeling better about Cabrera's presumed innocence, decided that he would confide in her about Torres when they met later. He suspected that she would be furious at him for spying on her, but that was something he would deal with when the time came. After she had left, he felt the throbbing slowly growing in his head again, so he decided to lie down and work the Torres problem once again. After what seemed like a couple of minutes, a rustling sound caused him to open his eyes, and he saw the Hospital Corpsman standing at the table with her back towards him.

"HM2? I didn't hear you come in. When did you get back?" he asked incredulously.

She turned and came over to the bed. "About two hours ago, Chief. You were out like a light when I came back, probably from the concussion."

Damion looked at his watch and was shocked to see that almost three hours had passed since he had lain down. A whole day wasted, plus the throbbing was coming back. Damion sat up, rubbing his eyes and focusing on the room. He needed to move around and maybe sneak out topside to get some fresh air.

"Hey, shipmate. You know I've been in this bed since yesterday. Any chance I could get out of here and go take a shower?"

"Of course, Chief," she chirped. "You aren't restricted to sickbay; we just had to keep an eye on you overnight. If you want to sleep in your own rack tonight, that's okay too."

"Outstanding," he replied, then added with a smirk, "*not* that I don't enjoy your company."

The Corpsman giggled again, "No worries, Chief. But if you feel anything more than what you are now, make sure you come back here. Senior Chief has duty today."

"Okay, will do."

Damion left sickbay and made his way towards the forward Chief's berthing. Fortunately, the passageways were empty, for a change, and he didn't run into any well-wishers or curious stares while he slowly made his way.

Damion stood in the shower and turned the handle to full. The water was hot. Very hot. Just short of scalding his skin, hot. Just the way he liked it. The sting of the heat wasn't painful; it was liberating. It reminded him that he was still alive, and the little boy was still alive. The hot water poured over his head and down his back, easing the constant throbbing and the pains in his shoulders and ribs. He rolled his neck slowly, each click and pop reminding him just how close he had come to being a Navy statistic. But it was all worth it, he thought, smiling at the memory of the little boy waiting to make sure he was okay.

Damion was feeling almost like himself again after the shower, so he decided to go to his office to see if there was anything he needed to catch up on.

As soon as he entered the office, the sound of light footsteps behind him caught his attention. He turned just in time to see Cabrera stepping in, leaving the door only partially closed behind her.

"I didn't expect you to still be on board," he said, surprised.

"I was waiting for you," she said, her voice soft but steady. "How are you feeling?"

Damion shrugged slightly while leaning on his desk. "I felt better earlier. But after you left... the headache came back."

Cabrera stepped closer, a faint, knowing smile playing at the edge of her lips. "Hmm...I know what'll make you feel better again," she replied suggestively.

Before he could say anything, she leaned in, lips locking in a slow, passionate kiss.

Suddenly, their whole world came crashing down as the office door creaked open, and a voice called out mid-step, "Hey, Salina, you got a min....oh!"

Both turned sharply and saw Ensign Stephanie Cheng standing in the doorway, eyes wide, her expression frozen in disbelief. Her gaze bounced between Damion and Cabrera; lips parted, but no words came out.

Cabrera gasped and instinctively stepped back.

The awkward silence was thick as molasses.

Stephanie blinked, seemed to regain her composure, then slowly stepped back and pulled the door shut behind her without another word.

Cabrera sank into the chair across from Damion, her face pale. She placed both hands over her face and exhaled into her palms.

"She's going to report us," she said quietly, not even looking up. "This is it. We are so screwed."

Damion remained standing, staring at the closed door. The look on his face didn't carry any hope at all.

"We'll just have to see what happens," he said after a long pause. "And own up to it."

Neither of them spoke after that. There was really nothing left to say.

Eventually, Cabrera stood and left the office without saying a word. The soft click of the door closing behind her was the only sound left in the room.

That night, neither of them got any real sleep. "Plan for the worst, hope for the best," Damion lay awake thinking. That's what he would always drill into each security team member. Except this time, it wasn't a security team member or a boarding mission, and no amount of planning could get them out of what comes next.

The night passed by at a snail's pace, like it usually does when something worrisome is on one's mind. At khaki call the next morning, Damion could see that Salina had gotten very little rest. To anyone else, she may have just looked a little tired, but to Damion, she looked entirely different. Worry lines across her forehead, slightly bloodshot eyes - possibly from crying, and then there was her posture; not standing tall and proud, but seeming a little bit diminished in stature. Damion, although not fully rested, had gotten a solid three hours of sleep, courtesy of his concussion. One minute, he was lying in his rack mulling over their predicament, and the next, he was waking up with a throbbing headache several hours later. Now, standing at khaki call, he closed his eyes for a moment and steeled himself for when the XO called them out. He glanced around at the assembled khakis, spotting Stephanie Cheng in the back row of officers. She did not make eye contact or look around, but kept her gaze straight ahead and her face passive.

As the XO was finishing up his notes, Damion felt as if the CSO was staring at him a little too much.

He knows, thought Damion. Then the XO's voice interrupted his thoughts.

"On a final note, as some of you may have heard, Chief Jackson was injured in a car accident while walking out in town the other day. Now normally, this would be cause for a *safety standdown and review of our liberty policy*," the XO quipped, surprising everyone by grinning and saying it as a joke. "However, Chief Jackson got injured *on purpose* while protecting a young child from getting run over by a car, which in all probability would have killed him. So, let's give a round of applause for MAC. Well done, Chief!"

The XO started clapping and was immediately joined by all the other assembled khakis. After the chorus of clapping, back-patting, and *way-to-gos* were finished, the group was dismissed to go to their separate divisions for morning quarters.

As Damion and Salina started to leave, the XO called out to them, "Ensign Cabrera, MAC, come see me in my stateroom after you finish quarters."

"Aye, Sir," they answered simultaneously, as the XO departed. Cabrera stood there for a moment, then glanced up to see the Combat Systems Officer glaring at her. Stephanie Cheng, her expression unreadable, was also looking from a distance, just before she disappeared inside the ship.

They walked in silence on the way to division quarters, each lost in their own thoughts and feeling like the weight of the world was on their shoulders. Just before they reached the space where their division of ten sailors was assembled, Damion stopped and told Salina that the crew would be concerned about the NCIS interviews, so they had to show up looking like everything was okay. Salina leaned against the bulkhead, looking at the deck with her hands behind her back.

"I don't know if I can face them right now; not with what we both know is about to happen," she replied, her voice breaking.

He stood there, wishing he could take her in his arms and comfort her, but they were already in enough trouble - no need to broadcast it further before its time.

He took a deep breath, trying to muster up the strength to give her the emotional support she desperately needed, and hoping that he would have some left for himself.

"Look, I will take care of division quarters. Why don't you wait for me in my office, then we can go face the music together."

"Thank you," she replied solemnly.

Damion watched her walk slowly down the empty passageway. At one point, she paused and looked up at the ceiling for a moment, then continued walking.

After another few seconds, he turned and proceeded to the compartment, opening the door to greet the waiting division.

Cabrera was just about to go up the ladder when suddenly she heard loud voices cheering and hands clapping coming from the compartment behind her. The division welcoming Damion back. *Well, at least there's that,* she thought to herself.

The division muster took longer than usual since everyone had lots of questions for Damion about the NCIS investigation, and also wanted to know everything about his accident. To put them at ease and not seem pressured or worried about anything, he took his time answering as many questions as he could, then dismissed them to go to work. By the time he made it to his office, Salina was pacing back and forth, looking as if she was about to explode.

Before he could say a word, she stretched out her arm towards him, holding a small piece of paper in her hand.

"What's this?" he asked.

"Before I came here, I went to my stateroom to get myself together. When I opened the door, this paper fell down. It was folded much smaller than that, and I think it was tucked into the top of the door jamb so no one else would notice it."

Damion unfolded the paper as Salina continued to pace back and forth.

"It must have been Stephanie who put it there. She's the only one who saw us. Unless...oh no," she gasped, sucking in her breath. "The CSO."

Damion said nothing, but stared at the three words scribbled on the paper – *I know everything.*

After a moment of silence, he turned to Salina.

"No, not the CSO. If it were him, he would have ratted us out in the most public way possible. I *know* he doesn't like me, and the way he addresses you...probably is just fallout from his hatred of me. No, this is someone else. The fact that they left a note may mean that they want to use this knowledge as leverage, maybe to get something from us later. Either way, the XO is waiting. May as well get it over with."

As they headed up to the Executive Officer's stateroom, Damion wasn't lost on the irony he was experiencing in this moment, feeling like a criminal in prison, being escorted to the execution chamber. Only, the guards were not physical military police, but the Navy Regulations (NAVREGS) and the Uniform Code of Military Justice (UCMJ), both of which defined every aspect of their professional behaviour.

When they reached the XO's open door, he was sitting at his desk, intently reading some type of report.

"Come in and shut the door," he said.

After he had finished reading, he looked at them, stood up, and came around to lean back against the front of his desk. Silence. Damion felt as if the XO was looking through them and trying to decide whether he should hang them or keel haul them. It seemed as if the bottom had dropped out of his stomach, and Damion was sure that he had heard Salina's as well. After a long pause, rubbing his chin, the XO began.

"So, what's going on?"

Cabrera and Damion, taken off guard by the question, stood there, staring and confused, a wave of emotions flooding over them. After a moment, Cabrera found her voice, although it was weaker than usual.

"Si-Sir?" she stammered.

"With our personnel? *Our boarding teams*. How are they holding up with these *interrogations* by NCIS?"

"Uh, I think they are doing fine, Sir. I haven't heard of anyone being put off by the interrogations, *I mean* investigation, Sir," she corrected.

He then turned to Damion.

"What about you, Chief? I know you've been indisposed for the last two days, but the boarding teams are a tight bunch. I know someone has been keeping you in the loop."

"I agree with Ms. Cabrera, Sir. Everyone seems to be doing fine."

"Good. I don't want any of them second-guessing their actions on every boarding we have to do after this *inquiry* is done."

"Aye, Sir," they said in unison.

The XO nodded, walking back behind his desk, then looked directly at Salina.

"Ensign Cabrera, are you feeling okay? Looks like you missed a few hours of sleep."

Cabrera stood straighter, feeling cold sweat running down her back, as her mind tried to fathom that *this* was the reason he wanted to see them, and not that they had been reported. Not yet, anyway.

"Yes, Sir, I'm fine. Just a little head cold, I believe."

The XO nodded, "Well, make sure you get some rest. The ship needs both of you at one hundred percent when we leave port. Okay then, that will be all."

As they turned to leave, he spoke again, "Ensign Cabrera, you go ahead. Chief, hang back a minute."

Salina promptly exited the stateroom and closed the door quietly behind her.

The XO waited a few seconds before speaking.

"So, what's the deal, Chief?

"Sir?"

"You and Ensign Cabrera work together very closely every day, and we all know how quickly relationships and protective feelings can develop."

Damion felt the bottom drop out of his stomach again.

"So, I need you to look me in the eye and tell me the truth: have you observed *anything* that supports Special Agent Torres' insinuations against Ms. Cabrera?"

Damion stood there, controlling his breathing after what he thought was the XO playing his final trump card to expose them. Then, after what could have been mistakenly perceived as a moment of intense thinking, he answered back.

"No, Sir. Not a thing. I'm not trying to protect her, but I do believe she's innocent of what Special Agent Torres is implying."

The XO slapped his hand hard on his desk, shaking his beloved model of an Arleigh Burke-class destroyer that he personally carved by hand out of Swiss pine wood.

"I agree. I don't know why, but this whole thing smells like someone is looking for a scapegoat. It just reeks of it. Well, not on my watch, and not with my crew."

The XO nodded to Damion, dismissing him, but before he exited his office, he added, "When Torres comes back on board, keep an eye on her. Quietly."

"Understood, Sir."

"And, Chief? Watch your back with that one. She's dangerous."

Chapter 19 - Crossing the Line

Damion exited the XO's stateroom to find Cabrera standing there waiting for him. He says nothing as she follows him down the corridor. Just as they reach the exit from Officer's Country, Stephanie Cheng opens the door from the other side and walks in first. They all stop in place. Damion and Cabrera stand there speechless, as Stephanie looks at both of them, her face as unreadable as it had been earlier at khaki call. After an awkward silence, Cabrera starts to speak, but Stephanie quickly raises her finger and shakes her head, prompting Salina to stop talking. She then brushes between them and heads down the corridor. Cabrera slowly shakes her head and glances at Damion. She then turns to call out to Stephanie, but is shocked to see the CSO standing at the end of the corridor watching them. She watches as Stephanie approaches the CSO, respectfully greets him, then continues down the corridor to her stateroom. The CSO looks one more time at Cabrera and Damion, then enters into his own stateroom.

Neither of them said a word until they were behind the closed door of his office again. Damion, sitting at his desk – eyes closed and his head leaning back against the bulkhead, and Salina sitting in the extra chair opposite him with her elbows propped on his desk.

"*What is she waiting for*?" she asked no one in particular.

"I don't know. Maybe she is thinking it through - waiting for the right time, or weighing her options."

"*Her options?*"

"Sure, especially if she's the one who left you the note. Maybe she plans on blackmailing you into giving her your nicer stateroom," he joked.

"That's not funny. *This is serious*, you know."

"I know, but she obviously has a reason for waiting, and that can be a good thing. Either way, whatever her reason is, I think we will find out soon enough."

Salina quietly leans back in the chair, her face deep in thought. After not saying anything for about two minutes, she abruptly stands up.

"You're probably right. *The hangman's noose is not tied yet, so I had better get back to work,*" she sang. Then, with a half-smile, "*Business as usual.*"

Damion sat up straight, "*Business as usual.*"

Slowly walking around the desk and leaning down with her lips close to his, she whispered, "*And until the noose is tied…*"

After Salina left his office, getting back into a regular work routine was exactly the distraction he needed. It didn't take long before thoughts of Ensign Cheng and Maya Torres had receded into the deep recesses of his mind, along with the throbbing headache he had been experiencing since the accident. Inspections, reports, and the accompanying paperwork were non-stop and piled up quickly if left unattended. Surprisingly, by the time lunch rolled around, he had not only gotten caught up on everything but also had time to develop two new training exercises to add to the boarding team's self-defense exercises. Depending on how the rest of the day played out, he would run them by Salina as well. He was not too proud to admit that she had a keen eye for detecting gaps in his coverage, even though she had less training and experience than he did. It was like natural intuition for her, which he found a little disturbing sometimes.

Locking his office and heading to the Chief's Mess for lunch, he felt unusually light on his feet, as if a heavy weight had been lifted from his shoulders. Maybe it was because they had dodged the proverbial bullet with the XO, or maybe there was the light of *negotiation* waiting for them with Ensign Cheng. Whatever the reason, he was going to enjoy it while it lasted, because with his luck, it most likely wouldn't last very long.

As he passed the mess decks, dodging sailors rushing to eat lunch before the next duty watch, he saw Ensign Stephanie Cheng standing outside the Chief's Mess talking to B.B. Slowing his pace, he approached the pair to within twenty feet when she turned and, with a big smile, yelled "Chief!" B.B. also turned and smiled.

"We were just talking about you," B.B. started. "The XO really put you on the spot at khaki call." "I'll bet you enjoyed that," she said, still grinning.

"Not really. You know me, B.B. – out of sight, out of mind."

"I know, but what you did out in town needed public recognition on the ship. There may even be something a little more formal coming later," she replied.

Ignoring the subtle hint, Damion asked, "So, you were talking about me?"

"Yes. I know being stuck on the ship is probably driving you nuts, but the doc wants you monitored regularly until your concussion is better. I also know that you do not want to be a *dragging anchor* following the other Chiefs around on liberty, unable to hang out in the pubs and have a few beers. "

Damion remained silent, knowing what she was saying was correct.

"So, to help with this little dilemma, Ensign Cheng here, and your Div-o have volunteered to be your *liberty buddies* today," she commented, as the Tennessee smile grew even wider.

"Excuse me, but you have got to be joking." Turning to Stephanie, "Not that I don't appreciate it, Ma'am, but I'm good. I don't need chaperones. I'll be fine staying onboard."

B.B. continued, "Well, the doc wants you to get off the ship and get some fresh air. She also needs someone to keep an eye on you, and they have offered to help."

Right on cue, Stephanie, all smiles, joined the conversation.

"I have a nephew about the same age as that little boy you saved, and my family would have been devastated if something like that happened to him. I know it's silly and has no connection to him at all, but I still want to show you that we appreciate what you did for that mother and her son." She then added, *"And I won't take no for an answer."*

B.B., towering behind the small Ensign Cheng, looked slightly disappointed that he had refused their offer.

However, Stephanie's face had somehow changed, exposing a very different look about her. Gone was the happy smile and inviting attitude, while the spark in her eyes had been replaced by something dark. So dark that it gave Damion a chill when he tried to maintain eye contact with her. Her last comment about not taking no for an answer was not innocent or idle talk. It had a specific message intended solely for him. *You don't have a choice. You either come, or else.*

Damion shook off the chill, then gave in with a slight nod.

The smile suddenly reappeared, her eyes sparkled, and the darkness faded away.

"Thanks, Chief! I'll let Ensign Cabrera know that we will be leaving together on liberty."

As she hurried down the passageway, Damion turned to look at the Master Chief.

"Thanks, B.B.," he said dryly.

"What are you so sore about, DJ? You get to get off the ship for some fresh air, and hang out with two beautiful women. What more could a single sailor ask for?" she laughed while heading into the Chief's Mess.

He stood outside the door for a couple of minutes thinking about what had just happened. He knew B.B. was just going along with the narrative, but Stephanie Cheng, well she had other plans in mind. At least Salina and he would get the chance to try and clear the air with her while no one else is around. One way or another.

There was also an extra worry he was trying to avoid. His fellow Chiefs. He hoped that they would have a little bit of understanding and not hound him after being *chaperoned* by two junior officers, approved by B.B. They could be merciless when they got their teeth into a good teasing, but there wasn't anything he wouldn't do for his khaki brothers and sisters in arms. And he knew that they would do the same for him. His stomach rumbled just loud enough to remind him why he was here, so he opened the door to go and get some chow. He had only taken three steps inside the door when he heard:

"Hey, DJ, I hear you got yourself a couple of hot dates, *lover boy*!" followed by raucous laughter and hands slapping tables around the room.

These guys suck, he thought as he headed for his favorite spot.

Damion leaned back with his arms crossed and looked around the small table as they sat in silence in the back corner of a small café far away from the regular tourist hangouts. The cafe was empty except for the owner, an older gentleman sitting on a stool at the cafe's entrance, listening to a Spanish talk-radio program. Stephanie chose the corner because it provided a moderate amount of privacy and also allowed them to maintain good situational awareness in case any newcomers arrived. The evening air was humid, causing streaks of water to run down the sides of their cold beer bottles, pooling in little circles under each one on the linen-covered table.

The tension in the atmosphere was reminiscent of an old spaghetti-western 3-way standoff, with each of the participants ready to draw their gun on the first one that flinched. Only in this case, Stephanie was the only one with a weapon; not a physical one, but she had them dead to rights in her crosshairs. With her finger slowly tapping the top of her opened beer bottle, she no longer looked like the fresh-faced, impressionable young Ensign straight out of the Naval Academy. No, she was something else entirely. There was a strength that radiated combat confidence, and a silent fierceness that dared anyone to cross her, at their peril. It was a trait he had seen only once before in one other person – Maya Torres. And right now, Stephanie was sizing them up.

And then, there was Salina Cabrera. Slouching in the chair to his left, she sat silently twirling a bottle cap between her fingers, with just enough reach to spin it every now and then on the tabletop. A mixture of anger and sorrow was etched across her face, and she had been understandably quiet since they had arrived, considering how Stephanie had *flame-broiled* them both after leaving the ship. Something that they were totally unprepared for.

They had met on the quarterdeck and departed the ship together as planned. Leaving the main gate, they walked past the roundabout and followed the road leading toward the coast. The streets were peaceful, with the gentle murmur of scooters in the distance. Drawn toward the coastline, the trio made their way onto the promenade near Playa de la Costilla. Along the boardwalk, families strolled, joggers passed by, and several couples relaxed on benches, watching the world settle into its evening routine.

Turning inland through a quiet residential street, they had reached the historic heart of the town. Suddenly, the stone façade of Castillo de Luna came into view; a 13th-century fortress nestled among narrow lanes and terracotta rooftops. A short walk further brought them to a small plaza where Iglesia de Nuestra Señora de la Expectación stood, its Gothic and Baroque architecture commanding quiet reverence. The scene was peaceful, with only the faintest sound of tourists' footsteps echoing off the cobblestones.

Walking past Torre de la Merced, the remaining tower of an old convent, they turned down a narrow street. They arrived at Parque El Mayeto, which displayed a rich tribute to Rota's farming heritage, with shaded pathways, old tools displayed as sculptures, and a central gazebo. Stephanie stopped and stood there in silence, admiring the park for about ten minutes. Under different circumstances, Damion would have enjoyed the leisurely stroll and sightseeing tour, but for the third time today, he felt like he was being led on a leash and had no control over his fate. Even so, he wasn't about to tempt it now by challenging Stephanie Cheng. Continuing on from the park, it appeared as if they had been walking for a while to no place in particular, until Salina had had enough and broke the silence.

"Stephanie, *where are we going?*"

Ignoring Cabrera's question, Stephanie picked up her pace and turned onto a narrow, deserted street. After Damion and Salina had followed her halfway down the street, she suddenly stopped and turned to face them.

"*Are you two sleeping together?*"

"*Wha...?* Uh, no," answered Cabrera softly, glancing at Damion. "*Not yet.*"

"Well, from where I'm standing, it sure looks that way. And *now*, I'm stuck in the middle of it!"

"I know. We're sorry about that, Steph, but you don't *have* to report us. We *promise* to be discreet."

"*Discreet? Are you kidding me?* I caught you guys sucking each other's faces off because you were *too sloppy* to close the damn door! What if I had been, oh, let's say...the CSO? Yeah, we wouldn't be having this conversation right now, would we?"

"You are absolutely right, and we are very sorry for putting you in this position. *Please*, don't report us. We *know* that we shouldn't be fraternizing...and I know that you were maybe a little interested in Damion, but we were already in this, and we *just*..."

Coming to a stop from worriedly pacing back and forth, Stephanie turns and gives Cabrera an incredulous stare.

"*Unbelievable*. Do you really think that I am this upset because *you two are together and want to break some rules?* I don't care if you make out in an office, in the galley, or on the flight deck! No, what I am upset about is much bigger than your...*whatever this is!*"

Cabrera looks at Damion, who has the same confused look on his face as she does. He finally takes a chance and enters the conversation.

"I don't understand. You are not interested in our...*relationship,* yet you brought us out here because you are *more interested* in something that doesn't have anything to do with us?"

Stephanie turns her gaze on Damion, and he could swear she had actual fire in her eyes.

"*Oh, no*. You two have *everything* to do with this. But as God is my witness, if you get caught and it interferes with my mission in any way whatsoever, the level of pain and suffering that I will cause to rain down on you both will be *Biblical*."

Damion snapped out of the searing memory when Stephanie let out a long, exaggerated sigh.

"Okay, let's get this over with," she began. "I know that I may have come off a little hard on you guys earlier, and I would apologize, *but you deserved it*. Now, I will tell you a little about me and why I brought you out here, but let me warn you. If either of you tries to corroborate what I'm about to tell you with anyone, or tries to search for *any* information about me, you are going to trigger certain protocols that will result in you receiving a visit from some very unpleasant people. That's a fact. Now, with that said..."

Stephanie tells them that her name is Stephanie Baheela Singh. Her mother is Asian-American, and her father was a Bahraini Public Security Force officer. Her parents met when her mother worked at the American embassy in Bahrain as a cultural liaison. The night her father was murdered, she remembered overhearing her parents talking about his concern that someone on the force may have been leaking information to a criminal organization of human traffickers. He felt that the criminals always seemed to be one step ahead of them. The PSF would receive reliable information from informants on the group's location and contraband, but whenever they arrived to arrest them, they would be gone. Her father thought that he had found the connection to the leaks, but he was killed before he could follow up on it. Her mother was devastated and did not accept the official report of his death, so she started using her embassy contacts and financial resources to try to track down the criminals herself.

After months of unsuccessful attempts at trying to find them, she was forced to stop the investigation or risk losing her job. Stephanie's mother later remarried to an American Naval Officer and resumed her life. Stephanie grew up, went to college, and majored in cybersecurity, but she never forgot about what happened to her father. Just before graduation, she was approached by a government recruiter for a job. After completing her training and having new resources to use, she revisited her mother's investigation notes and discovered that she had narrowed the leak down to two people. Ironically, both had been in the American military at the time.

Stephanie paused and looked at her drink, then continued.

"After further investigation, I ruled out one of the two suspects due to the fact that, *one*: he killed the man who murdered my father, and *two*: he did not disappear afterwards. He remained in the military, went through psychological counselling, and continued with his career." She let the words hang in the air, then turned to Damion.

"Thanks for that, by the way."

Damion, stunned, replies, *"Your father...was the Bahraini PSF officer killed the night of the raid on the docks?"*

Stephanie nods, looking at him closely.

"And your name...*Baheela Singh* is Bahraini?"

She nods again. "Baheela is Arabic for beautiful woman or one who is beautiful. My father used to call me his *little baheela*."

"So, the other American in the raid that you and your mother suspected was leaking intelligence is...."

Cabrera finished the sentence for him, "Special Agent Maya Torres."

A long silence passed between them, then Cabrera turned to Damion with fire in her eyes.

"Why didn't you tell me that you knew that witch? Not only that, but you've known her for a *very long* time and said nothing! No warning, no heads-up, nothing!"

Damion, at a loss for words and head spinning from the new revelations, stared at the table as she continued to roast him; her voice low, but hitting hard like a ton of bricks.

"That woman is threatening to ruin my career, my family, my life, and you knew the whole time about her and what type of person she is! And to top it all off, *she was with you when you killed someone?"* As the tears welled up in her eyes, Cabrera sat back in her chair, arms folded, shaking her head.

"I thought we were..." she stopped abruptly, quickly glancing up at Stephanie, then remembering that she already knew about their relationship.

After a few moments, Stephanie chimed in, her voice absent of any ounce of sympathy.

"You may want to think about reeling in some of that aggression, Salina. In all fairness to Damion, he was under orders not to tell you anything." She paused, then continued. "Just like *you* were under orders not to tell *him* anything."

Cabrera and Damion both stared at Stephanie, shocked by the surprise revelation.

"*How do you know about that?* There was no one else present at the café when that witch ordered me not to say anything," Cabrera replied.

"Yes, there was. You just didn't know it, and neither did she."

"Wait, *what*? *You met Maya at a café? When*?" Damion asked.

Cabrera, looking at Stephanie, turned to Damion.

"Two days before the ship pulled back in. After I got out of the hospital, she approached me, not the other way around."

Damion, now deep in thought, replied, "She came to the ship *two days* before we pulled back in, to brief the CO & XO. She specifically requested that the CO have *me* help her with her inquiry. *Jeez...*"

"Yep. She played both of you, trying to get you to turn on each other. The question is...*why*?" Stephanie asked rhetorically. "We had nothing solid to justify continuing our surveillance of her until she contacted you," nodding towards Cabrera.

They sat there, each in their own thoughts, until Cabrera spoke next.

"You really have everyone fooled, you know. Thinking that you are some new Ensign who parties a little too hard early in her career and can't hold her alcohol. I guess they teach you how to *drink like a sailor,* too? And all of the questions about Damion were just part of your digging to make sure he wasn't somehow involved?

Stepanie nodded, "Yes and no. First, *no*, we don't get trained on how to drink. Have you ever heard of *the so-called hangover pill*? It's supposed to help you recover quicker by absorbing most of the alcohol a person drinks. Well, we have something better, and it's government-patented, so it's not on the market. A proprietary combination of Metadoxine plus Benzodiazepineimidazole. You take it thirty minutes before you drink, and it absorbs one hundred percent of the alcohol. The downside is that it only lasts three hours before you have to dump it out of your system, *or else*. And second, *yes*, the questions about Damion were all part of my *digging,* so don't go getting your panties all twisted up in a knot, *he's all yours*."

After spending several moments quietly venting, Cabrera continued. "*Wait a minute.* If you are NCIS, shouldn't the CO and XO have been informed about all of this with Torres? It could have saved you from all of this cloak-and-dagger nonsense."

Tilting her head and observing Cabrera for a moment, Stephanie replies, "Whoever said that I was NCIS?"

Damion and Cabrera looked at each other, both thinking the same thing: if she wasn't NCIS, did they really want to know who she actually worked for? They took a long look at Stephanie, neither one offering to ask the question. With a chuckle, Stephanie grabs her beer bottle and puts it up to her smiling, mocha-painted lips.

"You two have that whole psychic connection thing down hard, don't you?" She let out a loud sigh after taking a long gulp of her beer. "Ah, yes! This tastes so much better when you don't have to take that pill before it."

Damion and Cabrera stared at her, still shocked by her unnatural change in personality.

"You want to know the answer to the million-dollar question, but you don't want to ask it. Well, we can come back to that later. For starters, I want you to fully understand what you have gotten yourselves caught up in, so right about now would be a good time to start drinking those beers."

Chapter 20 – Oaths and Orders

Stephanie casually pulled out her mobile phone while looking directly at Damion and Cabrera, her eyes sparkling with a mischief that didn't quite match the weight in her voice.

"Here's where it starts to get interesting," she said, her tone carrying the promise of something equally exciting as it was serious.

She rotated the phone sideways and double-tapped the upper right corner of the blank screen. A thin purple line emerged from the corner, tracing the perimeter of the display like a laser-guided sentinel on patrol. As soon as it completed the loop, enclosing the screen, it flashed once, and Stephanie pressed four fingers of her left hand flat against the surface. Instantly, the display went dark purple and icons lit up in response, like a classified operating system booting up from sleep.

Her fingers danced across the glowing interface, tapping a precise sequence that clearly wasn't meant for everyday users. A fully rendered 3-D image of the Earth sprang into view, rotating with crisp clarity and impossible fluidity. She gave Damion and Cabrera a quick side glance, and the look in her eyes carried a jolt of adrenaline.

"This is like Google Earth riding a cheetah on steroids," she said, barely hiding her excitement.

She tapped another icon without hesitation. *"Operation Phantom Tide."*

In a flash, the globe vanished, replaced by five equally-sized squares, each holding a subject ID tag. She selected one. The Mediterranean Sea materialized in ultra-high detail, crawling with icons: ships, aircraft, mapped-out sea lanes, air routes, even a few symbols Damion and Cabrera didn't recognize. Those were the ones that caused them to feel uneasy since they were both familiar with reading a variety of classified overlays.

Then came the voice command.

"Zoom in, Western Med. Isolate North Africa."

The screen came alive, shifting, zooming, sorting data faster than either of them thought possible. Damion leaned forward slightly, unconsciously holding his breath, while Cabrera sat frozen, eyes locked on the screen, absorbing the visual symphony of intelligence data being streamed in real time. It wasn't just a display; it was a window into a world they had no business seeing, a level so far above their security clearance it may as well have been a myth. And in that instant, they didn't just *know* everything had changed... *they felt it*.

Stephanie didn't look at them as she covered the screen with her hand. The deliberate tone of her voice, however, cut a clean path through to her words' unspoken meaning.

"Do I need to remind you that seven percent of all military personnel deaths overseas are *non-combat related*?" she said, eyes finally lifting to meet theirs. "You know, accidents, muggings, hit-and-runs, food poisoning..."

237

Cabrera blinked rapidly, her face registering a mix of disbelief and confusion. She opened her mouth, then closed it again.

Stephanie added, deadpan, *"What? Food poisoning can happen."*

Damion shook his head, the barest hint of a grin on his lips as he broke the silence.

"We get it," he said. "Don't say a word. Don't even dream about this conversation... *or else.*"

Stephanie's face lit up with a wide, satisfied smile. She didn't speak right away. She didn't need to.

"Outstanding," she finally said.

With a single fluid motion, she removed her hand from the phone and placed it in the center of the table between them, still pulsing with raw data and classified images of the hidden world around them. Damion and Cabrera stared down at it in stunned silence as Stephanie began her briefing.

"Several key regions between the Middle East and Western Hemisphere have emerged as significant corridors for arms dealers, drug and human trafficking, and migrant smuggling. North Africa is the primary corridor, serving as both a destination for migrants from Sub-Saharan Africa and a major departure point for migration to Europe. Tunisia's transients are up to more than two hundred percent since last year, which supports intel from several reliable sources that Tunisian authorities are selling intercepted migrants to Libyan militias for pocket change – about 25 euros per person."

"Now, there are three sea lanes that matter. The central route: consisting of Libya, Tunisia, Algeria to Italy, and Malta. *Big* money, hundreds of millions in U.S. dollars every year. Then there's the western route: Morocco and Algeria to Spain. And finally, the eastern route: Turkey to Greece, consisting of sixty thousand-plus illegals last year alone. "Sometimes we get lucky and are able to shut down one of the smuggling routes. However, when we cut off one line, the flow just shifts sideways until a new route can be established to replace the lost one."

"The networks are like thousands of little Lego pieces that can snap together any way they need them to. They move drugs, guns, people - whatever sells. They are mostly family-run cells and not large-scale cartels. "We have evidence of their latest tactic - conscripting regular people. Port guards, customs officials, ferry drivers, cops, and maybe even military personnel, using blackmail or threats. If your paycheck can't be squeezed, then they'll leave a package with your kid's school photos instead."

"Which brings me to these. One of our guys in Cádiz found them during a raid. He sees these weird-looking goggles, puts them on, looks at a Guardia Civil truck, and *bam* - strange blue symbols all over the chassis. Totally invisible to the naked eye. We swiped the paint and sent it to the lab. Results came back as an unknown compound. They never saw anything like it. They did their tests, tried mixing it with other elements, the whole shebang. Now here's something interesting: when it was mixed with water and left to dry on a surface, it disappeared. That police truck was hauling fentanyl precursors and digital maps of stash pads in

Valencia. The smugglers could have driven that vehicle anywhere, and no one would have been the wiser."

Her voice drops. "Bottom line: the smugglers aren't always sneaking *past* law enforcement – we think they're developing ways to ride *along* with it. Until our scientists figure out how those lenses work and duplicate them, we are shooting in the dark on this.

Damion and Cabrera sat in silence. They had been purposely drawn into this world by Maya Torres, and they still didn't know why. Then, along comes Stephanie Cheng/Singh, who turns out not to be some newbie, fun-loving Ensign, but a death-threat-slinging psycho working for God knows who. As he sat rubbing his head from the information overload, a thought suddenly came to him.

"This has serious national security implications," he said to himself.

"Now you get it," replied Stephanie. "That's why I'm here."

Cabrera, joining the conversation, sat back in her chair.

"And who exactly *are* you, Stephanie? You say that you aren't NCIS, but you managed to infiltrate our ship as a Navy Officer, a cybersecurity expert at that. You have access to tech we have never heard of before, and you've managed to mislead everyone from the CO on down about your true identity. So there, now I've asked."

Stephanie took another gulp of her beer, only much quieter this time. Looking at them both, as if she is trying to decide whether to let them borrow her new

Porsche or not, she tips the beer bottle towards Cabrera.

"I'm OGA."

Cabrera looks at her with a blank expression and says, *"Is that supposed to mean something to me?"*

She then looks at Damion for support and sees that he has his head down, rubbing both his temples with his thumbs.

"Salina," he begins slowly, "OGA stands for *other government agency.* It's what people so far above our working level call themselves when they can do things like: create sanctioned front companies to move money, or help a deposed president escape his country after a military coup, or even create a fictitious background with official orders to place someone on a Navy ship, specifically for one purpose."

When she didn't respond, Damion glanced up at Cabrera and saw that all of the fight had gone out of her like a hot-air balloon, as the realization of how deeply they were involved finally settled in.

"Hey, Salina, you still with us?"

Cabrera, not looking up, started talking as if to herself.

"I was just thinking, what if they targeted a disgruntled sailor on one of our ships during a 6-month deployment? Maybe they are fooled into thinking they are going to get rich quickly, or it's a case of blackmail, as you said earlier. Either way, the package or packages get picked up sometime during a port visit and smuggled onboard. Then, when the ship returns home, it is offloaded sometime during standdown for delivery and distribution. Think about it. We deploy, and when we get back, customs comes aboard, checks the paperwork, and asks some questions. They don't have the time or resources to search the entire ship for contraband in spaces they know nothing about."

"And you, Damion, conduct random urinalyses underway and maybe a locker search for contraband, *if* you have enough probable cause, but even with that, you need a command authorization for search and seizure from the CO. And let's be realistic, as awesome as the military working dogs are, how likely is it that if they were brought onboard, that they would find a sealed package the size of a shoebox, full of some synthetic drug, on an active ship our size?"

"Granted, I believe that 99% of our service members would not willingly do anything like that, but *honor, courage, and commitment* only go so far. It's that last 1% that would keep me up at night."

"Now, let's not go all DEFCON ONE just yet, okay?" Remarks Stephanie. "We believe that these families currently are only focused on the regions mentioned earlier, but these people are long-term planners – real forward thinkers. It wouldn't surprise me if they tried expanding their reach by marking active military vessels with that stuff a few years from now, after they have compromised some key personnel. But we don't think they are anywhere near that kind of deployment capability yet. Plus, for them to try and expand to the US or Canada would be tantamount to suicide."

"Only if we can see them coming," Damion said sarcastically.

Ignoring his comment, Stephanie continues. "Everything we know about this network has a motivation we can understand - power, control, and money. The only discrepancy I still can't figure out is the two of you. Why did Torres get you involved in this?"

Cabrera's head suddenly pops up.

"Hold up. You think that Torres is having me targeted to blackmail me into using the ship as their mule? And Damion is supposed to be the one who takes me down?

Damion, quietly listening, suddenly curses and slams his fist on the table, causing them both to jump.

"The pictures," he remarked blankly.

"What pictures?" Asked Cabrera cautiously.

"She had photos of us standing at the lighthouse, just before that crazy bird flew over us. She used them as leverage to get me to cooperate."

"But we didn't do *anything* at the lighthouse."

"Perceptions," Damion replied, cursing under his breath.

"What kind of *perceptions* are we talking about?" Asked Stephanie.

"How did you put it? We were about to *suck each other's faces off*, but a seagull flew overhead and yelled at us."

Stephanie looks up at the sky while laughing, "I guess it was trying to warn you that you were being watched!"

Silence falls again on the group for a couple of minutes, then Cabrera speaks up.

"So, what do we do now? Is there a plan to catch Torres?"

Before anyone can answer, their attention is drawn to the entrance when the owner suddenly hops off his stool and, with a charming smile, beckons in several new customers. After quickly scrutinizing the new arrivals and determining that they aren't a threat, Stephanie pockets her phone and stands up from the table.

"Now, we get out of here."

The trio arrived back at the ship just as the last traces of daylight surrendered to night. The glow from the quarterdeck lights gave the non-skid a muted shine, and the shadows cast by the watchstanders stretched like sentries across the brow. Damion was last in line as they stepped aboard, his mind still unwinding from the day's events.

The Officer of the Deck, a fellow Chief in his khakis, greeted them with the casual nod reserved for those who had known each other's temperaments for years. But his tone shifted as his gaze fixed on Damion and Cabrera.

"The XO wants to see you two," he said, pointing toward Cabrera first, then Damion. His voice carried no urgency, but there was weight behind it, a subtle gravity that set Damion's senses on alert. Stephanie glanced between them, her expression unreadable. She had a gift for keeping her emotions behind a steel curtain until she needed them as leverage. Cabrera didn't react much at all, maybe because she'd already been through more than enough these past weeks. One more meeting wouldn't make any difference.

"Aye, Chief," she said evenly.

As Cabrera and Stephanie began to walk toward the passageway door leading below, the OOD leaned slightly toward Damion. His voice dropped to a whisper.

"The ship's not getting underway in two days as scheduled. Don't know why."

Damion nodded but didn't stop walking, filing the information away like a live round in the chamber of his favorite M5 carbine.

He caught up with the two women just as they reached the ladderwell.

"That was fast," he said, his tone measured.

"What was?" Cabrera asked, glancing over her shoulder.

"She already got them to change the ship's orders," Damion replied.

Stephanie stopped and turned toward him with a sharp, assessing look.

"What are you talking about? I haven't been in contact with my people yet."

Damion slowed his pace for half a step.

"Then something else must be happening without us."

Stephanie's eyes narrowed, and for a fleeting moment, the three of them exchanged the kind of silent look people give each other when they suspect that someone else might be working behind the scenes trying to manipulate events.

When they reached the XO's stateroom, Cabrera was called in first. The hatch closed behind her, and Damion leaned against the bulkhead, his arms folded loosely, but his mind was anything but relaxed. He started running scenarios in his head — orders delayed, NCIS involvement, Torres still somewhere in the mix. The ship was a self-contained ecosystem, and every ripple meant something.

Five minutes later, Cabrera emerged. She came out with an expression that told a different story. Her eyes were wet, but she wasn't crying.

"I've been restricted to the ship," she said, her voice brittle, "and to Officer's Country. No contact with the enlisted crew - especially the boarding teams. XO says it's by request of NCIS."

Stephanie's brow tightened, but she said nothing. Damion could see the questions forming behind her eyes.

Cabrera then walked past them quickly, head down, with her hand covering her mouth. Damion and Stephanie, shocked, looked at her but didn't say a word as she hurried down the passageway.

Then it was his turn.

As he entered the stateroom, Damion could feel the aura of electricity in the air. The XO wasted no time and delivered his speech like he was reading it off a teleprompter.

"Chief, since you were brought into this by Special Agent Torres, I'm going to give you an update on what's going on. You will no longer be participating in the investigation. There have been some new...*developments*. Ensign Cabrera has been temporarily relieved as ATFP Officer effective immediately. The crew is not to be informed under any circumstances, and for all intents and purposes, it will be business as usual until everything is concluded. You will, however, maintain official contact in a limited capacity with Ensign Cabrera to prevent any rumors from starting about why she is not interacting with the crew. And, there will be zero unofficial contact between the two of you. NCIS will be back in a couple of days to conclude their investigation."

Conclude. The word had a finality to it, like a guilty sentence, already decided.

"Sir, what are these new developments?" Damion asked. It wasn't a plea. It was a statement of operational requirement.

"Any additional information is on a need-to-know basis," the XO said. "And you don't need to know...not yet. Also, you are not to get further involved unless NCIS requests it. Look, Chief, I know how much you respect Ensign Cabrera, but orders are orders. Understood?"

Understood. Another word with finality that signals - the discussion is over.

Damion exited the XO's stateroom and saw Stephanie waiting for him further down the passageway.

"What's the situation?" she asked in a low voice.

"Salina has been temporarily relieved of duty, but from the sound of the XO's tone, it's about to become permanent. I am only to have limited official contact with her to keep the rumors from forming, and no unofficial contact. Crew stays in the dark. NCIS will be returning in a couple of days to finish their massacre."

Stephanie's mouth made a line that didn't move.

"Torres is two steps ahead of us. She's isolating you two while she's away on another op. A real chess player, that one."

"Maybe you should talk to the XO?" Damion remarked without thinking.

The glare that radiated off of Stephanie's face could have burned the paint off of the bulkheads.

"Right," he said flatly, lifting a palm towards her.

"I haven't been ordered to stay away from Cabrera yet," she said. "That window of opportunity is going to close very quickly, so I had better take the chance to talk with her while I still have it." She then turned and left without waiting for a reply.

Stephanie knocked on Cabrera's door once – a professional courtesy, not a question – then entered the compressed privacy of a junior officer's stateroom. Cabrera was curled in a ball on her rack, knees drawn up, and the dim light casting dark shadows that accented the profound exhaustion in her face. She looked like someone who had been weathering a major storm for days, not minutes.

"This is Torres," Stephanie stated in a low voice, sitting on the edge of the bed next to her. "She made a preemptive move to keep you off balance until she gets back."

"She's already won," Cabrera whispered.

"No, she hasn't. Not yet. I'll do some digging to see what she has done to make this happen. You just have to keep your head above water until we can figure this out and take the fight to her, okay?"

Cabrera didn't answer, nod, or show any sign of acknowledgement. Stephanie stood and gave her one last look before leaving, a look that was neither laced with compassion nor cold as ice. It just was.

Chapter 21 – A Not So Simple Truth

The next morning, Damion was having breakfast in the CPO Mess, the familiar background hum of casual conversation washing away his troubled thoughts. Another Chief suddenly plopped down in the seat across from him, making small talk that led inevitably to the question Damion had expected.

"XO tell you why we're staying inport?"

"No," Damion said without missing a beat. "He just had some follow-up questions on that car accident with the kid." The lie slid out smoothly because he knew that someone would want to know what his late-night meeting with the XO had been about. He couldn't tell them the truth, so he had to fill the space so the shape of the conversation didn't draw attention.

"Ah," the Chief said, content with the explanation, then he hurried off. However, not everyone was so easy, such as EWC(SW)Sylvia Beechum. She had a real talent for getting under his skin, and her voice cut through the background conversations of the Mess like a scalpel.

"Soo...how was your hot date with the two little Ensigns?"

Damion slowly set his fork down, turned his face to hers, and drew a steady breath.

"Sylvia, I would rather paint your toenails red and kiss your cruddy feet than ever have another night like that."

He reached for his coffee, with eyes focused on hers, and took a drink as if he were cooling a volcano about to erupt.

"Wow," she said, not laughing. "*That bad*?"

"You can't even imagine," he replied. The finality in his tone was the kind that makes even a seasoned Chief draw back and let it be, which she did.

Damion left the Chief's Mess and returned to his office. He barely had time to get settled in before a knock came at the open door. A young engineering seaman poked his head in.

"Good morning, MAC. When you have time, the MPA would like for you to come to MER one and inspect the security locks on one of the main reduction gears. Nothing serious, but she thinks it may need replacing."

Damion nodded once. "Tell her I'm on my way."

Grabbing his cover, he locked the door again and headed towards engineering. The route to Main Engineering Room number one was all muscle memory. Ladderwells, constricted passageways, and the occasional need to step aside for a sailor hauling work gear. He walked the passageways with the determination of a man who belongs where he's going - neither hurried nor slow, ducking the way sailors do when the overhead reminds you that the ship was built for machinery first and men second; something that every sailor who has ever tested that truth has found out the hard way. *Nothing serious*, the sailor had said, but a request from the MPA for a security lock inspection on an MRG - there's a seriousness in that even when someone says "nothing serious." You don't call the

Chief Master-At-Arms to look at security locks because you're bored.

The main reduction gear, or MRG, is a critical piece of equipment that most people, even sailors, don't usually see or think about, but without it, the ship wouldn't go anywhere. The ship's four jet-aircraft engines are designed to run at very high speeds, but the two propellers don't work well at those speeds. They need to turn much slower, but with a lot more force, or torque, to push the ship through the water effectively. The MRG takes the fast, high-energy spin of the engines and slows it down while increasing the torque, resulting in smooth, controlled propulsion. Without the MRG, the engines might be running, but the ship wouldn't be going anywhere. It's one of those behind-the-scenes systems that keeps everything functioning as it should - reliable, powerful, and absolutely essential. The MRGs are so critical to the ship's function that they warrant having 14 high-security locks around the casings, checked several times daily by security watches.

Damion reached the access door to MER one and stepped through into the space. The air was warmer here, combined with the low, constant vibration of machinery readiness. Every bolt, every lock, every danger tag was a silent affirmation to the precision demanded in keeping the ship ready for combat deployment on a moment's notice.

Damion saw that Stephanie Cheng was there, speaking with Ensign Donna Reed, the new Main Propulsion Assistant, or MPA. He stood back to give them privacy til Ensign Reed waved him over.

"Thanks for coming so quickly, MAC," she said, almost apologetically.

"No problem, Ma'am. What's the issue with the security locks?"

"Well, the issue is that I don't know if it *actually* is an issue. I may be jumping the gun, and I don't want to say that the locks were tampered with, but I noticed some scratch marks, and I need an expert assessment to rule out any potential foul play."

Donna Reed's speech pattern was fast in a professional way, not nervous, pointing two fingers at the securing points and the locks she'd flagged for inspection. After she finished giving him the rundown, Damion knelt in low, using his eyes and fingertips to check the texture of the hardened steel casings of the security locks. He took out a small mirror and a pen light, focusing his attention on the slight markings on the locking hasps. The fine scratches said that a tool probably slipped there at some point, and a tiny scratch at the edge of a retaining ring suggested a past overtightening was made by someone who probably didn't know their own strength.

Halfway through what he already knew was going to be a useless inspection, a junior sailor popped around the casing to alert the MPA of a valve alignment issue on the other side of the large space. She excused herself with the speed that suggested a major catastrophe might happen and moved off, clipping the edge of a steel table with one knuckle and not even acknowledging the sting.

Stephanie waited until Donna had disappeared behind some equipment, then slid into the conversation like she'd been there all along. "I got something," she said.

Damion didn't look up immediately. "About?"

"On Cabrera," she said, her voice pitched to stay below the natural hum of the room. "My people intercepted communications between the smugglers that line up with the allegation. Product lists. Shipping manifests. And a document with a suspicious account at the Central Bank of Tunisia. Payments were being regularly made to a person identified as *Banya el-Jazeera*. The island girl."

Damion let the mirror freeze. The polished rectangle held a fragment of his eye like a shard of glass with memory in it.

"You think it's legit," he stated.

"I think it's clean enough for an inquiry," she said. "And I think it could be Torres. Leak forged comms, seed falsified documents into official channels through an intermediary, and make it look unassailable. You want to call it elegant? Fine. It's elegant."

He breathed once through his nose, steady and quiet.

"And now, you are going to ask me if I still think that she's not involved?"

"I'm asking if you can see what I'm seeing," Stephanie said, not unkindly. "Because if you can't, then we have an internal problem that I can't fix alone."

Damion set the mirror down and finally looked at her. "What I see is a frame that fits too neatly. And, I know the target. Cabrera's a lot of things, but she's not a traitor."

"Maybe, you knowing the target is part of the problem," Stephanie shot back. "Blind faith in someone makes for a poor shield."

"Sometimes it's the only one you've got," Damion said defiantly. "And it's not blind."

Finished with his inspection, he stood, secured the mirror and pen light, and closed the case with the quietness of a man who had decided something he didn't plan to write down. He took two steps, then turned back.

"Regardless of what you *believe*, let's make sure we scour every tooth and nail first, before we jump to any conclusions. And until we know otherwise, keep your *protocols* holstered. We don't need 'accidents' to the presumed innocent while the adults argue."

She didn't smile. She didn't frown. Her eyes gave the barest signal of acknowledgment, a micro-nod you could miss if you blinked. He moved away, found Donna Reed, and delivered his assessment: some misplaced wear and tear, but nothing that crossed the line to disciplinary action. Donna accepted it with a professional's gratitude, and he left.

The moment he stepped out of the engineering space, his mind kicked back into investigation mode - back to the basics. One of the first investigative techniques he learned before he even earned his rating badge was to *always consider the source of your information*. No matter what it was or how reliable it appeared to be. Damion smiled to himself as he thought of his old MAA instructor's favorite analogy for processing crime scenes.

"How does a mouse eat an elephant? One small bite at a time."

In this case, Torres was the elephant and Damion was the mouse. He began by using his 5WH approach. The who, what, when, where, why, and how of every investigation. Then he sorted his primary thoughts into containers.

Container one: Torres's deceptions – having him and Cabrera spy on each other. Container two: the investigation, insinuations, then accusations.

Container three: Cabrera's restriction and the smugglers.

Container four: the XO's tone and specific use of "conclude." Container five: Stephanie, and everything about her.

By the time Damion reached his office, he knew the order he'd work them in. Torres's endgame was coming soon, and he needed to keep the ship's rhythm in him so that when the next attack came, he'd feel the tremor before he saw the wave.

The next couple of days dragged by in a fog as Damion tried to maintain a regular routine so that he didn't draw any unnecessary attention. He avoided the enlisted rumor mills without making it obvious that he was avoiding them. The crew didn't need a distraction; they needed leadership, stability, and confirmation that everything is as it should be. He began each day reviewing current geopolitical threat assessments for different regions the ship would be operating in, as well as any potential dangers related to military members in port. He walked the weapons magazine corridor, checking two-person integrity controls, access checklists, and whatever else he could think of to keep his mind busy. Some of the security checks were not even directly under his purview, but no one dared challenge the MAC for ensuring everything was secure.

During one of his rounds, he stopped to observe a boarding team operational briefing being conducted by one of the boarding team leaders, a First Class Petty Officer, explaining and asking questions about a scenario where the team would experience opposition from the target ship being boarded. Damion was proud of his team leaders, all of whom were very capable and highly experienced. Then he would think of Salina. Stuck in limbo while Torres played her game.

"Stephanie's been by," Cabrera would say almost at every visit. "Keeping me updated, but nothing new."

Damion nodded in silence. He wanted to tell her that everything would be okay, but "okay" had left the building a long time ago. So, he did the only thing he could do at the moment: stay as long as possible without going too far over the "official update visit" limit.

"The teams have been asking about you and your *condition*," he started.

"My *condition?*"

"Yeah. Apparently, you are sick with a serious case of pneumonia or something. That's why you are staying away from contact with the crew. I don't know exactly what it is due to medical patient privacy and all that. I just know that it's not contagious," he smirked.

Cabrera, half-smiling, "Right. And how long will that weak story last?"

"Not long. I also heard someone else say that you are staying away from the crew because you are pregnant and the command doesn't want anyone to know."

Cabrera let out a genuine laugh, although somewhat sadder than usual, thought Damion. Regardless, he missed hearing it.

Slowly shaking her head, Cabrera sighed, "I really do love this crew. Any mention of who the father is?"

Seeing her like this, fighting so hard to hide the pain, Damion had had enough.

"No. Okay, I had better go. The CSO probably has a hidden camera somewhere in the passageway monitoring visitors and how long they stay," he said, trying to lighten the mood.

As he was about to open the door to leave, Cabrera stopped him.

"Hey. I don't know if I will get the chance again, and right now I don't see any way out of this situation, so," she slowly stood up and closed the distance between them. Gently pushing his back against the door, their lips locked, a sudden blaze of desire - unexpected, uncontained, and long overdue.

When Damion left Cabrera's stateroom, his mind was racing, not from the burning kiss that she had given him, but from something Stephanie had said earlier about

Torres being a real chess player. If she was already calculating their next response and moving her pieces to block them, then it was time he went on the offensive and played his game too. He'd given Stephanie space to hunt her quarry, and he knew she'd hunt. But there's a point where a man in his position has to put his own knight on the board, and he knew exactly what to do.

He hurriedly went back to his office and, after about three seconds considering the ramifications, he pulled the one thread he knew would make a noise. He reached out to the Guardia Civil lieutenant from the warehouse raid. The one with the hard eyes and the dislike for cooperation that wasn't his idea or that included outside law enforcement, which he deemed an intellectual challenge to his authority. Damion kept the call inside the lines of professional courtesy and curiosity, even complimenting the lieutenant on how professional his men were while conducting the search. He kept it short, asking for any additional information they had on the raid, including any equipment or chemicals that may have come to their attention that might be of interest. The lieutenant didn't offer much, as expected. But the call did what Damion expected. Unknown to him, somewhere, a note was being written: *The MAC is asking questions*. A note that quickly walked itself to Torres with a smile.

Damion sat with his head back and his eyes closed. He knew that he hadn't won the war; he only knew the little piece of relief that comes when you refuse to sit and wait for the axe to find you. He wasn't ignorant of the risk. Making a move without approval is how you write your invitation to a meeting in which someone uses the words "obstruction" and "disobeying a lawful order" while spelling your name when they do it. He weighed it and did it anyway, because leaving Cabrera with a bullseye on her head inside a narrative built by other people felt not only like betrayal dressed as patience, but it felt like cowardice. Neither of which sat well with him.

He saw Stephanie twice more in passing and once on purpose. The passings were a handshake of eyes, the kind of professional glance that says "still checking." The on-purpose meeting was in an alcove outside a repair locker where conversations go when they need to look like they didn't happen.

"A little heads-up would have been nice. Your call to the Guardia Civil pinged," she said without preamble. "One of their informants belongs to the other side, and he flagged it. Torres will know by now."

Damion folded his arms because it kept his hands from making gestures. "Good," he said.

"*Not good*," Stephanie corrected. "She'll use it."

"She was going to use something. Let her use that. At least this time, I picked the terrain. And now that we know she is directly involved with the smugglers, we can feed her some bogus info."

"Obstruction," Stephanie replied flatly. The word had a sterile sound to it.

"They'll say that you are contaminating their investigation."

"I only asked for any new information, since I was part of the raid," he said. "I didn't ask for favors, didn't share anything classified, didn't misrepresent my status. Call it: professional curiosity."

"They won't care what you call it," she said. "They'll care that you moved without permission, and she'll present it as a pattern of insubordination."

"She's already doing that," Damion said. "Salina and I are not some pictures on her wall; we are moving targets."

"And she's a better shot than most," Stephanie added. "Look, I'm working the Tunisian angle. The bank account is clean enough to stand up to a general audit, which I will not be doing. If it's forged, I will know that it was done with access through the bank. If it's real..." She let the rest of the sentence hang.

"She's clean," Damion said. No hesitation.

Stephanie studied him. "Belief, as armor again."

"You have yours," he said. "And it's been working for you."

She didn't argue. She didn't agree. She shifted her weight, turned, and glanced through the metal mesh that partially hid the alcove.

"NCIS arrives tomorrow," she said. "Torres moved up her timetable."

"Of course," he said. "She wants this concluded while the crew's still in 'what happened' and not yet in 'why.'"

"I pulled a thread," Stephanie said. "The Tunisian account shows transfers from a non-profit shell company in the Seychelles, and the shipping manifests match shipments transiting from Almería. Also, the comms we intercepted mentioned an island reference twice in a way that feels like someone is trying to be very clever for an audience."

"Banya El-Jazeera," Damion said. "The Island girl."

"Yep," she said. "It's smart-dumb. Smart enough to pass casual scrutiny. Dumb enough to tell a pro that someone fabricated it."

He nodded, and for a moment, the quiet between them felt like a plan trying to gain its footing. He didn't ask her what she planned to do next because he knew he wouldn't get the answer, and because it would be a stupid question from a man who knows better than to ask an operative to narrate their operation.

He headed back to the privacy of his office to focus on his next move. He set his elbows on the desk and linked his fingers, and let the image of Cabrera on her rack, devastated, play over and over in his head. He filed it in the back of his mind, then closed the drawer on sentimentality because sentiment doesn't play well in war.

The day progressed slowly, and before he knew it, he had already drunk four cups of coffee. In the CPO mess, Damion noticed that Sylvia was keeping her distance. She kept eyeing him like an insecure hunter, unsure if she would end up as predator or prey. She opted for the latter and didn't ask him any more questions. Not feeling an obligation to appease her curiosity, he ate, stood, and left without a word.

Returning to his office, he occupied his time with some "busy work." He wrote three emails. One to a department head correcting a berthing compartment inspection schedule. One to the MPA, thanking her for the alert on the locks and confirming the maintenance window plan. One to the OOD watchstanders, a reminder on quarterdeck military bearing and professionalism. He sent all three. Maintain the appearance that everything is in order and keep the crew in the dark. Business as usual. Just as he hit the 'send' button on his last email, the phone rang.

"MAC."

"I just received notification that Torres is back in town," replied Stephanie. "She's not wasting any time, but my gut says that she will wait until tomorrow before she comes on board. Make sure you are on your game. She'll probably try to play the ally, while maneuvering you and Cabrera to slip up."

"Of course she will," Damion said. "That's where she's the most dangerous."

"Your call to the Guardia Civil will be the spearpoint to claim that you are interfering or leveraging your position to derail the investigation. Maybe even include an insinuation about an improper relationship. Remember, she doesn't need hard proof, just the *perception* of something that will reflect negatively on the command. And her finishing touch will be to wrap it up in a nice Navy Regulations and UCMJ package with Cabrera as the lace holding it together."

Damion wasn't fond of her analogy using Salina, but he kept his tone neutral.

"Then we give them some crumbs. I'll stay in the lanes, no additional movement. You do your digging. I'll hold the line here."

Stephanie didn't respond right away. Damion could sense through the phone that something else had her distracted, and her mind was trying hard to solve it.

"You still there?"

"Yes. Just thinking about how none of this makes any sense. I can't wrap my head around Torres's motive, and it's driving me insane. I have looked at this from every angle I can think of, but my intuition tells me that this is personal - that Torres's interest in you has something to do with Bahrain. Unfortunately, there's still a lack of a true motive or proof to take her down." As the line became quiet again, Damion waited for Stephanie to finish processing the thoughts racing through her head.

Finally, she spoke again. "I need to be in that room during your interview."

Damion grunted, "Right, and your justification for being in Torres's interrogation?"

"I don't mean physically, only that I need to hear what's happening."

"Okay. How do you plan on pulling that off?"

"That's the easy part. Just promise me that you won't go into that interview before I see you again."

"Okay. So, that's the easy part. What's the hard part?"

"The hard part is making sure you don't go in there like Cabrera's knight in shining armor, lose your composure, and screw everything up."

"Thanks for the vote of confidence," he replied dryly.

"Do I need to remind you of your Guardia Civil call?" When he didn't answer, she continued. "Do whatever you need to do today, but stay under the radar. I recommend not even leaving the ship. Get some rest and prepare for when she comes on board. Now, I have one more errand that needs to be taken care of.

Chapter 22 – Echoes and Reflections

When Torres and her team arrived, she lined up her face the way a hunter lines up his sights on a deer, smiling as if she was there to fix something broken. Damion met the smile with the same neutrality that said he'd do and be whatever was needed to get to the truth. The board was set. The pieces were in motion. And this time, he would not let anyone else write a scene in this story without his fingerprints being all over it. He squared his shoulders, took a deep breath, and stepped into Torres's world.

The overhead light in the commandeered ship's classroom hummed faintly, casting a dull white halo over the table. Two video cameras with attached microphones had been set up by the time he entered the space. The large lenses reminded him of the mythical cyclops looking hungrily down at who it was going to devour, and in this case, him. He knew that the two cameras were a bit overkill and part of a tactic - Torres's attempt to intimidate him, and Cabrera, when it was her turn, with the knowledge that they were being recorded and that "others" would see it as well. She had played the game well, but now it was his turn, and if they were going down, then he was going down fighting.

His eyes focused on Torres. Her projected movements were slow, deliberate, and mechanical. Damion had seen her technique many times when they had worked together, dragging out the preparation to make her prey uncomfortable. She sat across from him with a legal pad, pen in hand, all business on the surface, but a fire burning beneath it. When the show was over, she looked up and locked eyes with him.

"Good morning, Chief. How are you doing today?" Torres asked, as if required by procedures and not out of any genuine concern.

"*It's a fine Navy day*," he answered.

She smiled thinly, "Hmm. You look a little tired. Uncomfortable. You sure you are up to this?"

Damion smiled to himself. She opens up with a carrot, then comes the stick. It didn't matter, though; he was prepared. He was, however, kicking himself mentally for showing how uncomfortable he was. Not because of the interview, but due to the Molar-Mic that Stephanie had loaned him. It was reasonably comfortable, if you liked having an extra tooth in your mouth. The molar microphone is a tiny device that clips onto a person's upper back molar and allows them to talk and listen without ever using their hands, or even making it obvious they're communicating. The device is both a microphone and a speaker, but instead of working like a regular headset, it picks up the natural vibrations in the user's jaw when they speak so that even in a loud, chaotic environment, words come through clean. When someone talks to the person wearing it, the device sends vibrations through the teeth and skull, and the user's brain does the rest, translating those vibrations into clear, understandable sound that's not heard through the ears like a standard headset.

Damion finally relaxed, "I'm good," he replied.

"Okay, then. Chief Jackson," she began, voice clipped, "explain your relationship with Ensign Salina Maria Cabrera."

Damion leaned back slightly in his chair, shoulders loose. "Ensign Cabrera is the ship's Anti-Terrorism Force Protection Officer, and since I train and run the boarding teams, that makes her my boss. She's professional and highly respected by the crew. Trustworthy."

Torres's pen scratched the page. "What are your feelings towards Ensign Cabrera? Strictly professional? Protective? Maybe a little personal? Do you ever *hang out* together, like go to clubs or grab drinks after work?"

Damion let a slight smile touch his mouth, taking a deliberate pause, refusing to be baited. She's going directly for the throat, already tasting blood in the water.

"We share long hours and bad coffee doing administrative work, planning boarding tactics, training exercises, etcetera. As far as being *protective* of her, she actively participates in our MIO boardings, so the entire team is protective of her. Just as they are of every other team member. We did happen to run into each other out in town while here in Rota, but then this place is not that big. Let's see, we also did a morning run together where she sprained her foot and was sent to the hospital for a month for rehab, but you already know all of that. I guess that's about it." Then, with the same easy tone, he added, "I guess our relationship is kind of like you and me working together in Bahrain."

Her pen paused, just for a beat, before continuing. "We're not here to talk about Bahrain."

"Of course not," he said casually, "but you remember those ops, right? The counterfeit ID ring, that fake passport factory out past the airport? You were the lead on that one. Ran it like clockwork."

Torres didn't answer, flipping a page instead.

"And that warehouse job in Mina Salman," Damion went on. "The one that turned out to be nothing but crates of bad-quality knockoff handbags allegedly en route to be sold on the base? I swear, we spent more time laughing about that in the truck than writing the report."

A faint twitch at the corner of her mouth. Not quite a smile.

"Getting back to Ensign Cabrera, do you ever discuss personal things like family, relationships, or personal problems?"

"Well, I think it would be inappropriate for my boss, an officer, to tell me all of her personal problems if she has any. That wouldn't exactly instill confidence in the person responsible for the ship's defense, and the care and well-being of the crew."

"Hmm," she began. "I'm going to share some information with you about your ATFP officer. After she was released from the hospital, we believe that she met with her contact in the smuggling ring. Our surveillance team followed her for several hours and observed her going into a concealed area in a park to conduct her business. When she went in, she appeared apprehensive about the meeting, but when she came out, she seemed very satisfied, even happy about the way it went."

"Is that all you've got? That she may have met someone in a concealed park? No video of an exchange, and no electronic surveillance mic of a conversation? That's pretty thin evidence, Maya."

"Special Agent Torres," she corrected him. "That place is the perfect drop spot. Completely surveillance-proof, which the smugglers know. What other reason could she have for going there and staying so long? Also, we have other evidence that points to her as working for them."

Damion did not answer as he studied her face. And then he saw it – her "tell." When they had worked together, Damion always knew when Torres was about to go in for the kill on a suspect she was interviewing. Whenever she was one hundred percent certain that she had maneuvered them where she wanted, she would get a slight twitch in her right eye, and her nostrils would flare ever so slightly, as if she were breathing in a rush of adrenaline. He even mentioned it to her once, but she laughed it off, saying it was her legal "high" from catching the bad guys.

Responding as if he didn't hear a word she said, Damion steered the conversation back to Bahrain, easing it in naturally as if it were just another memory.

"Wow. I just thought about that night on the docks," he began. "Now that was a mess."

For the first time, her hand stilled completely. The pen hovered above the page.

"Messy how?" she asked, her voice flat.

Damion shrugged lightly. "For starters, bad intel and two casualties. Granted, one of the casualties was a low-life dirtbag, but it still shouldn't have happened. Plus, most of the big targets were gone before we even got there. Funny thing about that night, like someone must've had our playbook. They moved like they knew where we were coming from, and how the leader got away Scott-free is still beyond me."

She tapped her pen twice, then shifted the topic back to Cabrera. "Tell me about why you interfered in an active NCIS investigation…"

"I don't recall interfering with an active NCIS investigation," he said, cutting her off without sounding like it. "You know, it's just the way the smuggler's leader disappeared off the docks, almost like he had help from the inside. Hard to pull that off with the tight security preparations you put into place that night."

Her jaw tightened just enough for him to see it. "A lot of people knew about that op, Chief."

"True," Damion agreed, watching her eyes, "but not everyone knew the leader liked to keep his shipments close to shore until the last possible second. That's not in the briefs."

Her gaze flickered for half a second, maybe less, and she took a barely noticeable, deep breath before locking back onto him. "Let's stick to the investigation at hand," she said defensively.

"Of course," he replied. "You were saying?"

From her workstation in the Ship Signal Exploitation Space, or SSES, Stephanie leaned toward a microphone, her voice low in the recording. "Got it. We've got her."

Cabrera focused on one precise spot on the bulkhead. Her target, her nemesis, her enemy. And it wasn't a photo of Special Agent Torres. It was a single, red bullseye she had made with a magic marker. This spot represented everything she needed to overcome today. Many people believe that when you train to confront an enemy, you condition yourself to focus on the image of that person, but Cabrera had learned differently. She was taught that if you concentrate on a person or a group of people, then it becomes emotional, and can sometimes be challenging to follow through. But when you turned that person or target into an inanimate object, then it was easier to eliminate them and get a good night's sleep afterwards. So, she decided that if Torres wanted to break her tomorrow, then she would be as ready as possible today. The last twenty-four hours had been a focused exercise in control; control of her body, control of her mind, and most importantly, control of her spirit.

She had raised and secured her rack immediately after waking up that morning to give herself space, transforming the small stateroom into a makeshift dojo. Bare feet pressed into the deck as she moved through the kickboxing drills her brother had taught her years ago. Each strike, pivot, and snap of her foot into the air wasn't about the enemy in front; it was about fighting the weight pressing down all around her from direct and indirect sources. Her fists cut through invisible resistance, sweat dripping steadily down her temple and into the neckline of her PT shirt.

When she began to feel the burn in her lungs, she switched to meditation. Sitting cross-legged on the cold deck, she closed her eyes, steadied her breathing, and forced the hum of the ship's ventilation system into the background. Inhale through the nose, slow, deliberate. Exhale, longer, softer. She held the image of a steady flame in her mind and matched its rhythm. Calm. Measured. Unyielding.

Full-length push-ups followed. Back straight, palms flat against the deck, arms pushing her weight in clean repetitions. She counted silently. Not just numbers, but resolve and perseverance. Each rep was another refusal to let Torres see her broken.

By the time the knock came on the door, her hair was clinging damp against her forehead and on the back of her neck. She rose, wiped a sheen of sweat from her brow with the back of her wrist, and opened the door.

Stephanie Cheng/Singh stood there, composed as always. Her eyes flicked once to Cabrera's damp shirt and face.

"You're sweating," she said flatly, stepping inside before Cabrera had finished moving aside. "Why?"

Cabrera closed the door behind her, then posed in a horse-stance. "Training. Kickboxing drills. Push-ups. Meditation. I want to walk into my interrogation tomorrow with my head clear and focused, not rattled like some terrified perp," she replied defiantly.

Stephanie gave a slight nod that revealed nothing of her opinion. Then, without preamble, she delivered what she had come to say.

"Something new has come up. Torres says that you met a smuggler/contact in a tree-lined tunnel not far from the base, after you were released from the hospital. No audio. No video. They don't know who you allegedly met, but she's pushing it hard. She's using this as another brick in the case that you're dirty."

Cabrera stiffened, hands curling at her sides. Stephanie's voice didn't change tone as she pressed on.

"Look, I'm taking a huge chance here at exposing myself, so if I'm going to help you, I need the whole story. Not some version you think sounds safe. Everything. I need to know why you went to that tunnel, what you did there, and whether you met anyone. And if so, who? Otherwise, I can't fight this for you."

Cabrera drew a long breath through her nose and let it out slowly. Her gaze drifted toward the deck, not out of guilt but because the memory weighed heavier than she wanted to admit.

"All right," she said quietly. "I'll tell you everything."

She began with the morning run. "Damion and I went out early for a normal morning PT run before the sun was fully up. We hit the midway point at the lighthouse, which you know about, then turned back. When we ran through the tree-lined tunnel, I slipped. Loose stone. My ankle went out, and I bruised myself up pretty good." She gave a rueful smile that didn't last. "I could barely stand on it, so Damion carried me over to this old wooden bench in the shadows. You could literally run right past it without knowing it's there. He then checked my foot to make sure that I hadn't broken anything. That's when..." She stopped.

Stephanie's expression didn't shift. She waited.

Cabrera forced herself to continue. "That's when we kissed. I'm not talking about a quick, passing brush of the lips. Not some mistake. A long, heavy... passionate kiss. Several, actually. We sat there a while, making out and talking. By the time we finished, my foot had swollen up very badly, so he carried me back to the main gate and base security transported me to the hospital."

Stephanie's face remained unreadable. Her voice, when it came, was a single word. "Continue."

Cabrera nodded once, eyes dipping before she pressed on. "After the hospital cleared me and I was discharged, I went walking in town. I didn't mean to end up there, but my feet carried me back to that same tunnel. When I realized where I was, I went and sat on the same old bench. I thought about Damion and what happened between us."

Her voice faltered, and she looked down, embarrassed. "Then... I vandalized the bench."

Stephanie tilted her head. "How?"

"Carving. Like a teenager. On the backside, where no one would notice right away." Cabrera hesitated, her face becoming slightly pinkish from blushing. "Chief Valentino has this... secret nickname for me, which he doesn't know that I know about - the *Red Light District*. Like...I'm trouble. Well, I guess it's accurate, because on that day, I felt like trouble. So, I carved it. My mark. Stupid, I know."

Stephanie's brows raised slightly. "That's it? That's what you did in the tunnel?"

"Yes." Cabrera's voice was firm now. "That's it. After I carved it, I left and went to the café. That's where Torres found me."

"Okay." Stephanie folded her arms. "Then I need to see this carving of yours. Evidence is evidence. Maybe I can use it. What did you write?"

Cabrera started to answer, then stopped. She studied Stephanie for a long moment, weighing something unspoken. Finally, she said, "I'm going to take a chance and trust that you are as good as I think you are. When you see it, I think you'll know."

Stephanie's face remained blank, but her silence told Cabrera she had heard exactly what she needed to.

As lunchtime approached, Damion, having just finished his marathon interview with Torres, felt that he needed to touch base with Stephanie to see if she was able to record the conversation. He figured that she would already be waiting at one of the pre-designated spots on the ship, which they had agreed upon to meet during the day, if they needed to exchange information. However, she was not at any of them. He decided to make another round through the checkpoints when he saw the ship's Intelligence Specialist approaching from the mess decks.

"Hey, IS1. Have you seen Ensign Cheng around?"

"She left the ship, Chief. Said she was going for a jog during lunch." Looking over his shoulder, he added, "Between you and me, no one would guess it by looking at her, but she's a little too gung-ho. Like, psycho-scary gung-ho. You would think she's training for a UFC fight as much as she works out."

"Yeah, she is kind of special," Damion added. "Thanks, shipmate."

"No problem, Chief."

Left the ship at lunchtime for a run? I wonder what that's about, Damion thought.

At that moment, exactly one mile from the Rota Naval Station main gate, Stephanie Cheng/Singh slowed to a walk as she entered the tree-canopied pathway. There, in the shadows, sat an old wooden bench, weather-beaten, but with a certain charm that she liked. She approached the bench slowly, taking in the surrounding details. The canopy of branches and leaves overhead, the thick sides of overgrowth providing near-perfect privacy, and the soft moss-covered path. Reaching the bench, she carefully studied the myriad of carvings and designs left to document the many visitors to this hidden oasis. Even though she found no personal satisfaction in leaving her presence engraved in any one place, she did appreciate some of the artistic work done on the old wooden surface. Halfway through the collage, one carving caught her eye. It looked much newer than the other engravings, but the inscription did not provide her with any earth-shattering revelation of who the artist was.

"Cabrera said that I would know it when I saw it," she mumbled to herself. As she continued to stare at the wooden bench, a smile suddenly parted her lips. There

it was, right in plain sight. She took out her phone and snapped a photo of the engraving.

"Good one, Salina. I might just be able to save your little butt after all." After taking several more photos of the surrounding area, she left the cool tunnel and ran back towards the base like a marathon runner seeing the finish line.

Chapter 23 – And Just Like That

Damion stood on the starboard weather deck watching Stephanie running down the home stretch of the pier at a full sprint. He had never seen her run before and was impressed by how fast she was. Her legs were a blur as she practically glided down the pier, showing no signs of physical exertion. He wondered if the thought of being an Olympic sprinter ever crossed her mind. As she completed her run and began several cool-down stretches, he wanted to get her attention, but made sure not to stare at her, as half of the enlisted males topside were doing. He casually looked around until she locked eyes on his position, giving him a slight nod to acknowledge that she saw him.

Damion then turned to look in the opposite direction, and stayed that way until he heard, "Hi, Chief! It's a great day for a run."

He turned to see Stephanie smiling at him, like a college cheerleader on steroids.

"Yes, Ma'am. Did you enjoy your run?"

"Yes, I did. I even found this cozy little tree-covered path that Ensign Cabrera told me about, with an antique bench that runners can rest on if they get tired. Maybe you should check it out sometime."

"Uh, yeah. I might do that on my next run if I have time," he replied hesitantly.

"Okay, then. I should probably go get myself cleaned up." Turning her back to him and lowering her voice, she added, "*I can only keep this fake smile on for so long.*"

Damion chuckled to himself as he listened to her footsteps fade away, followed by the opening and closing of a watertight door. Only then did he stand up straight and head back inside the ship.

About an hour later, a single knock on the steel door announced Stephanie's arrival. Without waiting for a response, she entered his office carrying a laptop computer and closed the heavy metal door behind her.

Placing the laptop on his desk, she said, "You handled that well."

"Well, it wasn't exactly a warm reunion."

While logging into the computer, the corner of her mouth curled up in what could have been mistaken for the beginning of a smile. "What did you expect? She's trying to destroy you and Cabrera's lives. But, she slipped up, just like I hoped she would."

"How? Where at?"

The computer screen flickered, and four separate windows appeared on the screen showing still video images from four different angles. The videos showed two angles from behind Damion sitting in a chair in the classroom, with Torres centered on both screens. The other two video angles showed Damion in the center while filming Torres from behind. The cameras covered the entire room in ultra-high resolution so that no matter which way anyone turned, they would always be facing at least one of the cameras.

"*What the...*" Damion began. "*You put cameras in there? What if she had seen them?*"

Stephanie paused and looked at him as if he had just asked the world's dumbest question, before pressing the spacebar to start the video playback.

"The docks in Bahrain." Stephanie tapped a key on the keyboard, replaying the moment on the screen. Torres's image flickered back to life, her hand freezing mid-scribble the second he mentioned the raid. "That pause wasn't just her thinking. You could see it in her breathing - shallow, quick. Plus, those cameras also record several biometric responses. She was back there, reliving it."

Damion leaned forward, elbows on the desk. "Then she went out of her way to explain a detail I didn't ask for."

"Exactly," Stephanie said. "That little nugget about 'a lot of people knowing about the op'? That's a tell. And when you brought up the smuggler leader's unexplainable disappearance, she deflected...for the second time. She didn't even blink at your questioning it. Why? Because she already knew the answer - and she shouldn't have."

Damion exhaled slowly. "So we've got a reaction, and we've got her volunteering operational knowledge that was never in the official brief."

Stephanie nodded once. "That's two threads. Pull them right, and we can tie her to the group."

"Problem is, she's smart and cautious. That was her slipping up without even knowing it. We try to force it, and she'll triple her situational awareness and lock down everything. She's already shown that she has a knack for decisive preemptive actions, intentional or not."

Stephanie's smile was thin but sure. "I don't know about all of that," she replied, letting the thought hang.

Damion leaned back, letting the silence stretch for a moment. "You know something that I don't?"

"Oh, lots," she said with a not-too-sarcastic smile. "Let's just say that I have put some things in motion that will let us know very soon which side of the coin she's on. We're about to give her enough rope to hang herself."

As they sat watching the video of Damion's interview with Torres, the phone rang.

"MAC."

"Hey, it's me."

Glancing at Stephanie, "It's Cabrera. Hi, Stephanie is here with me. How are you holding up?"

"I guess I'm about to find out. Torres has moved up my interview to 1500 today in the Wardroom. I guess burning me at the stake couldn't wait another day," Cabrera replied, voice choking.

Gesturing for the phone, Stephanie gets on the line. "Hey, Salina. Listen very carefully. I went to your bench, and I believe you. No matter what Torres says or does, keep your head up and stay focused. You are getting out of this." She then hands the phone back to Damion.

"I don't know if my plan will take effect in time, and I don't have any cameras in the Wardroom. I need to try at least to get some microphones in there." Stephanie grabs the laptop and quickly leaves the office without a word.

Damion pauses, then puts the phone back up to his ear. "What did you tell Stephanie?"

After a brief moment of silence, Cabrera answers, "Everything. I told her everything."

At precisely fifteen hundred hours - three o'clock sharp in the afternoon - Cabrera entered the Wardroom in her service khaki uniform. She walked with measured steps, her shoes clicking faintly against the polished deck, and slid into her assigned seat at the far end of the long table. The room felt colder than usual, the air heavy with the faint hum of the ship's ventilation system. She sat upright, hands resting neatly in her lap, though her stomach churned beneath the surface.

Moments later, Special Agent Maya Torres strode in with one of the agents close behind her. She carried herself like a predator on the hunt, the corners of her mouth curling into a smile that looked less like courtesy and more like a shark circling a wounded seal. Torres didn't even need to speak; her presence alone projected itself like a living entity, reminding everyone in her orbit who was in charge here. Without any sense of hurry, Torres set her folder, pen, and legal pad on the table, arranging them slowly and deliberately as though each movement was designed to test Cabrera's patience. The other agent set up a video camera at the far end of the room, making adjustments to capture every detail of the interrogation. Cabrera felt her shoulders stiffen, but willed herself to relax as Stephanie's words echoed in her head.

The agent finished his preparations and gave Torres a thumbs-up - time for the execution to begin. Just as Torres opened her mouth to speak, the door opened again. Another agent eased inside, leaning down to whisper something in Torres's ear. Cabrera's gaze stayed fixed forward, but her hearing sharpened, straining to catch even a fragment of the interruption. She couldn't hear the words, but she saw the effect immediately: Torres stiffened, her jaw tightening. Whatever was whispered wasn't good. Torres turned and leaned closer to the agent, her voice sharp and clipped, irritation dripping through even though she kept it low. For the first time ever, Cabrera saw the stone mask crack.

A flash of anger, raw and unfiltered, shot across Torres's face before she caught herself. Her eyes darted toward Cabrera, as if checking to see if she had noticed. Cabrera kept her expression neutral, though inside her pulse quickened, her instincts telling her something had shifted. Without explanation, Torres snapped her folder shut, rose to her feet, and swept out of the room. Both agents followed close behind, the door clicking shut behind them.

The sudden silence was deafening. Cabrera stayed seated, hands clasped tightly in her lap, the tension creeping into her knuckles. She thought about standing, about pacing, but forced herself to remain still. She could feel her heartbeat thumping as if it were going to hop out of her chest. What was going on? Had something gone wrong in their investigation - or worse, had they discovered something that made her situation even more damning? She swallowed hard, reminding herself to concentrate on breathing evenly and focus on maintaining her composure.

She had learned discipline and patience in the military, but now it felt more like a punishment. With every passing second, her nerves twisted tighter and her imagination wandered further.

Finally, after nearly fifteen minutes, the door opened. The same agent who had whispered to Torres stepped inside. His face gave away nothing.

"You can leave for now," he said flatly. "We'll contact you if and when we continue the interview."

For a moment, Cabrera didn't move, the words taking time to register. When they finally did, she blinked, almost disbelieving. Relief began to slide into her chest like a quiet tide, releasing the crushing weight that had pressed against her all week. It wasn't freedom - not yet - but it was something. And for the first time in days, her heart stirred with the faintest pulse of hope.

Cabrera rose slowly, straightened her khaki uniform with steady hands, and walked out of the Wardroom without looking back.

Cabrera sat on the edge of the bed in her stateroom, waiting for the call to return to the Wardroom for her NCIS interview. She had done everything she could to prepare herself, both physically and mentally. Now, all that remained was to see how it would all play out.

The phone rang, causing her to jump. She took a steady breath, picked up the handset, and heard the XO's voice instructing her to report to the Commanding Officer's inport cabin. As she set the handset back in its cradle, her thoughts quickened. *Why the CO's cabin? The interview hasn't even started yet.* If Torres was bypassing procedures, then Cabrera was resolved to fight her every step of the way. Guilty or not, she wasn't going down without a fight.

She made her way to the Commanding Officer's inport cabin and knocked firmly. When ordered to enter, she stepped inside and paused, finding the CO, XO, and Torres waiting. Cabrera closed the door behind her, came to attention, and faced the CO.

"Good afternoon, Sir. Ensign Salina Maria Cabrera reporting as ordered."

The CO told her to stand at ease, then shifted his attention to Special Agent Torres.

Already standing in a corner of the room, Maya Torres cleared her throat before speaking. She began by saying that there had been an egregious case of incompetence in how intelligence information received from outside sources had been parsed and not thoroughly verified, before being acted upon. Embarrassed, she admitted that NCIS had dropped the ball during the investigation. She added that she could not go into many details but explained that the misinterpreted intelligence had identified the term *island girl* as Cabrera. Only later was it clarified as the name of a commercial RORO vessel – a Roll-on/Roll-off vehicle transport ship.

As Torres spoke, Cabrera's heart was racing, but she remained silent, her expression disciplined and unreadable. The CO, however, leaned forward in his chair, his jaw set and eyes narrowing with each word that flew out of Torres's mouth. The XO's hand twitched against his armrest, knuckles tightening, as if holding himself back from doing something that he might regret later. Torres continued to speak, her words careful but unsteady under the weight of the Commanding Officer's glare.

Torres stated that she was presenting a formal apology to Cabrera on behalf of the service, and a personal one from her if Cabrera felt that she had stepped out of line at any time during the investigation. She added further that Cabrera had conducted herself as a true professional throughout the process, was an officer of high quality, and a credit to the naval service. Torres concluded by saying that Cabrera was cleared of any suspicion of wrongdoing and recommended her immediate reinstatement to all previous duties.

Cabrera stood in silence, too stunned to respond. She could feel the CO's simmering anger in the room, his expression betraying how close he was to erupting. The XO didn't even bother to hide the look of utter disdain he shot at Torres, his glare sharp enough to cut steel.

"Do you have anything to say to *Special Agent Torres*, Ensign Cabrera?" The CO asked.

Cabrera raised her chin a little higher and answered, "No, Sir."

The CO then dismissed her to leave, his voice tight and measured.

She quickly exited the room, closed the door behind her, and took a deep breath as she walked down the passageway. Almost immediately, the CO's voice boomed inside the room, tearing into Torres over the harassment of one of his officers and the disruption to the ship's mission. Cabrera kept walking. By the time she reached the end of the passageway, she could still hear the CO's anger roaring like a tsunami, spilling out from behind the closed door.

A smile spread across her face as she stepped out onto the weather deck and breathed in the fresh, liberating air.

Cabrera, Damion, and Stephanie stood together near the quarterdeck entrance, quietly discussing the abrupt end to the NCIS ordeal. Their voices were low, but their expressions still carried the weight of the last couple of days of intense and unpredictable drama. Cabrera, though relieved, had yet to relax fully.

From down the passageway, Torres appeared. Her pace was slower than usual, her once sharp confidence dulled. When she reached them, she gave a half-smile and said, "Well, I think it's safe to say that I've worn out my welcome here. The Captain made it very clear he wants me off his ship as soon as possible. Like, yesterday."

Her tone carried an edge of humor, but her eyes betrayed the sting. She went on, "My boss isn't too happy either. Headquarters is calling this a waste of time and resources, so I won't even be flying commercial. They've got me booked on a late MAC flight to D.C. tonight for a full debriefing tomorrow on what went wrong." She gave a dry laugh. "If I'm lucky, maybe I'll only get reassigned to someplace remote, like Diego Garcia. Either way, I'm glad things worked out the way they did."

None of them spoke. Cabrera's gaze stayed steady, Damion's jaw tightened, and Stephanie tilted her head ever so slightly, but no one believed the act Torres was trying to sell. The silence stretched, heavy with unspoken truth.

Torres suddenly clapped her hands lightly, breaking the stalemate. "Anyway, I'm pretty sure that the CO wants to get this ship underway first thing tomorrow, so tonight might be the last chance for me to set things right. Let me buy you both dinner. A local restaurant, my treat. Consider it a personal apology."

Cabrera didn't move, and Damion's expression didn't change. Neither looked interested. Torres raised her eyebrows and added quickly, "Well, if you change your minds, I'll be at La Flor Del Barrio all evening, most likely drowning the embarrassment of my team's blunder with a lot of beer."

For a split moment, it seemed as if that was the end of it. Then Stephanie, in her gentle, unassuming way, spoke up. "Maybe you two should go. It wasn't her fault she got bad intel. It could happen to anybody."

Cabrera and Damion turned and stared at her, as if she had a horn sticking out of her head, but Stephanie's face remained neutral and unreadable. After a long moment, Damion finally broke the pause.

"We'll see."

"Great," Torres said, forcing a smile as she backed away. "Then I had better get off of this ship before the Captain comes here and personally throws me overboard." With that, she turned and left them standing there in her wake.

As her footsteps faded in the distance, Stephanie spoke again. Her voice was lower and sharper now, and her words carried a weight that the others did not miss.

"Now," she said, "we'll see what's on the other side of that coin."

Chapter 24 – Checkmate

The walk through Rota Old Town felt different to Cabrera. The streets were the same, the lights no brighter than any other night, yet everything seemed fresher, sharper, alive. It wasn't the city that had changed - it was her. Each step fueled the sense of freedom washing through her after weeks of suffocating tension.

When they turned down the narrow street where the café was tucked away, Cabrera suddenly let out a laugh.

"What's so funny?" Damion asked, glancing at her.

Looking down the dim stretch ahead, she replied, "I was just thinking about those ridiculous British crime shows where someone wanders into some creepy, empty place, calls out, 'Is anyone there?' and then gets taken out by something absurd—like a giant block of cheese falling on their head."

Damion looked down the street, then back at her. "Well, there are plenty of people out here tonight."

She grinned. "Yeah, but if there weren't, I was ready to ask. And don't even try to tell me the thought didn't cross your mind - that Torres might be setting a trap for us."

"It crossed my mind," he admitted, his voice level. "But it looks like everything here is business as usual."

When they reached the entrance of *La Flor Del Barrio*, they shared a subtle smile, a silent nod to their earlier joke about this being "*not a date.*" A small sign reading

Abierto hung in the glass. They opened the door and stepped inside.

The café was quiet, almost empty except for in one corner, where an elderly man and woman leaned close over their plates, eating what looked like braised oxtails. At the back, Torres sat where Damion and Cabrera had once been, waving with the familiarity of an old college friend meeting them after years apart.

They crossed the room and took seats at her table. A young waitress appeared, smiling, and handed them menus. After taking their order for two beers, she disappeared into the back.

Torres wasted no time. "Thanks for coming, guys. I really wanted to clear the air between us," she said, her tone polished. "I know things weren't handled in the best way, but sometimes we have to play hardball when chasing *alleged* suspects." Her eyes flicked toward Damion. "I'm sure you understand what I mean."

He didn't answer.

Torres pressed on. "But now that this chapter's behind us, maybe we can let bygones be bygones. At least share one last meal together."

The evening moved on with little change in the social atmosphere. Cabrera and Damion ate quietly while Torres filled the silence with idle talk. Spain's beauty, her career, and the toll of the job on personal lives. If she noticed their silence, she didn't show it.

When dessert was offered, Cabrera excused herself to go to the restroom, leaving Damion alone at the table with Torres. He shifted slightly, frowning. The room suddenly feeling warmer as if someone had turned on a giant heater.

Torres tilted her head. "Are you alright? You look a little warm. Maybe we should move closer to the window so you can get some fresh air."

"I'm fine," he muttered. "I just need to get some ice water from the waitress."

He rose to his feet but swayed almost immediately, the floor seeming to tilt beneath him. Dizziness then nausea overcame him, and his body suddenly felt like a wet towel, collapsing hard onto the tiled café floor. The room spun in violent circles, his vision doubling, blurring. After a few moments that seemed like an eternity, several out-of-focus shapes closed in quickly around him - four pairs of shoes.

Straining his eyes upward, Damion saw the elderly couple, the young waitress, and Maya Torres, all looking down at him.

Torres's head was tilted, revealing blank eyes, and studying him the way a cat looks at a dying mouse it has been using as its chew toy. Slowly, she leans in closer, her mouth forming a razor-sharp smile as her voice cuts through the haze just before the darkness swallows him whole.

"Checkmate."

The warehouse smelled of dead fish and sea rot. A single bulb swung lazily from the rafters, its pale light crawling over stacked crates, rusted barrels, and old fishing nets. Outside, the water lapped against wooden pilings, the sound faint but steady, like the slow tick of a clock counting down to something inevitable.

Damion slowly regained consciousness with his blurred vision starting to clear. He immediately became aware that his hands were secured in front of him, and he was lying on his side on a damp stone floor in what appeared to be a large room. Turning his head, he saw that Cabrera was beside him in a kneeling position with her hands also secured. With some effort, Damion pushed himself up to a kneeling position. He had a pounding headache that seemed suspiciously like an alcohol induced hangover, and his wrists were burning from zip ties biting into his skin. He glanced at Cabrera kneeling beside him, bound the same way.

"Where are we, and how are you awake before me?" he asked lazily.

She didn't look at him when she answered. "I didn't get drugged, I got hooded. I guess they thought I was less of a threat than you. Her breathing was steady, and her eyes were staring straight ahead as she continued. "As for where we are, I'm sure that the creepy person lurking in the shadows can answer that one better than me."

Damion turned and locked onto the shadowed figure silently moving behind several dilapidated shelves. When his vision finally cleared, he saw Torres step into the light with a pistol in hand. Her movements were unhurried, like she had all the time in the world.

"Glad you could finally join us," she said with a sneer on her face.

"What's all this about, Maya? Why have you brought us here?"

"We'll get to that in a minute. You know," she said, circling them, "I used to be exactly like you two. I believed in the mission. The uniform. The flag. Until I learned the truth."

Damion kept his voice flat. "And what truth is that?"

She stopped behind him. He could feel the gun's presence before she even laid it against his shoulder. "That loyalty means nothing when you're disposable."

She moved in front of them and squatted down with a smile on her face.

"You know, I really thought that I had you two all wrapped up with a tidy little bow, ready to be shipped off to who knows where. But, apparently not. Just as I'm about to close the deal on you, I suddenly receive orders to terminate my investigation due to *unreliable* intelligence information. Allegedly, an informant who also works for one of the *international export families* was discovered embedded in the Guardia Civil. He was conveniently caught using unauthorized access to documents and digital files that revealed his connection to my associates. Now, how could the intelligence information have been unreliable, I asked myself, when I was the one who fabricated it?" She stood and walked to an old table with her back to them.

"So then, it occurred to me that one of two things was now in play. Either you, Ms. Cabrera, had some friends in *very high* places looking out for you, or another unknown player was in the game and they were coming after me." She turned abruptly and looked directly at them.

"That means that I am now forced to up my timetable and adjust my plans for both of you.

Torres's gaze drifted, not around the room, but somewhere far beyond, as if she were replaying a memory.

"*Enough* with the maniacal genius speech, Maya. What's this really about?" Damion snapped.

Torres came out of her trance and focused her attention back on them. "The first time I met him was on a raid, years before Bahrain, in some backwater swamp of a country not worth remembering. I chased him on foot for thirty minutes and thought that I had him cornered, but it was a trap. I was outgunned and captured. The gang leader was going to kill me on the spot, but not before sharing the details of how he was going to do it. Just as he pulled out a machete, he..." she smiled faintly, "...*he* stopped him. Said I deserved better. Promised to prove it."

She began pacing again, the pistol still loose in her grip but never pointing far from them. "They let me walk with two thousand euros in my pocket. At first, I thought it was a cruel trick, expecting to be shot in the back while walking away, but it wasn't. Later, the money started coming. Then the jewelry. No conditions. Just because...he loved me."

Cabrera's eyes narrowed. "*Traitor. You betrayed your oath and fed them intel.*"

Torres glanced at her, unashamed. "I gave them the locations of supply shipments and planned raids. Sometimes I delivered the goods myself. I was happy. Appreciated. And then..." she turned and looked directly at Damion, her voice sharpening to a blade's edge, *"you took him away from me."*

Bahrain. The smuggler. The struggle with the knife-wielding attacker that had ended in his accidental death. Damion felt the full weight of Torres's revelation settle in his chest.

"I did everything I could to make sure his death was erased from your record," Torres said, almost proudly. "So, I could write the ending myself when the time was right. And then, in Rota, I saw her." She nodded towards Cabrera. "The way you looked at her. I knew exactly how to hurt you."

Her voice was nonchalant - each word like tossing dirt on the ground. "Frame her for working with smugglers. Frame you for helping her. Simple. But, since my agenda has been altered, I will have to do things the old-fashioned way and get my hands dirty. Finally, justice will be served."

She leveled the gun at him.

"So, all of this is just part of some twisted, petty revenge scheme? And, how are you going to justify us being shot and left in a warehouse when we have witnesses who know that we left the ship to meet you?" Damion asked.

"Oh, that's easy. By the time they find and identify your bodies, I will be in the good 'ole U.S. of A. The autopsy will show that you had a very high blood alcohol level and were possibly mugged. There may be some suspicion of some other type of foul play, but it won't go anywhere. Not with the local police's lack of resources, and especially not with the Navy, after the glowing compliments I gave her in front of that annoying CO of yours."

Torres moved nearer, to about eight feet from them. "Don't get any ideas about last-minute heroics," she said. "I'm not coming any closer. This is goodbye, Damion," as she pointed the pistol at his head.

From the darkness, a voice cut through the tension, dripping with sarcasm. "My God, I thought you would never shut up!"

Stephanie.

Blinding beams of tactical spotlights suddenly bathed the warehouse as figures in black fanned out from the shadows. The crack of boots on concrete echoed through the space.

Torres's reaction was instantaneous. She dove to the floor in a forward roll and slid behind Cabrera, wrapping her arm around her neck in one smooth motion while simultaneously yanking her in front of her as a shield.

Damion tensed, his eyes flicking to the jagged edge of a crate beside him.

"Put the gun down, Torres," Stephanie called. "You've been blabbering for ten minutes. Every word's been recorded. Every confession."

Torres's jaw clenched. "You think this is gonna' end with me in cuffs?"

A metallic clang rang from the far side of the warehouse - one of Stephanie's team breaching through a side door. The distraction was all Damion needed. He shifted, bringing his wrists against the crate's edge.

But Torres fired first.

The muzzle flash lit the air for a fraction of a second. Cabrera gasped - her body jerking violently as the round tore through her back shoulder. She fell forward as the impact of the bullet spun her sideways before she hit the ground and went still.

Damion's world turned red as he tore his wrists free, lunged, and slammed into Torres with the force of a sledgehammer. The gun slid across the floor as Stephanie's team swarmed in, weapons raised and racing towards Torres.

Damion dropped to Cabrera's side, his hands already pressing against the wound. "Stay with me," he muttered, though she didn't respond.

Torres, bleeding from a split lip and grinning like a wild animal, stared at him from across the floor. "This isn't over," she hissed.

As two armed agents stood over Torres with weapons aimed at her, she suddenly rolled on her side and kicked one of them in the groin. As he doubled over, she used her legs like a giant pair of scissors, violently crossing them and catching the other agent's left knee in a bone-splitting vice. As the second agent yelled and fell to the floor clutching his knee, Torres scrambled to her feet and ran full speed through a boarded-up doorframe. Without hesitation, she vaulted over the rusted metal pier railing and plunged into the black water below. The Mediterranean swallowed her whole, muffling the chaos above. Torres descended quickly, her legs kicking and arms knifing through the water with practiced control, until her hands found the thick wooden pylons supporting the pier. Just as planned.

Stephanine and several armed agents stood on the pier looking down at the murky water.

"Should we go after her?" one of the agents asked hesitantly.

"No, let her go," Stephanie replied. "We'll get her."

Inside the warehouse, an EMT was stabilizing Cabrera and reassuring Damion that she would survive, but he barely heard her. His eyes stayed on Cabrera, her face pale under the flickering light, as the sound of the waves outside carried on, steady and indifferent as if nothing had happened at all.

Torres swam deeper without any worry of being followed or shot at. This was not some testosterone-fueled action movie where agents fired blindly into the water, hoping to hit their target. In the real world, there were things in the water that didn't react well to bullets, such as underwater fuel lines, insulated power cables, and who knows what else. No, they would want to catch her and debrief her at some secret black site to find out everything she knew. Well, she had a little something to say about that ever happening. Torres continued to dive until she reached the spot. Tied to the beams, thirty feet under, her salvation awaited. She worked quickly, fingers fumbling against the cold knot of nylon rope until at last, the scuba gear slipped free. She pulled the regulator into her mouth and took one deep, steadying breath. After strapping on and securing her air tank, she pushed off from the pier and disappeared into the underwater darkness.

Her strokes were smooth and efficient, steadily increasing the distance between her and the compromised warehouse. Soon, her thoughts returned to the sudden interference by the unknown strike team. Damion had gotten away tonight, but she would track him down later when he least expected it. But for now, she would have to disappear within the network. She obviously was burned with NCIS, so at least she didn't have to play the loyal agent game anymore. As her mind returned to the effort at hand, she measured her progress in heartbeats, the muffled thrum of her pulse syncing with each exhale of bubbles that trailed to the surface. At 500 yards from the pier, she could feel the excitement of escape growing in her chest, victory almost within her grasp—

Then, the water shifted. A strange vibration pulsed through it, low and steady, like the growl of some unseen seabeast beneath her. She froze. Another vibration followed, stronger this time, rattling through her ribcage. Ahead, a dark shape materialized out of the gloom - long, sleek, and mechanical.

A ROV.

The remotely operated vehicle's four 20,000-lumen underwater searchlights snapped on without warning, slicing through the black water like white-hot blades. Its propellers churned the sea with an angry hum as its camera lens locked onto her, unblinking, merciless. She kicked backwards instinctively, bubbles spiraling around her mask, but the ROV pivoted effortlessly, tracking her every move.

Before she could adjust, a fifth beam of light speared her from behind - another ROV.

Her chest tightened with a sickening realization: the reason they hadn't chased her into the water was because they had been waiting for her there the entire time. The gear that she thought was her secret escape hatch had somehow been compromised and tracked. They knew her plan before she even jumped.

She kicked hard, twisting to break away, but the nearest ROV extended a mechanical arm. The Kevlar net shot forward, blooming open with terrifying speed. It tangled around her legs first, yanking her into a violent spin. She clawed at the mesh, bubbles exploding from her regulator, but the fibers tightened with every struggle, cinching around her arms and chest.

Her oxygen tank jerked backwards, pulled by the ROV's motorized winch. The water filled with the unsettling whine of the mechanical beast's motor as she was dragged thrashing helplessly toward the surface, trapped like a fish on a line. Or more accurately...a net.

For the first time since that night she was lured into the criminal gang's trap, Maya Torres panicked.

Chapter 25 – Always Darkest Before the Dawn

The night air outside the warehouse carried the sharp bite of an incoming cold front. There were no fancy blue and red police lights pulsing against the corrugated steel warehouse or washing the dock in flashes of color. Nor any video cameras blasting the nightly news with a raid by clandestine law enforcement units. Only the rhythmic thump of a medevac helicopter's rotors as it descended toward the landing zone, illuminated by Stephanie's team, marked the presence of anyone in the area.

Damion walked beside the stretcher with one hand on the corner. Cabrera's face was pale and her breathing shallow, but steady. An oxygen mask covered her mouth and nose, and an intravenous tube ran down to her left arm. The EMT continued to monitor her vital signs as they moved her towards the helicopter.

"She's stable," the medic shouted over the noise. "Through-and-through. Missed anything vital. She's tough."

Damion didn't answer. His eyes stayed locked on her, as if sheer will alone could keep her from slipping away.

Stephanie came up beside him while the EMTs prepared to load Cabrera onto the helicopter. Her expression was unreadable as always.

"She almost killed Cabrera," Damion said, his voice tight. "And…she got away."

"No. She didn't," replied Stephanie, as if she were talking about the color of the sky.

Damion turned and looked at her in surprise. *"What? You got her? How?"*

Stephanie, still looking at the stretcher, replied, "We had a little surprise waiting for her. When the time was right, we snatched her out of the water like a flailing tuna in a Kevlar net and dropped her traitorous butt onto the cold, hard deck of one of our boats. We left her in the net for about ten minutes, watching her squirm. The video is pretty funny. You should see it."

After a moment of disbelief followed by the exhilaration of picturing Torres's capture in his mind, Damion replied, "Thanks for sharing that with me. I know you didn't have to."

Stephanie didn't reply, but simply nodded.

"So, what happens now?" asked Damion.

"We will...*debrief* Torres, find out what she knows, and then she will pay for what she's done. But right now, your priority is making sure Cabrera sees a friendly face when she pulls through." She paused. "We're sending her to Rota Naval Station hospital. Best trauma care you're going to find on this side of the Atlantic. And don't worry, we'll straighten things out with the ship."

After a couple of moments contemplating his next question, "And then what?" asked Damion, looking at her cautiously.

"Then," she replied, glancing at him, "a regular debriefing will take place. Afterwards, you and Cabrera are going to return to your world, and I will return to mine. You know which one I'm talking about, right?"

Damion looked straight ahead as the medics lifted the stretcher into the helicopter.

"I have no idea what you are talking about," he answered, then climbed in after them without hesitation.

Stephanie stood on the tarmac, the downdraft whipping her hair as the bird lifted off. She watched the lights disappear into the night sky over the water, her jaw set. Even though they had captured Torres, Stephanie knew that this kind of game didn't just end with one arrest.

Still, for now, the board was clear, and a win was a win.

Somewhere over the dark Atlantic coastline, Damion sat in the hum of the helicopter, his hand resting on Cabrera's. Her eyelids fluttered briefly, and for the first time since the shot, he let out a long, pent-up breath.

She was still in the fight. And so was he.

The holding cell was cold and damp, its concrete walls sweating from the chilled night air. Torres sat on a metal bench with her wrists cuffed behind her. The agent who secured her made sure that the handcuffs were a tad bit too tight, causing the dull metal to bite into her skin. She ignored it.

Across from her, the two black-clad guards assigned to transport her kept their eyes focused on the wall behind her, while deliberately avoiding hers. She smiled faintly. They'd been told not to engage. Smart.

Somewhere down the corridor, a door buzzed open, then clanged shut. Footsteps echoed in the stone corridor, measured and unhurried. A tall man of European ancestry wearing dark civilian clothes appeared at the bars, his hands tucked into the pockets of a matching dark trenchcoat.

"You're a hard woman to get on the calendar," he began in a casual tone.

Torres leaned back, the faintest smirk curling her lips. "And yet... here you are."

He didn't change his position, but the way he glanced at the guards was enough to make her pulse quicken. They didn't even notice it.

"Sometimes, an opening just suddenly presents itself," the man said. "And when it does, business opportunities must be taken advantage of."

Torres tilted her head. "You're speaking like someone who's used to doing a lot of business. Let me guess...international trading? Import and export?"

His mouth curved slightly, just enough to show he appreciated the recognition. "Let's just say that my family's businesses are well represented throughout Europe and the Middle East, especially in Bahrain."

The name of that place hung in the air between them, heavy with unspoken meaning. Torres could see the faint scar along his jawline - a mark she remembered from grainy surveillance photos of the smuggler network many years ago.

"I've always wanted to work in a family-owned business," she said quietly.

He gave a slight nod, a movement so subtle that one would have to be looking directly at him in order to notice it. He then turned to go. "Then maybe you will someday," he replied. "Maybe...sooner than you expect."

The sound of his footsteps faded down the corridor, followed by the buzz and clang of a metal door closing. Torres sat in the dim light, her smile lingering long after the distinguished gentleman had departed.

The game wasn't over yet. Not by a long shot.

Epilogue

Damion stood on the weather deck, watching the calm, blue, glass-like surface of the Mediterranean slip past the ship. The sea-spray brushed his face and, for a moment, it felt like he had returned to an old and trusted friend.

It had been three weeks since his debrief with Stephanie – or *whoever* she was. The meeting had been short and to the point, focusing only on his and Cabrera's direct interactions with Torres. Whoever Stephanie really worked for, they had about as much interest in his and Cabrera's forbidden romance as a snail had in quantum physics. Perfectly fine with him.

He chuckled to himself, remembering his parting words to her. He had tried to be professional, even empathetic: *"It was nice working with you, Special Agent Singh. I hope your family can get some closure, now that Torres is behind bars."*

She had glanced over her shoulder, given him a sly smile, and said, *"You don't actually believe that's my real name, do you?"* Then came the wink, as she walked away without another word.

Damion shook his head now at the memory. It was probably safer not to know her real name - or anything else about her. People like *Stephanie* lived in the shadows, and shadows were safer left alone.

Still, the atmosphere had changed when he came back aboard. He had expected a flood of questions. Where had he been? What about Cabrera? Did he know anything about Ensign Cheng suddenly transferring off the ship? Instead, he got silence. Not exclusionary silence, but something closer to quiet respect.

Every officer and Chief in khakis treated him differently. The CO and XO both gave his hand a firmer shake. His fellow Chiefs offered fist bumps paired with silent nods, as though sharing an inside joke no one would explain. Even Sylvia - his rival and constant thorn in his side - looked at him with something he could only describe as admiration. Nobody ever said a word, but somebody, somewhere, had spoken. *Don't worry, we'll straighten things out with the ship,* echoed in his mind.

And then there was Salina. The surgery had gone well, and her spirits were high when he left her in Rota's naval hospital. She would remain there until her transfer stateside, where convalescence leave and more questions from the brass awaited. She had mentioned visiting her family in Puerto Rico if she got the chance, and had left an open invitation for him to join her when the ship returned. No one there would report them. She had left the rest unsaid.

The thought of seeing her again was something to hold onto, but for now, his focus had to remain on the deployment. Damion took one last look at the Mediterranean before turning back inside.

Paperwork, inspections, training schedules - it all had piled up in his absence. For the next three hours, he worked steadily through reports until a new message flashed in his inbox. It was from QMC(SW) Valentino.

Damion clicked it open, glancing at the last stack of reports on his desk, then his screen went black.

His pulse jumped. Had he been hacked?

Then the display brightened. A video played, shaky and deliberate. The camera pointed towards the ground before rising slowly, pulling him forward into the scene. His breath caught when he recognized the setting - the tree-canopied path.

The camera followed the walkway, turning slightly to reveal the old bench. The lens drew closer, sweeping over the carvings cut into the wood over decades. Then it stopped.

One set of marks stood out, fresh and sharp. Two hearts, interlocked, pierced by an arrow.

Inside one heart were the letters - *M.A.C.*
Inside the other heart was - *R.L.D.*

The video lingered for about five seconds, holding him in place. Then the screen faded to black, replaced by four words:

Do the right thing.

Damion unconsciously leaned forward, staring, waiting for something more, but the screen stayed dark. He exhaled slowly, realizing only then how hard his heart was pounding.

A knock came at his door.

QMC(SW)Valentino stepped inside with a big smile on his face.

"Good timing," Damion said, forcing himself to smile. "I just got your email."

Chief Valentino frowned. "What email? I didn't send you an email. I just came by to see if you wanted to grab some lunch."

Damion rechecked the laptop, but the inbox was empty. No message. No trace. He checked his trash, his history, and even his spam folder. Nothing.

Valentino chuckled. "You've been working too hard, brother," as he turned to leave.

Damion closed the laptop, stood, and followed him out. Before locking the door, he took one last look at the computer sitting there, silent, the empty black screen staring back at him like a premonition...or a warning.